It is only when Father and I are back out on the road, getting wet again now that it has begun to rain in earnest, that I allow myself to let my breath out in a whoosh. It's ridiculous, but I feel as if I've been holding it in since I heard about the Guardians.

"You knew about the Guardians?" I ask after a moment, squinting to see him in the light of the small lantern we borrowed from the Alders.

Father doesn't look at me. "Wait 'til we're home," he says shortly, quickening his pace with an audible squelching of mud.

I sigh. "But—"

"Ellin!" he snaps. "Be still, and obey me without questioning, for once."

I nod and look at the ground, stung until it occurs to me that it wasn't anger I heard in his tone, but fear. The idea of my father being afraid makes me shiver. It takes quite an effort not to look over my shoulder or jump at shadows and regular nighttime noises.

The walk home seems to take longer than it ever has, and I breathe another sigh of relief when Father unlocks the door and we step inside. I don't even have time to enjoy being out of the rain, though, before he speaks.

"Yes," he says, sounding tired and holding his coat in his hands as if he's forgotten where to hang it. "I knew about the Guardians. I had hoped I wouldn't have to tell you yet."

From **NORTHLANDER**

NORTHLANDER
Tales of the Borderlands · Book One

Brown Barn Books
Weston, Connecticut

Brown Barn Books
A division of Pictures of Record, Inc.
119 Kettle Creek Road, Weston, CT 06883, U.S.A.
www.brownbarnbooks.com

NORTHLANDER
Tales of the Borderlands, Book One
Copyright © 2007, by Meg Burden
Original paperback edition

Library of Congress Control Number 2007928597
ISBN: 978-09768126-8-5
Burden, Meg
NORTHLANDER: Tales of the Borderlands, Book One

Printed in the United States of America

For my brother, Matt, always willing
to go on journeys with me

ACKNOWLEDGMENTS

THIS BOOK WOULD NOT EXIST without the wonderful people in my life. The following individuals believed I could when I didn't think so, read scenes and chapters as I wrote them, encouraged, supported, and inspired me. Sincerest gratitude to:

My husband, Nick Leonard. Thank you. For everything.

My parents, Brad and Diana Burden. Thank you for your unfailing love and support, for believing in me, instilling in me a love of reading, feeding my book addiction, making me coffee, and being my friends.

My family: Matt and Annie; Ken, Ruby, Deb, Justin, Dan, and Amy; Jan and David. Thank you for being there for me.

Nancy Hammerslough, editor extraordinaire, thank you. You changed my life and made my dream come true. Your suggestions made this book so much better. It has been a pleasure working with you, and I can't thank you enough.

Idella Bodie, friend and mentor, thank you for giving me the confidence to try.

Beth and the Black Phoenix Alchemy Lab crew, you inspire me. Thank you.

And lastly, to the secret sisterhood (you know who you are): thank you for always being there for me, believing in me, teaching me, and cheering me on. Special thanks to Jenna, Raphaela, Min, Jo, Kim, and Diana.

CHAPTER ONE

THEY SAY WINTER IN THE NORTHLANDS can chill the skin right off your bones. That Northlanders have ice in their veins, hearts of cold stone, and they can freeze you where you stand with one long, frigid look. Of course, hardly anyone from the village of Harnon in the Southland has ever crossed the river that divides us from the Northlands, so they wouldn't know for certain. But I have. And I know these things are true.

"Papers?" asks the bearded, blue-coated guard in front of me, his tone flat as he holds out a meaty hand. There are guards posted at the city gates, both the big one with the paved road for Northlanders and the narrow, muddy track for visiting Southlings like me. The guards don't care much who goes out of the city, but getting in—for Southlings, at least—is another matter entirely.

"I don't have any," I reply, forcing the words past my chattering teeth. "I'm underage."

"What's your name, Red?"

"Ellin Fisher. My father is Rowan Fisher, and he's up at the college. We're boarding there."

The guard scratches his head. "Gate's closing soon, and it's quite a walk to the college. Would take awhile for me to find someone t' fetch your da."

"I know." I shift from one foot to the other, wishing I had thick boots like the Northlanders wear. "And I'm sorry, I know it's late, but I didn't expect to take so lo—"

"What's this all about, then?" asks another, younger guard.

"No papers," replies the first. "She's underage and says her da's up at the college."

The new guard glances at my face and then looks away as though the sight of me is distasteful. Typical Northlander, I think. Blond, with an arrogant set to his shoulders, probably wanting to spit at me just because my hair is Southling red. "Pity," he says after a moment. "The gates are now closed. You're in for a chilly night, Southling."

For a moment, I can only stare at him in disbelief. "It's hardly my fault I'm sixteen and don't have papers yet!" I exclaim at last. "You don't understand; I have to take—"

I clamp my lips shut, catching myself just in time. The last thing I need is for him—for any Northlander, except the college physicians—to know what I was doing out in the forest. If either of these guards knew I was gathering supplies to help my father heal their stupid king, getting locked out would be the least of my worries.

The younger guard raises one pale eyebrow. "I think *you* are the one who doesn't understand," he says with a sneer. "We require papers to keep track of the Southling trash coming into the city. That, of course, includes you. And if you're careless enough to come in so late, without arranging for your father to meet you, then it's your problem, not mine." With that, he turns on his heel and walks away.

It's still snowing, as it has nearly every day during the few weeks my father and I have been here. Tonight, the snow is the sort of hard, gritty stuff that stings, though the flakes seem to be getting bigger and wetter by the minute. The wind howls, bringing in dark. I have only the basket of herbs on my arm and my big woolen shawl, which, though warm enough for winters back home, offers little protection against the biting Northlands wind. I have no boots, no food, and nowhere to go.

"There now," the bearded guard says. My despair must be apparent because he claps his hand on my shoulder and gives it an awkward pat. "I'd let you in anyway, but if Garreth says I can't, then…well. Tonight's not a good night to argue," he adds cryptically. Then he clears his throat. "It's near dark, so you'd best get on, girl. Sorry."

I gape at him, fighting a growing panic. "But the gates weren't closed when I got here! If you'd just go and find my father—"

He shakes his head and gives me a last, regretful look before he begins to push the gates shut. I can't believe it, not really, until I hear the bar drop on the other side with a muffled thud. The sound smacks me like a fist, and I'm breathless for a moment before my chest heaves, and my lips shake, and I feel tears threaten. With a groan, I lean back against the wooden gate and close my eyes.

I hate the Northlands. Before my father and I came here, I didn't like the idea of this place, where Southlings are treated worse than animals: sworn at, spat at, and required to have papers and a curfew. But I didn't ever really think much about it. Safe at home, the Northlands were none of my concern. And then, a little more than a month ago, Master Willem, Chief Physician at the Northlands College, came. And everything changed.

He needed my father's assistance, he said. The king of the Northlands was ill, beyond his or any of his colleagues' ability to help. And Master Willem, old enough to remember when the Northlands and the Southland were easy with one another, remembered, too, the skill and power of Southling healers. The physicians were desperate, Master Willem said, and he begged my father to come and teach them, to brew Southling remedies for the king. But in secret, of course.

Of course. Because King Allard the Prudent of the Northlands deserves the best, and Rowan Fisher of Harnon in the Southland is a better healer than all of the Northlander surgeons and physicians put together. But, of course, the stupid, wretched Northlands laws forbid my father, Master Healer in the Southland, to lay so much as a finger on the stupid, wretched Northlander king.

King Allard would be healthy by now if only my father had been allowed to treat him instead of being forced to try and teach the Northlanders what he knows. As it is, Father and I have known all along that the king is probably going to die anyway. The simple fact is that no Northlander can heal like a Southling. And now, tonight, he will certainly die if I don't take the ingredients in my basket to my father. The king took a turn for the worse this morning, and the brew my father had in mind was his last hope.

I'm going to die, too, I realize. The horrible thought makes me hug my arms to my chest, my basket digging into my ribs. I'm going to freeze to death, right here in front of this gate, and the wolves and snow cats are going to come and eat my frozen body. Worse, the wolves and snow cats are going to kill me *before* I freeze. Either way, they'll find my remains in the morning, in a mess of bloody, trampled snow, but no one will care because their king will be dead, too. Not that anyone besides my father would care about me anyway, I note with another stifled sob. What would *they* care if a Southling died? That pasty guard would probably even be glad.

It's getting darker by the minute, and snowing harder, and I can barely see my shoes when I look down. The ground is a lighter gray than the sky, the wall a dark, hulking mass. The guards must be up there somewhere, but when I look, I can't see their lanterns. The wall and the wind mute the sounds of the city, too, making me feel even more alone.

I sniffle and wipe my face, then dry my hand on the edge of my shawl. "I don't want to die," I whisper. I try to remember everything my father told me about the Northlands. But I hate the Northlands, so I didn't ever listen.

"Well," I say softly, hoping the sound of my voice will scare off—and not attract—any wolves, "I'll be fine without food or water or sleep, for one night. I just have to stay warm." And not get eaten, I add mentally, not wanting to push my luck by speaking the words aloud.

I'll go toward the forest and get a stick, I decide. Then I can stand right here by the gate. I'll huddle against the wall for shelter, and if I have to, I can dump the silverleaf, roperoot, and garlic that I purchased from the apothecary into my basket and use the cloth bags to cover my ears and fingers. Being mixed up with the twisted elm bark and juniper berries I gathered can't hurt the more expensive supplies much, after all. I can jump and run in place to warm myself and keep from freezing solid, and, if I see any wolves or snow cats, I can hit them with my stick.

I frown. Maybe I'll get a few sticks: some to throw, and one to hit with. Some rocks, too, for that matter.

I only go as far along the road as I need to find some twigs, bent double and squinting, nudging lumps on the ground with my foot in hopes of finding rocks. The sticks I find are too thin and feel too dead to do much good, and the rocks are too small, but they're better than nothing.

I keep turning to walk backward as I return to the gates, figuring that any beasts will come from the forest, not the city. I'm stumbling along that way when I bump into something big and solid that sets a paw on the back of my neck.

I scream and drop the bundle of sticks from my numb fingers, too terrified to move.

"Whoa, there! Sorry, girl!" The hand—oh, not a paw, but a *hand*—moves to my shoulder and pulls me about. I blink into the sudden light of a lantern as the big, bearded guard gives me a crooked, apologetic smile. "I was looking for you, but I didn't mean t' scare you."

"It's all right," I manage. I'm surprised that I can force words past my heart, which seems to be pounding right in the middle of my throat. "But why were you looking for me?" I ask, hardly daring to hope that my father came to the gates looking for me. It isn't very late, yet, and I'm sure he's still patiently waiting. "Did that other one—Garreth?—change his mind?"

"No. I've not seen him since." He sighs. "But still, I got t' thinking about it, and I'm not about to let a little slip of a thing like you stay here, Southling or not. Come on." He leads me back up the road to a tiny hut set almost against the wall, outside the Northlanders' gate.

"What is this?" I ask quietly.

"Shush!" He unlocks the door with a furtive glance, shielding the lantern with his coat. "You can sleep in the gatehouse," he says when he has shepherded me inside. "It's not much, just where we catch a meal out of the wind or stay when we're shut out, but you'll be safer here. With the gates closed, no one will be in 'til sunrise."

I take a deep breath, feel my knees almost give out with relief, and smile at him gratefully. "Thank you!"

"Don't thank me yet, girl," the guard says. "It's safer, but you'll be cold. Don't light a fire. I'll give you my lantern, but keep it away from the window. I'll have hell to pay if someone finds you. " He presses the handle of the lantern into my hand. "Goodnight."

I stand in the doorway and watch him walk out of the circle of light. And then I am alone.

CHAPTER TWO

THE WIND RATTLES THE LONE windowpane of the gatehouse and shrieks down the chimney. I huddle in the corner wrapped in my shawl and a coarse blanket I found. My hands are still stiff, and now they shake and tingle as I cup them around the lantern.

My father must be worried about me by now. And angry. He trusted me to get the supplies he needs, and now, if the king dies, it will be my fault. Mine, and that haughty Northlander guard's. I hate the Northlands with every frigid bit of my being.

Lost in my thoughts, I almost don't hear the sound of footsteps outside the door. But when someone fumbles at the doorknob, my heart leaps into my throat again. There's no time to douse the lantern, so I leave it where it sits and dart to the far, shadowed corner of the room. I scramble to pull the blanket over my head as the knob turns, hoping I won't be noticed. It's a foolish hope, though. What sort of idiot would fail to see a lit lantern on the floor and a girl-sized lump beneath a blanket?

But the footsteps enter without pause. Whoever it is stomps his boots just inside the doorway, then goes to sit at the table. There is a muffled thump, followed by ragged breathing. A sniffle.

I frown. One of the stern, rugged Northlander guards is *crying*? It doesn't sound like he's going to stop soon, so I dare to peek out beneath a fold of the blanket.

I swallow a gasp. It's the second guard! I'd recognize his skinny shoulders and silvery blond hair anywhere. Serves him right, I think. I hope he's hurt.

After a few moments, though, when his sobbing hasn't let up, I'm afraid he actually might *be* injured. Much as part of me would enjoy that, for Rowan Fisher's daughter to ignore someone in need would be unthinkable. I make a face, shrug off the blanket, and go to him.

"Are you all right?" I ask, touching his shoulder gingerly.

"AUGH!" The guard—Garreth, I remember—whirls so fast he almost falls off the chair. "What are *you* doing here?" Even red-faced and with his nose dripping, he looks furious. "How *dare* you spy on me, you Southling bitch!"

"I wasn't spying, you stupid goat!" I snap. "I was just staying the night here because *you* wouldn't let me through the gate. How could I have known you'd come here and blubber? And I thought you were hurt," I add, seriously regretting my decision to help him. I narrow my eyes at him. "Are you?"

"No." He stares at me, seeming vulnerable with his pale eyelashes wet with tears, and I realize with a jolt that he's barely older than I am. "I wasn't blubbering," he mutters, looking away. "And you've no right to be here."

Strangely unafraid of him now that I've seen him crying, I shrug and pull out the other chair. "Oh? And what are you going to do about that?" I ask. "Call the guard?"

Garreth seems startled. "Are all you Southling trash this impertinent?" To my surprise, his face looks almost pleasant now, even tearstained and blotchy red.

I fight a smile. "Are all Northlanders so arrogant?"

He snorts, sounding amused, but does not answer. Then a shadow passes over his face, and he looks down at his hands.

"Why were you crying?" The words escape me before I have a chance to swallow them. It's none of my business, and anyway, I don't care.

Garreth sits motionless and silent for a long moment, as if he didn't hear. "What do you care?" he mutters at last, sullenly, clasping his hands so tightly I'm surprised I don't hear his white knuckles cracking. He's obviously miserable, and he looks terribly lonely, and I feel even more of my anger draining away as I watch him.

"We're both here, is all," I say with another shrug. "I thought you might prefer talking with someone to crying about it alone."

"As if talking to some dripping little Southling chit would make me feel better."

"And blubbering like a snot-nosed child *was* helping?"

"I wouldn't have, but thought I was alone!" he exclaims, smacking the table. "And I wasn't *blubbering*. I just—" Garreth breaks off with a ragged gasp and scrubs his palm over his face. He's silent again for a moment.

At last, he takes a deep, shaking breath, sighs, and gives me a bleak look. "My father is sick and dying. Probably tonight."

"Oh." I swallow, wishing I hadn't asked. "I'm sorry," I add uselessly.

He shrugs and nods, his face going all tight and puckered again.

"Why here?" I press, wondering why I can't stop asking these questions. "I mean, don't you want to be with him?"

"I'm on duty tonight." Garreth's mouth twists in a bitter half-smile. "And if my father knew, he would be furious if I went home to be with him. My brothers are there," he adds, as if this should make a difference.

I try to imagine knowing my father was dying and not needing to be at his side, and fail miserably. "You should be there, too," I say. "You aren't doing much good as a guard in here anyway, are you?"

"You're right." He wipes his eyes on his sleeve before he stands. "I should resume my post."

I bite the inside of my lip as I watch him put on his coat, straighten his shoulders, and head for the door.

"Wait!" I exclaim, before he's halfway across the room. Garreth turns and raises an eyebrow, icy and indifferent again. I force myself to continue. "Maybe I could help your father."

"You," he says skeptically, though he has gone very still and watches me warily.

"Well, I couldn't *heal* him, of course, but… maybe my father could."

He snorts. "Your father would use illegal Southling witchcraft to help a Northlander, simply because you asked him to?"

I look down at the floor, afraid, suddenly, that I've misjudged him and have just condemned myself and my father. "Not because I would ask him to. Because your father shouldn't have to die, just because he's a Northlander. Just because of your king's stupid laws."

"What has the king to do with this?"

"Everything!" I close my eyes and shake my head, realizing all over again that if King Allard is dead by morning, it will be my fault. I start to shiver, more from fear than from the bone-aching cold, and look up at him, feeling helpless.

"My father is here to heal the king!" I burst out, throwing caution to the wind. "Would have healed him already, if it weren't for his laws. Laws which your physicians have come near to breaking, by the way, because at least some of *them* are willing to admit that they need help. Father's brewing medicines for the king's physicians to give him, but he needed these supplies, and now I can't bring them to him because of *you*. So if the king dies tonight, it will be my fault! Don't you see?"

Garreth stalks toward me, and for a moment I worry that he's going to grab me and haul me out before the city officials at once. Instead, he fumbles for the back of his chair and clutches it as though he thinks it's going to run away. "Your—your father is here to heal the king," he repeats, sounding strangled. "And I prevented you from helping him."

"Yes." His face has gone pale as salt, and he looks like he might vomit. I lean away, just in case, and frown at him in confusion. "That bothers you? Are you going to report me?"

Garreth drops into the chair hard, making it skid against the floor. He looks at me, wide-eyed, and there is something in his expression that makes the back of my neck prickle.

"Garreth," I say, my voice trembling a little, "what's wrong?"

"You don't know who I am, do you?" he whispers.

"I—" I shake my head, even more confused. "You're Garreth. One of the guards. Are you all right?"

"I'm the king's youngest son."

I understand, now, that sick look on his face. "Oh," I breathe.

Garreth's head jerks in a nod. "I've done this," he says quietly. "I've killed him."

"No!" I jump to my feet, thoughts racing. "No. Garreth, it might not be too late."

"But how? You said—"

"I know what I said," I snap, grabbing a handful of my hair and worrying it between my fingers as I think. "But that's with the medicines alone. My father is one of the best healers in the Southland. If he could just see the king—examine him in person, touch him—then maybe it isn't too late at all."

Garreth shakes his head, the silvery strands glinting yellow in the light of the lantern. "That's against the law. His advisors would never allow it."

"Are you his son or not? Don't you out-rank them?"

"I'm his *youngest* son," Garreth repeats, sounding bitter. "You don't understand. I count for nothing."

"Your brothers, then? The oldest one, Prince Alaric?"

He pushes a hand through his hair. "I don't know! Perhaps."

"Well, come *on*, then. We have to try." I pull my shawl tighter about my shoulders before going to get my basket and the lantern.

"I don't suppose you have a plan?" he asks from behind me, sounding as if he hopes I do.

"Well," I say slowly, thinking, "I assume you can get us back into the city, even though the gates are closed?"

"Of course."

"Good. We'll go straight to the college and get my father." I give him the lantern. "We don't have time to convince your brothers first. Then we'll all go to the castle, and… and you can try to talk some sense into someone," I finish lamely.

"That's all?"

"That, and hope that we're in time," I snap. "Now, come *on*."

I start to head for the door, but Garreth's hand closes on my arm and pulls me back. "Wait," he says when I turn and glare. "It's gotten bad, outside, since we spoke earlier. Have you ever been out in a storm like this, Southling? You don't understand. You can get lost a few steps from your front door, nights like this, and they find you stiff, blue, and frozen in the morning."

"You were going to leave me out in it, remember?" I sigh and jerk my arm away. "Do you want your father to live, or not?"

Garreth stares. "You're willing to risk your life for him. For a king who hates your people."

"I've been trained as a Southling healer," I say flatly. "We don't let people die if we can help it. Even when they hate us." I shake my head, unable to explain it better than that. "Besides, my father would never forgive me if he knew I hadn't tried."

He looks at me for a long moment before he nods. "Get that blanket, then, and use it as a cloak," he says, gesturing at the rough blanket I left in the corner. "You're not dressed for the cold, South—" He shakes his head, seeming more than a little dazed. "I don't even know your name."

"It's Ellin."

Garreth gives me a small, hesitant smile when I come back. "Come on, then, Ellin," he says. "Stay close behind me. Do as I say when we reach the gates. And let's hope we're not too late."

"For both our sakes," I agree. I surprise myself by hoping this, very much, as I follow him out into the cold.

CHAPTER THREE

I COME OUT OF MY FATHER'S tiny bedroom at the college, heart as numb and heavy as my frozen feet. Garreth looks up hopefully, and I shake my head. "He's not here." My voice catches, and I wipe my dripping nose with fingers that feel like icicles.

"Well, he can't be long gone," Garreth points out as he looks around the main room. "The fire hasn't gone out. His cup is still warm, too," he adds, putting reddened fingertips against the side of my father's mug.

"Do you think he's been arrested?"

"Perhaps, if the wrong person found out what he was doing," he says. "More likely, he's out looking for you."

Though he is obviously trying to reassure me, his words do anything but. "In *this*? He could die!"

Garreth looks away, and I realize that this means death for his father, too. Maybe. I take a deep breath, wincing as it warms my lungs, and look at him. "Take me to the castle," I say quietly. "I'll do what I can."

"You?" He shakes his head. "I thought you said you couldn't—"

"I'm not a Master Healer, but I'm not stupid, either," I retort as I begin to add packets of herbs and instruments from my father's makeshift worktable to my basket. "Surely I can do *something*."

"Ellin—"

"Get that book, would you? No, the one with the green cover." I point, noticing that my skin is an even brighter pink than his. "That little silver knife, too."

Garreth brings them to me, along with my father's thick-sided cup and Father's old coat, which I would have worn out today, had I known the weather would be so bad. "Drink this," he says, pressing the mug into my hand, "and wear this. You look as if you need them both."

My fingers curl reflexively around the mug, trying to leach the warmth from it, and my hand shakes as I bring it to my mouth and drink. My father's leftover tea is lukewarm and bitter and too strong, but after being out in the storm, the warm drink in my mouth is so comforting that it almost overwhelms me.

"We should go," I say with reluctance as I set the cup down and begin to shrug out of my shawl. Sighing, I pull on Father's old coat and fumble with the buttons. It's too long, with the color-less faded wool frayed and thinning at the edges, but at least it's dry. For now. The idea of going back out into the cold, of getting soaked again, slogging through the snow when my feet have only just begun to tingle with feeling, makes me want to cry.

I could tell Garreth to go, I think. And he would leave, and I could trust that Father would be all right, and I could strip off my wet, clammy clothes and socks and sleep wrapped up in my own blanket, with a cup of hot, sweet tea by my hand and a warm brick at my feet…

With a groan, I shake some of the melting snow off my hair and cover myself once again with the blanket from the gatehouse.

"It isn't far," Garreth says. That might have reassured me once, but it wasn't far from the gates to the college, either.

I sigh again, resigned, and lower my head as he pushes the door open and the storm swallows us whole.

"I thought you said it wasn't far," I mutter a short time later, stumbling along in Garreth's wake.

He turns and squints at me, his features sharply shadowed by the lantern's light. "What?" he asks loudly.

"I said, I thought you said it wasn't far!" The wind seems to rip my words away, cackling and shrieking as it races down the street.

"It isn't! But we're pushing against the wind."

As if I didn't know that. The wind keeps pushing my makeshift hood back and creeping past my coat collar to whisper coldly in my ears. Or it did, when I could feel my ears. I sniffle and lower my head again, feeling the wind and snow snake down the back of my neck. At least now I have pockets to burrow my frozen hands into.

I don't try to talk anymore and instead concentrate on plodding through the snow. I don't know how Garreth manages to move so quickly in those thick, heavy boots of his. My feet, in only socks and thin shoes, feel like they're made of stone.

As before, I lose track of time. It seems like we've been walking in the darkness forever, with the wind whistling and howling and wet, stinging snow prickling my cheeks. I watch the bobbing yellow circle of light in front of me and tell myself it will only be a few more steps. And then only a few more. I've forgotten how many times I've promised myself that.

"Ellin!" Garreth's muffled shout causes me to look up, and I stumble and almost fall as my mind tries to react before my body is ready. The castle looms before us, a few of its windows shining with warm, golden light.

"We're here," I breathe, my lips stiff and clumsy on the words.

"We're here," Garreth grunts a few moments later as he pushes a small side door closed behind us. My eyes are dazzled from the light after so long in the dark, only watching the lantern, but I have the impression of gray stone walls, tapestries, and heavy, dark furniture. Despite providing shelter from the wind, this place is as cold and forbidding as the Northlands themselves.

Garreth turns and beckons with a nod of his head. His hair, I can see now, is soaked and dripping down his forehead. "Follow me."

I do, and he leads me up stairs and down hallways that seem strangely quiet and empty. I don't know what time it is, but the stillness here tells me that it must be very late. At last we come to a hallway that is still well lighted, and I can hear the murmur of voices as we approach.

The murmur of Northlanders' voices, of Northlander physicians and Northlander princes keeping watch over their king who despises my people. All at once, I feel very small, with my wet, stolen blanket and squelching shoes and bright red, Southling hair.

"Garreth!" I call softly, hurrying to catch up. "I can't do this."

He looks at me, surprise and irritation and disappointment obvious. "What do you mean?" he whispers back. "I thought you said you could."

"It's not that! It's illegal. I'm going to be in trouble just for *being* here."

Garreth shakes his head. "You won't. Just...be quiet. And put your hood back up." He flushes slightly and looks away. "I don't want anyone to see that hair of yours until I've explained."

"Fine." I barely have the blanket pulled over my hair again when another blond boy pokes his head out of the room at the end of the hall.

"Who's out—Garreth!" the boy exclaims, hurrying toward us. "What are you doing here? And who's that?" he asks, stopping short when he sees me.

"Is Da all right?" Garreth asks.

Now that he's closer, I see that, despite being short and slight, the other boy looks a bit older than Garreth. He frowns and shrugs. "He's worse than before, but still here, at least."

Garreth exhales audibly, shoulders sagging, and I try not to let my own relief show. We aren't too late.

"Who is this?" the boy asks again, taking a closer look at me. His eyes widen. "It's a girl!"

"My *name* is Ellin," I say stiffly. Even dressed in a coat like a man and bundled in a blanket, surely he should have been able to tell.

"And I'm Erik." His sharp face is lit with curiosity. "And *you're* a Southling!"

"Shh!" Garreth hisses. "Look, Erik, I'll explain. Where's Alaric?"

"With Da, of course."

"And Coll?"

Erik nods.

"The lords and Master Thorvald?" Garreth asks.

"Of course."

"Damn!"

"Why?" Erik sucks in a breath, and his eyes widen as he stares from Garreth to me and back again. "The Southling? You're not!"

"I need to talk to Alaric," Garreth says firmly. "To all of you, without anyone else there. Will you help?"

Erik doesn't hesitate before he nods and hurries back into the sickroom. A few moments later, several robed men come out. I keep my head down and attempt to look as much like Garreth's servant as possible as I follow him in. I don't even know if he has servants of his own, but at least none of the lords or physicians tries to stop me.

The room reeks of unwashed body and the sweetish, disgusting smells of decay and impending death. Above that, it stinks of the perfume the Northlanders use in their medicines to mask less pleasant scents. I can smell the ingredients beneath the perfume, though, enough to tell me that they've been using typical Northlander brews. Rotted stuff, nasty parts of dead animals, urine... I shiver. I can just barely smell the fresher herbs Father uses, and I'd be willing to wager everything I own that his medicines, given to the king in small, secret doses, are the only reason King Allard is still alive at all.

The room is large. It must be the king's bedchamber, I assume, noting that it's richly decorated. It is not the furniture, though, that draws my gaze. It is the people in it. A few men are gathered around the bed, and they all look at Garreth and me as we enter.

"What is this, Garreth?" asks the handsome, bearded man sitting at the side of the bed. "Erik said you wanted the family to be alone with Da, but I know you're up to something."

"He's going to die if we don't do something," Garreth says.

"He's going to die anyway, boyo," the very fat man standing behind the handsome man says, but not unkindly. "There's nothing any of us can do."

"Garreth thinks he has a plan." Erik straddles a chair backward and leans his elbows and chin on the top. He smirks mischievously, as if anticipating trouble. "Don't you?"

"Well," Garreth begins, his voice uncertain. He toes the floor with his boot and looks nervously from the fat man to the nice-looking man and back again. "I—"

The king moans, then, and I truly look at him for the first time. I can't see him very well across the dimly-lit room, but what I can see alarms me. His skin is a pale grayish yellow, and his mouth is slack, hanging open as he gasps for breath. I bite the inside of my lip as I watch him.

I could kill this man, I think. Not with poison, or with my hands, but simply by doing nothing. By turning back and going to our rooms at the college. I could wait for my father there and never tell him what I hadn't done.

I join Garreth in looking at the handsome man across the room. Though I have not seen him before, I know him by his deep yellow hair and beard that gleam orange in the firelight. He is Prince Alaric. They call him Alaric the Golden, not only for his hair. It is said, here in the Northlands, that everything he touches goes well. That he is unusually blessed. He looks kind, if sad, and I wonder as I look at him if he would be fair and good enough to abolish his father's stupid laws banning Southling healing. The laws that cause people here to spit at me because of the color of my hair.

Alaric looks up as if sensing my gaze, and I meet his eyes from within the shadows of my hood. I could make this man king tonight, I realize, and the power in that thought makes me shudder. Then Alaric looks away, at his father lying on the bed, and I shiver again, this time at the direction my thoughts dared take. What would my father think of this? But I don't really have to ask myself. I know he'd be disappointed. Ashamed. Maybe angry, too.

The king moans again, and I take a step closer to the bed. "Garreth," I say quietly, when he still has not continued.

Garreth nods and squares his shoulders. "This is Ellin," he says to his brothers. "She says she is Da's only hope."

"A girl?" The fat man shakes his head and sighs. "*That's* why you've come back in this storm, boyo? On a fool's hope?"

"He's not a fool," I reply, voice shaking a little. My entire body is shaking, I realize, from the shock of being indoors again after so long in the cold.

Alaric looks at me again, sharply. "Pull back your hood."

I do, fumbling a little as I push the sodden cloth down with tingling, painful fingers.

"A Southling," the fat man says into the sudden silence, distaste thickening his words. "You've brought a Southling witch-girl."

Garreth sighs. "Coll—"

"A half-frozen Southling witch-girl, it seems," Alaric adds as he stands. He comes over to loom before me, and I crane my neck to look up, trying not to flinch.

"This witch-girl—" my mouth twists at the insult, "—might be able to keep your father from dying. *If* you'll let her get to it, instead of standing here until it's too late."

"A feisty witch-girl," Alaric observes mildly. "Why?" he asks me.

"Because..." I look to the bed again, where the king has gone very still and even paler. I bite my lip again, doubting I'll have enough time as it is. I resolutely do *not* think about what will happen to me if I try and fail. "Because I have to." I swallow. "Please."

"Please let her try!" Garreth bursts out, stepping to my side. "We walked all the way from the gatehouse!"

"We'll have to talk," Alaric begins.

Suddenly angry with all of them, I shrug the wet, heavy blanket off, followed by my father's coat, and hand them to Garreth. "There isn't *time*," I snap. "Can't you see? He is going to die if we don't do something *now*." I glare up at Alaric. "If you want him to live, either help me, or get out."

Before anyone can stop me, I slip around Alaric and go to the other side of the bed, opposite the fat man—Coll—and place my cold hand against King Allard's forehead. His skin is dry and burning beneath my touch.

I'm conscious of the princes' raised voices, but barely, as I focus my attention solely on the king. I sit on the edge of the mattress, wincing as weight is taken off my frozen feet, and take one of his hot, wasted hands in mine. I keep my other hand on his forehead, fingertips brushing his temple. Then I close my eyes and concentrate on breathing slowly, like my father taught me.

Fear, exhaustion, and this sudden moment of stillness bring tears prickling behind my eyelids. *Father*, I think, desperately needing him beside me. *I can't do this alone!*

Something agonizingly sharp breaks in my mind, and I gasp and go stiff, clenching my fingers around the king's hand. All of a sudden, I can *feel* him—feel his body with a sense that is like touch and smell and sight, but is none of these things. It is how a healer feels. Like my father has taught me about, but has said I am not ready to try.

And I know, immediately, that Father is right. I am *not* ready for this. With this new sense, I can feel the sickness in the king. I can see it with my mind like bruised, tangled spots squirming around his body. I take my hand from his forehead and reach out to touch one of these spots, then almost gag when I seem to smell the vileness of it.

I don't know what to do, and that knowledge sits like a lump in my stomach. I'm afraid, not to mention ashamed that I dared presume to heal this man.

"He's cold," I say, as much to myself as to anyone else. Opening my eyes, I look at his face, scarcely remembering that this sick man is the king. "I need hot water. Two bowls of it. Clean cloths, too."

You'll be all right, I think, not even bothering to be surprised that my thoughts, as well as my body, feel ragged and sore. *I'll do what I can. You'll be all right.*

I open my basket and begin to do my best, using my training and what I can feel from his body with this new healer's sense. Crushed juniper berries dabbed beneath his nose and above his eyebrows, to help clear congestion. Pressing his temples to relieve headache. Rubbing his chest with more juniper and roperoot pulp to help him breathe.

"Here," a soft voice says at my side as someone lightly touches my shoulder. I take one of the steaming bowls of water without looking up. "I wish there was something I could do to help," the boy adds.

"Bathe his forehead, chest, throat, and hands with the other bowl of water and a cloth," I say as I begin to shred some of the silverleaf into my own bowl. My throat hurts when I speak, but I ignore it. "Dry him before moving to each part, though. You want to warm him, not wet and chill him."

We work together in silence, and I concentrate on dripping the silverleaf tea into the king's mouth and on his dry, cracked lips. I have the vague impression that the boy helping me is tall and blond, but he is not Garreth. It shouldn't surprise me, I suppose, that the servants, too, look like typical Northlanders.

The king begins to groan and sigh before we're done, but I continue to murmur comforting things, both aloud and in my thoughts when my throat hurts too much to speak. Even though I know the king can't hear me, I hope some part of him understands.

At last, and all too soon, I've run out of things to do. I sit back as the realization that I've done my best hits me, leaving me breathless and at a loss. King Allard's face is blurry as I blink at him with scratchy eyes, still holding his hand.

The bed seems to tilt, and I squeeze my eyes shut. "I don't know what else to do," I whisper. The words echo in my head, mocking me.

"Drink this," says the servant boy, at my side again. He presses a warm cup into my free hand. I take it and drink, though I hardly taste it.

The warmth and comfort and sudden calm loosen something within me, and I feel myself start to shake yet again as tears finally overflow. I keep my eyes closed and bow my head as my face crumples, hoping my hair will curtain my cheeks so the boy won't see.

I try to stop crying when I hear the door open behind me, but I'm sobbing too hard to even look up as someone takes the cup from my hand and sits on the bed beside me.

"Oh, Ellin. Brave girl," my father murmurs, tucking my hair back behind my ear. My breath catches, and I look up, scarcely daring to believe it.

"Father?" I croak. "How—?"

"Shh, we'll talk later. I'm here now."

My mouth trembles again. "I was so *afraid*—"

"I'm here now," Father repeats. He smiles and brushes some of the tears from my cheek with his thumb. "You did well. Now, go warm up and try to sleep. Your friend Prince Garreth has some blankets for you by the fire, there." He points. "I'll wake you when I've finished."

I stand and stumble a little as the floor seems to sway beneath me. "I'm not dreaming?" I ask, noticing distantly that Father and the king and the whole room, in fact, look strange and unclear.

"You're not dreaming." Father squeezes my hand.

With that reassurance, I make my way to the fireplace and sink to my knees in the warm nest of blankets. I should remove my wet shoes and socks, I think as I lie down and pull some of the blankets over myself. I've only toed one of them halfway off, though, when I decide I don't care and let sleep claim me.

CHAPTER FOUR

SOMEONE IS COUGHING INCESSANTLY, a deep, wet-sounding rasp. I pull my blankets over my head and try to go back to sleep, but it is no use. The barking cough continues, dragging me back to consciousness even though I squeeze my eyes shut and burrow my face into my arm. Now that I'm awake, I'm aware of the stiffness of my body, of my hip digging into the floor even through the blankets, and of the fact that I'm thirsty. I remember, after a confused moment, where I am and who must be coughing. With a groan, I sit up and push my tangled hair off my cheeks.

"You're awake," Father observes from his chair beside the king's bed.

"Mmm." I blink at him before scrubbing at my face in an attempt to clear the stuffiness from my head. "Is it morning?"

"Almost dawn, I think. You haven't been asleep long."

I go to him, clutching one of the blankets around me like a cloak. "How is he?" I ask with a nod at the king.

"It's too soon to say," Father replies. "The coughing is a good sign, though." He sighs and reaches up to rub the back of his neck. When he turns his face toward the fire, I can see how exhausted he looks. He must have been out in the cold almost as long as I was, I realize.

"How did you find me?" I ask, perching beside him. "I mean, what happened?"

"I went to the gates after dark, when you hadn't come back. One of the guards told me he'd sent you to the gatehouse," he says. "But he couldn't open the gates to let me out."

"But why weren't you at the college when we went looking for you?" My eyebrows draw together in confusion. "That was long after dark."

Father pulls a face and shrugs. "I got a little lost in the storm. I walked into a inn—literally, walked into the wall—by accident, and decide to wait it out there."

"Then how did you know to come here?"

"I just knew," Father says slowly, but he doesn't meet my gaze. I open my mouth to ask him what he means, but he raises a hand, forestalling me. "Then, once I arrived, Prince Garreth explained what had happened. It seems you made quite an impression," he adds, smiling a little.

"I think I shouted at all of them," I reply, though I can hardly remember. It seems like a dream. "And I think some of the advisors tried to make me leave, at one point." I know I remember the princes yelling. Maybe at each other? "But Alaric—I think it was Alaric—told them I could stay."

"King Allard is fortunate that he did. That *you* came when you did. He would have died, had you not been here." Father smiles again and squeezes my shoulder. "I'm proud of you, Ellin."

I start to reply, but my words are swallowed by a jaw-cracking yawn.

Father chuckles tiredly. "You should go back to sleep."

"I don't think I can. Do you think I could get a drink?" I can tell I'm getting sick, myself, and I can't help hoping that a warm, strong cup of tea might clear my nose and soothe my sore throat.

"Tonight, I think you could have the castle, if you wanted it. As I said, you made quite an impression on your friend Prince

Garreth," Father says. "He let me in at once and practically fell over himself being polite, when I told him who I was."

"He's not my friend," I say as I stand. I don't know why it irritates me to hear my father refer to Garreth that way, but it does. I can't help seeing Garreth's sneering face in my mind, all of a sudden, and remembering the disgust in his voice when he called me Southling trash at the gate. "Tonight was strange," I say slowly, "but he's still a Northlander. They're all Northlanders. Nothing has changed."

"No," my father agrees. "It hasn't. But that doesn't mean it can't."

"Hmm." I shrug, not sharing his optimism. I know Father doesn't feel the same way about the Northlands that I do, but then, he's always willing to look for the best in people. Even when there's nothing good there to find. "I think I will go see about that drink," I say, not wanting to discuss the Northlands anymore.

"All right."

I give Father a quick, impulsive kiss on the cheek before I go out, and smile at his surprised look. "I'm proud of you, too," I say. "And glad you came."

It is only when I'm out in the colder hall, away from the fire, that I realize I'm still only wearing one shoe. Rather than go back to get the other, I push this one off with my toes and leave it in the hall, along with my socks. I can get them later.

I'm not sure where the kitchen is, but I assume it's somewhere near the entrance, so I attempt to retrace the way I took with Garreth. The castle is still mostly dark and very quiet, and I'm soon glad I left my shoes behind. The stone floor is like ice beneath my bare, sore feet, but at least I'm able to walk softly. My own silence unnerves me a little, though; I keep expecting Northlander advisors to burst out of the shadows and arrest me for daring to be here. I shiver and pull the blanket more snugly around my shoulders as I peer into shadows and doorways.

I've barely reached the top of the stairway when one of the doors behind me opens with a creaky groan. I jump at the sound and whirl, hair flying.

"Oh, it's you!" I exclaim, pressing my hand to my racing heart. I feel my chest sag with relief as I blink in the light of the candle the tall, blond boy is holding. I *think* it is the servant boy from earlier, at least.

The boy gives me a nod and steps closer, and I look down, a little embarrassed at acting like such a ninny.

"Sorry," I say. "I'm a little nervous, being here. And it's dark, and..." I shrug when I realize I'm only making myself look worse. "Anyway, I'm glad you're here," I continue. "I wanted to thank you for helping me." I look up and smile, scarcely knowing how to tell him how comforting it was not to be alone, for that.

He shakes his head and gives me a puzzled sort of smile. I frown in confusion.

"You *are* the one who helped me earlier, aren't you? With the king?"

"Ellin?" I turn to see Erik behind me, coming up the stairs with another candle in his hand. "I thought I heard you," he says. "Who're you talking—oh! Finn!" He takes the rest of the stairs two at a time and goes to stand by the servant boy, who gives him a grin and some strange sort of wave.

"He helped me earlier. I think," I say. "I was just thanking him."

Erik laughs. "That'll do no good."

"What?"

"He can't hear you. He's deaf," Erik explains. "And it's too dark where you're standing for him to see from your mouth what you're saying."

"Oh!" I look at my feet, embarrassed. "I didn't know. But why didn't he say something?"

Erik shakes his head. "Oh, Finn can't talk, either."

"Are you sure?" Even as I speak, I realize that's a stupid thing to ask.

Erik huffs a laugh and wiggles his fingers at Finn in the same odd, graceful-looking wave. "I'd better be sure," he says. "He *is* my twin."

"Your—oh." I'm suddenly thankful it's dark so that they can't see how red my cheeks must be. I'm also very glad I didn't ask if there are any other servants who look like Finn, as I was about to do. "It must not have been him, I guess," I say with a shrug. "I talked with the boy who helped me."

"Ellin?" Erik says a moment later, sounding strange. "Finn says it was him. You must have imagined you heard him talking to you."

"I'm sure—" I begin to say, and then I shake my head. Tired as I was, maybe I *did* imagine our conversation. "And how do you know?" I ask, looking curiously from one of them to the other. "I thought you said he can't talk."

"Like this." Erik lifts his free hand and wiggles his fingers at me.

"You can *talk* like that?"

"Sure."

Finn touches Erik on the shoulder and moves his fingers so fast I can hardly see them, and Erik laughs. "I told Finn a moment ago that you just wanted to thank him. He says he thought you were asking how to get to the privy."

Finn, obviously catching my gaze, gives me an embarrassed smile and claps his hand to his forehead. I can't help grinning back as I realize that my stammering and shuffling must have made me look just like someone badly in need of relieving their bladder.

"No, I just wanted a drink," I say. It occurs to me that he might not be able to see my mouth, so, after a second's hesitation, I raise my hand and pretend to drink from a cup.

"We were heading to the kitchen ourselves," Erik says as the boys step beside me. "Come on. We'll find you something to eat, too, if you want."

The kitchen, I'm surprised to see, is already well-lit with both a fire and lanterns. I'm even more surprised to find that we aren't the first ones here, even though the sky out the window has not yet begun to lighten.

"Ellin!" Garreth smiles and jumps off the woodbox when Erik, Finn, and I enter. "You've seen your father? And slept a bit?"

"Yes, to both." I reach up and push my palm over my wildly tangled hair, suddenly conscious of the fact that I'm barefoot, bedraggled, and wearing my bedding over my wrinkled skirt and blouse. In a room full of wide awake and apparently washed and dressed princes.

"She met Finn, too," Erik says over his shoulder as he goes to rummage in a cupboard.

"You did? Good." Garreth apparently doesn't notice or is too polite to mention my rumpled appearance because he pulls out a chair at the table for me with a small, formal bow. "Please."

I blush and shrug the blanket off to drape over the back of the chair.

"And you know Erik, of course, and our brothers Alaric and Coll?"

I look at the two older princes across the table from me and try to smile, still struggling to remember what, exactly, I said to them earlier when I sent them from the room. Now that I'm not so worried about the king, I feel entirely out of place being in the same room with them. Not to mention horribly embarrassed that I wasn't more respectful. Alaric and Coll are grown men, after all, not boys like the others.

"Um," I murmur at last. "We didn't meet. Officially. I mean, I saw you, and we spoke, but—" I suppress a wince, realizing that I'm babbling like a fool.

Alaric's white, straight teeth flash in a grin behind his beard as he rescues me from my own stupidity. "I'm Alaric. And this is Coll."

Coll nods curtly behind his mug. "Witch-girl," he grunts, by way of greeting. I'm not sure if he's teasing or not, but even if he is, I don't think it's funny.

I don't know what to say. Were I not a little afraid of Coll, three times my size and dangerous-looking, I'd be tempted to snap at him and call him 'Nasty Fat Northlander,' or something equally rude. Instead, I attempt another smile aimed at Alaric, clenched jaw protesting, and nod politely.

"It's nice to meet you." It isn't entirely a lie. Alaric seems pleasant enough, and he has a kind smile. He doesn't seem to have anything more to say to me, though, nor I to him, and an awkward silence falls.

"So," Erik says as he flops down beside Coll, a hunk of buttered bread in hand, "Garreth said he locked you out, and you broke into the gatehouse?" He grins at me over his bread before taking an enormous bite. "How'd you manage that?" he asks thickly.

"I—" I start to say that I didn't, but then it occurs to me that I might get the kind guard at the gate in trouble if I admit that he let me in. I close my mouth, shrug, and start over. "I just saw it there," I lie. "And I didn't want to freeze. I figured being inside would at least keep me alive."

Erik nods his approval. "Smart."

"She has good instincts." Garreth smiles at me almost proudly. "For a Southling, I mean."

I stare at him in disbelief. Garreth is the reason I was locked out, the reason I could very well have frozen to death. And now he thinks he can grin at me, looking smug, as if I'm merely a curiosity he brought home to show his brothers. Good instincts! Like I'm some sort of animal.

I'm sure my wordless fury must be apparent, but Garreth seems not to notice as he comes to stand at my side. "Would you like something to eat, Ellin?"

With an effort, I separate my gritted teeth. "Well," I say pointedly, "the 'Southling trash' was wondering if she could have a cup of tea. If such a request wouldn't be too impertinent. I'm not sure. You see, I might have good instincts, but—"

"Southling trash?" Alaric interrupts, looking at me sharply. "Did one of the maids call you that, Ellin?"

"It's nothing—" I begin, wishing, now that his piercing blue eyes are on me, that I hadn't been so petty. Not that I regret what I said, but I wish he hadn't overheard.

"No," Garreth says heavily. "I did." He sighs and shoves a hand through his hair. "I'd just received the message that Da was worse, and I was upset, and…I apologize."

"We're all in your debt, and your father's," Alaric adds, shifting his gaze to his youngest brother. "And we all should—and will—remember it."

Garreth nods, pink-cheeked. "I know. But I didn't know what you were like, at the gate," he adds, sounding defensive. "I didn't realize what you could do."

I want to tell him that no Southling deserves to be locked out in the cold, but instead I only nod, accepting his apology.

Someone brushes my shoulder, and I look up to see Finn holding out a steaming mug. "Thank you," I say in surprise as I take it.

Finn smiles and sits, and he says something with his hands to Erik, making him grin.

"He says one of us ought to have some manners."

"Indeed," I murmur into the cup, arching an eyebrow at Garreth over the rim. He groans as he wedges himself between Erik and Coll.

"*Are* you going to rub that in indefinitely?" he asks, helping himself to a piece of Erik's bread.

I shrug and fight a smile. "I don't know. Are you going to continue to need the reminder?"

Across the table, Alaric makes a choked sound and rubs at his mouth with the back of his hand before resuming some conversation about horses and saddles with Coll.

"You'll have to excuse Garreth," Erik says confidingly, his eyes sparkling with mischief. "Being the youngest, he's had no time to learn good manners. And I've heard some of his brothers are bad influences."

"Not all, though," I say, smiling at him and Finn. Finn shrugs and looks away, seeming pleased, and I find myself wondering if all Northlanders would be so charming if they couldn't talk.

"I shouldn't defend the Youngest," Erik says, "but in truth, you've hardly seen any of us at our best."

"And you've seen me at mine." I reach up self-consciously to touch my hair, wincing when I find it every bit as bushy and knotted as I feared.

Again, Finn touches my shoulder. Surprisingly, I find that I don't mind this, though normally the idea of being touched by a Northlander would make me shudder. When he has my attention, Finn waves his hands at Erik.

"You look like you might be getting sick," Erik translates. "She does?" He peers at me. "You do! You're white, and your nose is all red, and there are big circles under your eyes."

I blush into my tea, uncomfortable with his close scrutiny. "I know," I say when I've swallowed. "But it's nothing. I was just out in the cold and wet too long, is all."

Finn touches his throat and gives me a questioning look, and I nod. "It's sore." I point to my throat and make a face.

He nods and points to my tea, then to the door, and I don't need any translation for "back to bed."

Garreth stands. "I'll take you. I want to look in on Da, anyway."

"It's not as if I'm going to faint going up the stairs," I mutter as I stand and gather up my blanket and tea.

"Yes, but—" Garreth glances down and sucks in a breath. "Ellin, your feet!"

"What?" I follow his gaze, and my eyes widen as I see my feet for the first time since our treks through the snow. They're white and bloodless, and it occurs to me, looking down at them, that they don't hurt and aren't cold anymore because I can't properly feel them. "Oh," I say faintly. "That's not good, is it?"

Finn grasps my elbow hard enough to slosh my tea. When I turn to him, he points to me and then makes a gesture at his head that says, very clearly, "Are you insane?"

"*Are* you?" Erik asks aloud. "Why didn't you *say* something?"

"I didn't notice!"

"This is my fault!" Garreth groans. "I made you take a blanket, but I didn't even *think* to ask if you had boots!"

"It's all right, though, isn't it?" I ask, because their concern is making me nervous. "I mean, I'll just go put some socks on and be all right."

"What's the matter?" Alaric asks, looking up with a frown. "What is it?"

"This one's nearly frozen her feet off, and she thinks *socks* will fix it," Erik says. He rolls his eyes. "Southlings!"

"And she's sick," Garreth adds.

"I'm not," I mutter. It probably doesn't make the lie more convincing that I sniffle and wince when I swallow a sip of tea, though.

Coll snorts. "Sick and frozen? Welcome to the Northlands, witch-girl."

Alaric bends to get a look at my feet and pulls a face as he comes back up. "Best get those taken care of."

"That's the plan." Erik takes the blanket and my cup from me. "Come on, witch-girl," he says, the name so obviously teasing that I can't be mad. "We'll see you up to your father."

Finn says something to Garreth, who nods.

"Right." Garreth steps up to me and holds his skinny arms out stiffly. "I'll carry you up. You shouldn't be barefoot on the cold floor."

I look from one of them to the other, fighting an almost uncontrollable urge to giggle. "You can't be serious."

Garreth frowns. "You're small!"

I refrain—with difficulty—from pointing out that, despite being tall, he's so scrawny that he can't weigh very much more than I do. "I'll walk," I say firmly. "They don't hurt," I add, addressing them both though I make sure to face Finn.

He rolls his eyes, and Erik shakes his head as we start for the door. "'Course they don't," Erik says. "But you should know better, if you're a healer."

"We don't have this in the Southland," I mutter, embarrassed. "Nobody ever freezes their feet."

Despite that, my father seems as alarmed as the princes when they see me back to my bed of blankets and tell him.

"I didn't even consider that you might be hurt or sick," Father murmurs, kneeling with one of my feet held up for inspection. My stiff, dirty skirt bunches up around my calves, and I wish the princes would leave instead of staring down at me. "You never get sick."

I sniffle. "I'm fine. I just need some twisted elm, maybe some honey for my throat, and a good sleep." I make a point not to look at my bone-white, dead-looking feet.

"You know this is serious," Father says. It's not a question.

I sigh and nod.

"Not as bad as it could be, though," Erik says, putting a hand on Father's shoulder as he peers over it. "Sven—he's one of the stable boys—got one of his fingers frozen so badly that it turned black, and he lost the tip of it."

I gasp. "What?"

Erik nods. "Oh, it's ugly, all right. I've even heard of men losing an entire fo—oof!" He grunts as Garreth elbows him.

I've heard enough, though. "Well," I say, breathing through my nose in an effort not to panic. "How do you treat it?"

Finn says something, and Garreth looks surprised. "Ice? Really?"

"*Not* ice," Father says firmly. "We'll warm them, first, and stimulate the flow of blood. After that, I'll do a healing to prevent permanent damage. You may require more than one," he adds. "I don't know."

Finn, kneeling on my father's other side, begins to flick his fingers at Erik, though he looks questioningly at my father.

"Finn says—"

"No need for that," Father interrupts Erik, smiling a little. "A woman I knew at college was like your brother. Your speech is a bit different," he says to Finn, "but I understand enough."

Finn smiles back and repeats whatever he was saying, more slowly, and my father shakes his head.

"No, rubbing them with ice or more snow won't do any good. I didn't realize you still do that here," Father says, looking surprised and a little disturbed. "In fact, chilling her feet would likely make them worse."

Finn nods slowly, seeming embarrassed, and a strained silence falls.

After a moment, Erik gestures to the king and asks what we've all been wondering. "Is he any better?"

Father takes a deep breath and lets it out slowly. "The king is resting," he says carefully. "And his fever is lower than it was."

"But?" Erik presses, and my father sighs.

"I—"

Finn touches Erik's arm and shakes his head, saying something, and my father nods.

"Yes, it is difficult to tell, at this point. And he may get worse before he gets better." Father gently sets my foot down and gives me a sympathetic look as he tugs the hem of my skirt back where it belongs. "As will you, I think."

"What do you mean?" I ask.

Father pats my shoulder. "Warming your feet is likely going to be painful."

"Oh." I shrug. "Well, it can't possibly be worse than how they felt out in the snow."

Chapter Five

M Y FATHER POURS MORE warm water into the basin around my feet. "Well?"

I press my lips together and nod. "It's fine," I grit through clenched teeth. Actually, it's worse, but I see little point in telling him that. By now, I've gathered that this thawing process is *supposed* to hurt.

He nods and straightens, wiping his hand on his shirt. "I'm going to check the king's fever and his breathing and then see about a cup of tea and some breakfast." I follow his gaze to the bed, where the king is still sleeping, a big, shapeless lump beneath the crimson bedclothes. "Keep moving your toes," Father adds. "And ask Prince Finnlay to find me if the pain gets too bad."

I nod and set about curling and uncurling my toes in the water again. Every movement sends cramping, tingling pain up the balls and arches of my feet, and I close my eyes and concentrate on breathing slowly, clutching the arms of my chair for all I'm worth. I can hardly believe how *much* it hurts to have my feet warmed. I thought nothing could be as bad as the bone-deep ache they felt last night in the snow, but I was wrong.

I hear Father go out, and, a moment later, footsteps approaching and the scrape of the other chair's legs on the floor. Finn pushes his hair off his forehead and tilts his head at me questioningly when I open my eyes. He points at my feet and raises an eyebrow.

"They still hurt."

Finn rolls his eyes and gestures, and I shake my head, not understanding.

"What?"

His eyebrows draw together in thought, and I wonder if he's as frustrated with our inability to communicate as I am. It figures, I think. One of the few Northlanders I've met who seems decent, the *only* one who's been pleasant to me and shown proper respect to my father—Finn offered to stay and help, after all—and it's just my luck that we can't even talk.

Finn pinches his fingers together to indicate something small, then holds his hands apart, to indicate something big, and points to my feet again.

I frown and look down into the basin, remembering as I do so that I'm still supposed to be moving my toes. "My feet are big? They're growing?"

He snorts with amusement, then shakes his head as if to say it doesn't matter.

"Ow!" I wince and flex my left foot as a particularly sharp pain shoots straight up my shin. "I'm sorry," I say when I've unclenched my jaw. "I just…don't understand. I wish I did."

Finn shrugs, and I have the feeling this must happen to him a lot. We look at one another blankly for a moment, and I wiggle my toes and swish my feet and realize that at least our guessing game was helping to take my mind off the pain.

I pry my fingers off the arms of the chair and clasp them in my lap. "You seem interested in healing," I say, just for something to say. "Do you want to be a healer—I mean, a physician?"

Finn looks surprised for an instant, but then he nods.

"Have you always?"

He nods again, holding his hand out a little above the arm of his chair, and I know he means he has since he was a small boy. I nod to show my understanding, and he looks pleased as he points to me.

"Have I?" I tap my thumbs together and look down at them, thinking, before I remember to look up when I speak. "I didn't really have a choice. I was helping Father when I was that big," I add with a small smile, holding out my hand to indicate a child.

"Why do you?" I ask, curious. After all, the Northlands are different. They don't value healers the way we do in the Southland, and anyway, surely a Northlander prince would have better things to do than brew medicines for old people's rattling lungs and run out in the night to help children with fevers.

Finn has his long, graceful-looking hands clasped in his lap, too, and they remain there for a moment as he studies me. Then he shrugs a little and gives me a wry smile as he points first to his ear, then to his mouth. I blush, realizing I've asked a very personal question.

"Oh," I say quietly. "Because they couldn't heal you?"

He stares for a moment, gray eyes wide, before he grins and shakes his head. Then he begins to gesture emphatically—first slashing, as if holding a sword, then at himself, then shaking his head in a vehement negative.

"You don't want to be a fighter?"

He points to his ear and mouth again, and shakes his head.

"Oh! You *can't* be a fighter." I realize that saying it so bluntly was probably rude, but Finn doesn't seem to mind as he nods. "Because...you couldn't hear someone yelling orders?" I guess.

Another nod. Then he points behind him and makes a walking motion with his fingers, over his shoulder.

"And enemies could sneak up on you!" I grin when he nods yet again, feeling as pleased as he looks.

Before I can ask anything else, Finn stands abruptly and goes to get the kettle of hot water. He comes back and gives me an apologetic look before pouring some into the basin. I hiss and clench my hands as the warmth makes my feet start to ache badly again.

Finn touches my shoulder on his way to replace the kettle in front of the fire. "I know it hurts," he says. "I'm sorry."

"What!?" I turn and stare as he goes to put his hand on his father's forehead before resuming his seat. He looks up and smiles at me, but his expression quickly fades to alarm when he sees the look on my face. He frowns and points to my feet, then fans himself.

"It's not too hot," I snap. Then I sniffle, hating the hot water for making my nose run. I wipe at it angrily and glare at him. "Why did you lie to me?"

Finn's frown deepens, and he shakes his head, either not understanding me or denying that he lied, I can't be sure. But either way.

"You lied about not being able to talk!" I'm furious, unable to fathom why he would do such a thing. I'm angry with myself, too, for trying to be friends in the first place. For making a fool of myself, apparently, attempting to understand him and make myself understood.

"I *knew* I heard you before, and I heard you just now! And *you* heard me when I talked to you, last night," I say slowly, as it comes back to me. "I remember! I wasn't looking at you when I told you to bathe your father, but you did it anyway."

Finn stares for a moment before he starts to gesture, but I look away, not wanting to play whatever game this is anymore. My feet hurt, and I just want him to leave me alone.

Finn sighs and comes to kneel beside my chair, where I can't help seeing him. I glare. "What?" I ask flatly.

He points to his ear, looking upset, and shakes his head vigorously. Then he points again, at his mouth, and chops his hand sideways hard, obviously saying, "No."

"I *heard* you. This isn't funny." I look away again.

He touches my hand, clenched once again on the arm of the chair, to get my attention. *"Ellin, look at me! I don't know why you'd think I'd lie about that!"*

I jerk my hand away—jerk my whole body away, in fact, and slosh water on the floor—and stare at him. "Because I heard you," I whisper, but I'm no longer angry. Just terrified, because I know, now, that I didn't hear him with my ears.

Finn shakes his head and stands, but his eyes, too, are wide and disbelieving. He points to his mouth and shakes his head 'no,' and I nod.

"I know you didn't," I say wonderingly. Then I grab his wrist. "Say something. Think it, I mean. Something I couldn't guess."

"*You're mad,*" he thinks immediately, then he shrugs. "*All right. Something you couldn't guess? I want eggs for breakfast.*" He gives me a look that clearly says he's humoring me.

"*I am not!*" I think back, grinning like a fool. "*And I want toast, but it'd hurt my throat.*"

Finn gasps and clutches my hand. "*You were right! I thought you were mistaken, but you can do it, too!*"

"Too?" I ask aloud, too startled to form the thought properly.

He nods. "*Erik and I can, but we thought we were the only ones. Because we're twins.*"

"*Then why do you use your fingers?*" I ask, confused. "*Isn't this easier?*"

"*We haven't told anyone about this. And it only works if we're touching. Or close, but then we have to shout, and it's difficult to understand. Besides, it gives us headaches. Talking with our hands is much better.*"

"*Hmm,*" I say, remembering…whatever he was trying to tell me…about my big feet.

Finn smiles. "*I was asking if the pain was greater or less than before.*"

"Oh." I blush, then frown as something occurs to me. "*Wait. How did you know what I was thinking? I didn't say anything.*"

"*Perhaps I'm just…better at this than you,*" he says slowly, sounding surprised. "*More experienced.*"

"Maybe," I agree, and I pull my hand away in order to wipe my nose again, wondering if the Northlanders have any handkerchiefs.

"Maybe what?" asks my father from behind me, causing me to jump. Finn steps back, too, looking vaguely guilty. I don't need him shaking his head or his half-warning, half-pleading look to tell me to keep quiet. Normally I tell my father everything, but somehow I know that this is different.

"It's nothing," I murmur, looking down at my hands. "Can I take my feet out?" I ask, hoping he won't press.

"Are you still in pain?"

"Not as bad. And they're getting wrinkled," I add, turning to look at him as he tends to the king.

"Go on, then," Father replies. "Dry them off, and we'll see."

Finn hands me a soft towel, and I dry my feet, wincing at the movement after sitting so long. My head pounds when I bend over, too, and I straighten with relief only to find both my father and Finn regarding me, wearing identically critical looks. It would be funny if I weren't the object of their scrutiny.

"You're ill," Father says. "It's not 'nothing.'"

There's nothing for it, and I nod, wondering when my neck started to feel stiff and sore. "I know." I notice, too, that my voice sounds scratchy and thick.

My father frowns and places a hand on my forehead. "You have a fever. Come lie down," he says gently, helping me stand. Putting weight on my feet makes them throb again, and even with my father's support, I limp as he leads me to the pile of blankets by the fire. "We'll see about finding you a proper bed later. For now, at least I can watch both you and the king."

"You shouldn't have to watch me," I protest, though I rest my head against the soft blankets gratefully. "I know you're tired."

Father smiles, making the lines by his eyes crinkle. "All the more reason for you to rest, so you can help me when you're well."

"But—"

"Ellin, shh," he says. He puts his hand to my head again, and this time, I feel the familiar tingle of power from his palm, the sensations of warmth and relaxation flowing over my body. I sag deeper into the blankets, too tired, suddenly, to argue anymore. "Rest," Father murmurs. "And heal."

Behind him, I see Finn lift a hand and smile, and there's a feeling of power from him, too—also warm, but strange and unfamiliar—but I'm too far gone to wonder about it. Instead, I just smile. And sleep.

CHAPTER SIX

"SHH! YOU'RE GOING TO wake her up!"

"Me? You're the one who's been making a racket over there."

Someone sighs, and the first voice laughs softly. "We know," he says. Then, "Hey, I think she *is* waking up. She just moved."

I smile, open my eyes, and blink into the bright, clear sunlight that streams in through the window. I find myself looking into three faces looming over me. Erik, with his sharp, pointy face and twinkling blue eyes. Garreth, taller, gawkier, and paler, with eyes like ice and hair that's nearly white. And Finn, taller still, blond, gray-eyed, and freckled. They wear nearly identical guilty expressions.

"Oh, we woke you," Erik says, his grin changing to a bland mask of innocence.

"I think you would've woken the dead," I reply, pleased to find that, though my throat is a little dry, it no longer hurts to speak. I push myself up against the pillows, then stop and frown when I realize that I'm no longer on my pile of blankets in the king's bedroom. I'm in a narrow bed with thick, soft sheets and a heavy blanket, in a small room with a woven rush mat covering the floor and crisp white curtains pulled back from the window. "Where am I?" I ask. "And what are you doing here, anyway?"

"In one of the maid's rooms," Garreth replies. He flushes when I look at him. "Sorry. Master Rowan said it would be good to find you a room, and—"

"No, I don't mind," I reply, wondering why my father would want them to find a room for me, just for one day, when we have our own beds back at the college.

"We were just looking in on you," Erik adds, perching on the foot of the bed. "We were starting to wonder if you were ever going to wake up."

"How long was I asleep?" I can tell from how much better I feel—and how hungry I am—that it must have been awhile.

"A little more than a day. It's midmorning," Garreth says.

"Midmorning *tomorrow*, as far as you're concerned," Erik explains.

Finn comes closer and makes his small-then-big gesture at me again.

"No, my feet aren't bigger," I reply, raising an eyebrow. At Finn's frown, and Erik and Garreth's confused looks, I can't help smiling. "Yes, I feel much better. Thank you."

Erik and Garreth still look puzzled, but Finn, understanding that I was joking, grins back and nods.

"We were hoping you would," Erik says. "Can you get up? Are you hungry?"

"Yes, and yes," I reply, and I smile again at his easy friendliness. There's something about Erik, I'm quickly finding, that makes it difficult not to like him. "But," I add, remembering that I haven't brushed my hair or washed in two days, "first I'd like—"

"Boys!" An older woman balancing a basket of clothes on one large hip stands in the doorway, looking stern. "Did you wake the girl when I told you not to?"

"Not exactly…" Erik begins.

"Not on purpose," Garreth corrects, pink-cheeked. "Sorry, Nan."

The woman rolls her eyes and sets the basket by the door when she comes in. "I thought all of you had better sense. Especially you," she adds, pointing to Finn. Without waiting for an answer, she walks over to the bed and looks down at me critically. "You look better. Feeling all right?"

"Er. Yes."

"Oh, I'm Nan," she explains, seeing my hesitance. "The Keeper."

"Whose keeper?"

"Well, ours," Erik says with a grin and a wink at Nan. "No," he explains, when I only look more confused. "*The* Keeper. She runs the castle. Don't you have Keepers in the Southland?"

"We don't have castles," I reply, thinking of the simple houses our village, and even city, elders live in.

"Well," Nan says, "that doesn't matter. I was coming by to leave you some things, but now you're awake, it'll save me the trouble of sending Bregid up later. Out, all of you," she says to the princes. To my surprise, they go meekly.

"Now," Nan says, after Garreth has closed the door, "I've brought you some clean, fresh clothes. They're just old ones of Bregid's, but I think they'll fit well enough. You might as well just keep them," she adds as she bends to sift through the basket. "She won't want them back, after… Well. Here."

After a Southling has worn them, I finish mentally, reminded yet again of my place here. I force myself to thank her. "Is there somewhere I could wash, and do something about my hair?" I ask.

"Next room," Nan says, pointing. "It's shared, of course, but the girls won't be in, this time of day. And take any brush—we've extras—but keep it for your own, please."

"Of course," I murmur.

"You know," she adds conversationally, hefting the basket onto her hip once more, "there are things that can help, with that hair. I even saw a girl once, like you, who'd used some. Stuff turned her hair a real nice yellow, and you could hardly tell."

I close my eyes and resist the urge to touch my hair protectively. I remember my mother brushing it, when I was small, and I remember her brushing her long, gleaming auburn hair. I'd sooner have mine fall out than drench it with the mixtures of old urine and harsh soap and the foul-smelling herbs they sell, even near the border at home, that promise to turn Southling hair into a more "acceptable" color.

"Thank you," I say at last, instead of clutching my hair and screaming at the unfairness of it all.

Nan gives me a pitying smile. "Think about it," she says kindly.

After she leaves, and after I've washed, shivering, with a cloth and a bowl of water, I try to be grateful for the clothes. They are a common Northlands style: a soft, creamy-white shift with long, tight sleeves, worn under a sleeveless blue smock-style dress that buttons in back. A red checked apron, thick patterned socks, and low boots complete the outfit. Though the shift, socks, and scuffed boots fit, and the blue dress is only a little too long, I feel lost in them. Dirty, even though they're clean and warm, because when I look down, I see a Northlander girl. It might be this that makes me brush my hair hard, until it shines like copper, before I go in search of breakfast.

Only Erik, a cook, and, to my disappointment, Coll are in the kitchen. "Where are the others?" I ask Erik, trying to ignore the way he stares at my hair.

"Master Rowan—I mean, your da—said he'd show Finn how to make something," he says with a shrug. "And Garreth's training with Alaric. Coll's here," he adds unnecessarily.

I refrain from asking how anyone could miss such a massive lump as Coll stands, leaving his mug on the table, and goes out without a word.

"Don't mind Coll," Erik says as he goes to scoop something out of one of the pots by the fire. He comes back to the table with two bowls and slides one to me. "Porridge."

"Mm," I say doubtfully, poking at it with the spoon. One thing I will never understand is why the Northlanders love a bowl of hot, wet, bland grain every morning, and sometimes at night, too. It is steaming, though, and I'm hungry, so I eat. "Don't worry," I say between mouthfuls. "I don't mind him. But is he always like that?"

"Mostly," Erik replies. He swallows. "But he's worse than usual today. One of the mares is due to foal and hasn't yet, and he's been in the stable waiting all night." He blinks at me, brightening. "Would you like to see the horses? Coll's are the best anywhere."

I shudder at the mere thought of going to the stables. "No," I say, more sharply than I intend.

Erik gives me a curious look, but he doesn't press. "Finn told me," he says a moment later. I nearly choke on my porridge.

"Told you what?" I ask, not meeting his eyes.

"About you. Of course." He grins when I look up. "And don't be mad. I could tell he was hiding something, and I pestered him until he told."

"For someone who can't speak, he's bad at keeping secrets," I mutter into my bowl, but I'm not really angry.

Erik laughs. "No, he isn't. But he knows he can trust me. And so can you." When I just look at him, he frowns, seeming older now that he's serious. "You don't, though," he says slowly, and I feel that tingle again, tickling in my head. I flinch and move away, trying clumsily to pull my thoughts away, as well.

"Stop that!" I snap. "I don't know what you're doing, but get out."

At once, I feel the sensation of pressure lift, and the tingling goes away. Still, though, Erik looks at me steadily, as if he can see right into me. "Why are you so angry?"

"I'm not." I drop my spoon with a clatter and shove my bowl away. "And what did you just *do*?"

Erik darts a glance at the cook and swallows a last mouthful of porridge. "Not here," he mutters as he stands.

He leads me through the hall Garreth brought me in and then into the castle's great room, where I stop with a quiet gasp and look around. I had thought this place dark and forbidding, but now, with sunlight streaming through the high windows, I realize I was wrong.

The darkness made all the furniture look black and heavy, but now I see that the large tables are deep red, with carved legs and polished to gleaming. The banners and tapestries are richly dyed, scarlet and deep green and dark blue and gold. And they're beautiful, worked with ornate pictures of wolves and horses and snow cats and other Northlands creatures. A fire crackles orange in the huge hearth, keeping the room warm despite its size, and benches and chairs are gathered in front of it, waiting for a storyteller and listeners to pass the cold nights.

Ahead of me, Erik stops and turns. "What's the matter?"

"This place," I say slowly, still dazzled. "It's beautiful."

He looks around, too, and shrugs. "This? It's not bad."

I shake my head, realizing that this room has to be larger than the main room of Alder's inn, back home in Harnon. "It's so big. How many people live here?"

"At the castle?" Erik's brows pull together in thought. "Well, there's Da, and us. That's six. Nan and her girls make ten, add the stable boys, Jana the cook, Lord Ivan, Lord Erfold the Wise and his wife, Master Thorvald the Physician, Master Fenrik the Smith and his family..." he shrugs. "Twenty-five? Thirty? Alaric would know exactly, and could tell you without blinking an eye," he adds with a grin. "I'm really not sure."

I nod, a little overwhelmed at the idea of living with so many people. "So, do they call you Erik the Uncertain?" I ask, teasing, as we leave the room.

He grins again. "Erik Archer. Actually."

"Because you're as quick to shoot with a bow as you are with your mouth?"

"Not as quick as you," he retorts, half-laughing. "Or as sharp, apparently."

"And the others?"

"Well, they call Alaric 'the Golden.'"

"I know that one."

He nods. "And then Coll Horse Master. Officially, at least," Erik adds with a wicked smile. "Everyone calls him Coll the Fat, though."

"And he doesn't *mind*?" I ask, trying not to giggle.

"'Course not. He is, isn't he?" Erik waves one hand dismissively. "Then there's me; they call Finn—actually Finnlay, by the way—'the Deaf,' of course, and Garreth the Youngest."

"I see Northlander names aren't always flattering."

"No. But they're always true." He turns, starting up a steep and narrow stairway, and talks over his shoulder. "What about you, Ellin Fisher? You don't look like any fisherwoman I've ever seen."

I'm not sure whether he's serious or not, but I can't help smiling. "I'm not. It's just my name."

"I thought Southlings called themselves after where they're from."

"Some do."

"Southlings are strange. Here we are," he adds before I have a chance to reply that Northlanders are even stranger. He leads me into a small, circular room, and I gasp again. The room is cold and very bare, with only a table, a few chairs, and a lantern, but it is not the furniture but the windows that shock me. There are five of them, evenly spaced around the wall, and I can see all of the Northlands from them, it seems.

"This is one of the towers," Erik says as he goes to lean his elbows on a windowsill.

"It's so white," I say stupidly, transfixed by the view. But it's true. Through the frost on the windows, I can see the city sloping away downhill. The pointed roofs of houses and buildings are covered with a thick blanket of snow, as are most of the streets, but I can see where the main roads have been stomped and scraped down to a dirty gray. Everything looks sparkling and still, and this high above the city, I realize for the first time that it is beautiful.

"We had quite a storm," Erik agrees. "Didn't stop snowing 'til sometime last night. And see?" He points. "Most of the streets are still heaped. Almost everyone's stuck inside, today. That's why it's so quiet. Garreth can't even get back to the wall. Well, couldn't even if he was allowed."

"What do you mean?"

He raises both eyebrows. "Oh, the Youngest is in trouble. Letting a Southling in *and* deserting his post?" He clucks his tongue, though he looks amused. "It's no wonder Alaric wanted to throttle him."

"Oh," I say, feeling as if this is my fault and hoping he won't be in too much trouble.

"It's not your fault, and he won't be," Erik replies, and I realize with a start that I can feel him in my head again. "Well, probably not."

"Would you stop *doing* that?" I turn from the window to glare. "What *are* you doing, anyway?"

"Sorry!" Erik holds up his hands, looking contrite. "I keep forgetting that you can feel me in there."

I frown more deeply when I understand what he means. "You do this to everyone?"

"Not everyone. And not all the time."

"Still!" I shake my head. "It seems wrong. And I don't understand," I add. "I thought it was just you and Finn. And he said only when you were touching."

"That's for speaking," Erik explains. He drops into one of the chairs and looks up at me, as if uncertain how to continue. "With this, it's like…listening. But the other person doesn't know you're there."

"It seems wrong," I say again.

"I don't hear the important things! Or anyone's secrets, usually. Just what's on the surface." He shrugs, looking as if he doesn't think it's wrong at all. But then, from what I know of Erik, I doubt he thinks real eavesdropping is wrong, either. "Anyway, Finn can't do it, except to me. He's as deaf to this as everything else."

"And the others?" I ask as I sit across from him at the table, interested in spite of myself.

Erik shakes his head. "We haven't told them, but you know that. Garreth's easy to read. Coll is sometimes. And Alaric…" he shrugs. "It's like there's nothing. Like a wall around his mind."

"And me?"

"I hardly even have to try. You think loudly." He grins.

"Well, try *not* to," I grumble. "I don't like not being alone in here."

"Sorry," he says again, though he doesn't look it. "You can try to do it to me, if that'd make you feel better."

I sigh. "I don't even know how."

"Just reach out and listen."

I doubt I can, but close my eyes and try to concentrate. It's like having an arm coming out of my forehead, and it is strange, but somehow I *know* how to reach out for him. I sense his mind, and I've almost touched it when the door opens. Without stopping to think, I reach out and touch the new mind, instead.

It's Finn. I don't know how I know, but I do. I sense deep quiet—that's not surprising, I think—and feel that strange warmth again, as well as his jolt of surprise, before I feel my mind…met. Like another thought-hand, gently but firmly disengaging itself from mine.

I pull my thoughts back at once and turn to look at Finn. He smiles as he touches my arm. "*I see Erik's been teaching you.*"

"*I'm sorry,*" I say, though it felt oddly wonderful, like stretching muscles I didn't know I had. "*I didn't mean to do that.*"

"*No matter,*" he replies with a small shrug.

"Well?" Erik asks me, moving his fingers for Finn's benefit. "I didn't feel you. Did you hear anything?"

"A little. From Finn."

Erik makes a face. "And here I was, thinking interesting thoughts."

"*That's possible?*" Finn asks with a wry look, flicking his fingers back at Erik. He adds something else, too, I think—at any rate, his hands move after his thought is finished—and when Erik laughs, I can't help wishing I knew how to do that, too.

"Really?" Finn looks at me in surprise, and I smile, though I'm a little embarrassed that he overheard.

"Of course. I'd ask you to teach me, if Father and I were staying longer." I'm startled to find that I'll actually miss him and Erik—and Garreth too, maybe—when my father and I go home. I won't miss the Northlands, though. It doesn't surprise me that just the thought of home makes me ache to be there.

Erik starts to say something, but Finn motions him to silence and gives me an unfathomable look. *"You should go see your da,"* he says at last. *"He was looking for you. And anyway, you shouldn't be up here in the cold."*

Without even trying—maybe without using my new talent at all—I have the sense that there is something he's not telling me. But before I have the chance to touch his mind again, or even ask, he pulls his hand away.

"I guess I'll see you later. Before we leave, anyway," I say to Erik.

Erik nods, though his eyes are on Finn's hands as Finn says something, and he looks troubled. "Right. See you," he murmurs. I'm hardly sure he heard, but the pitying glance he gives me sends a chill of apprehension slithering down my spine.

CHAPTER SEVEN

I LOOK FOR MY FATHER FIRST in the kitchen and great room, thinking he might be at lunch but also needing those familiar places to get my bearings. When I don't find him, I head for the king's room. I look around the hallways with interest until I find Nan, who gives me a sharp look and tells me I'd best stop gawking and get about my business.

"Father?" I say quietly as I open the king's door. Though I doubt King Allard is awake, there's a heaviness in this room—as there is in the houses of people who are very ill—that makes me feel hushed and stifled. Especially now, when I can see cracks of daylight where the heavy scarlet curtains meet, when I think of the cold, bright whiteness outside and compare it to this hot, still, stinking place.

The stench is at least a little better, now that Father has cleared out some of the Northlands medicines and given King Allard clean blankets and pillows. The room still reeks of sickness, and the stink of the Northlanders' brews lingers, but now, over that, there are the fresh, familiar scents of my father's herbs: the pungent sharpness of juniper and the warm, spicy smells of silverleaf and roperoot.

My father is nowhere to be seen, though I peer carefully into the dimness in case he's fallen asleep and didn't hear me come in. But the sleeping, quietly wheezing king is the only one here, besides me. All the chairs are empty.

I step closer to the bed, curious. Despite healing the king, I was so exhausted when I did, and concentrating so deeply on the task, that I can scarcely remember what he looks like. If indeed I even noticed at the time. I have a vague recollection of a big, blond man...but then, that could be most Northlanders.

King Allard looks ill. His skin is worn and grayish and papery, his cheeks sunken, his hair lank and damp on the pillow. He's a large man, built like Alaric, with broad shoulders, big hands, and arms that, though wasted with illness and relaxed in sleep, look strong. Unlike Alaric, though, the king's yellow hair is darkened and threaded with gray, and his beard is scraggly and unkempt. Even asleep, his face looks stern, and I know instinctively that his eyes must be icy blue, like Garreth's, not gray and gentle like Finn's.

I lean closer, searching for any sign of kindness and finding none in the harsh, deep lines by his mouth. So different from my father, whose lines are from smiling and reading and worry, and whose hands are callused from his work, not from the hilt of a sword.

"What sort of man are you," I whisper, "whose laws let things *be* this way?"

The king's eyes snap open without warning, and he shouts and sits bolt upright. I yell and stumble backard, feeling my heart leap into my throat.

"They're coming!" he exclaims, reddened blue eyes wide and staring. "They're coming!"

It takes me a moment to start breathing again, but when I do, I'm trembling so violently I can't speak. I can only press my hand to my heaving chest and gape at him.

"They're coming," the king repeats, seeming oblivious to my presence. "I feel them. They're coming. Soon!"

I shake my head, at a loss. "I—"

Footsteps pound on the floor behind me. "Ellin!" my father exclaims, panting, as he arrives at my side. "What happened?"

"I— the king—" I point unnecessarily at King Allard, who's still clutching the bedclothes and staring like a madman. "I didn't do it!" I add desperately. "I was looking for you, and he just started shouting!"

"The silverleaf," my father murmurs in explanation, touching the king's throat with one hand and his forehead with the other. The king seems not to notice. "And his fever is high again. He's delirious. It's nothing you did."

I nod, still jittery and breathless. "Should I get some cool water?"

"In a moment," Father says over his shoulder. For the first time, I can feel the tingle of power from him when he does a healing on someone else. "Sleep," he says to the king, gently pushing him back onto the mattress.

The king lies back, and his eyes close. They flutter open again an instant later, and he lifts his head and seems to actually see me. "I know you," he whispers hoarsely, sounding confused. Then he sags against the pillow and closes his eyes again, leaving me more shaken than before.

"What's going on?" I ask, once the king is asleep and we've bathed him with cool water to lower his fever. "Finn said you were looking for me."

My father sighs as he sets his bowl on the bedside table, but once he has, he spreads his hands and doesn't look at me. "Ellin, I don't know how to tell you."

I feel a stab of apprehension as he takes a deep breath. His thin shoulders slump, pulling his shirt tight and tense across them. "We won't be leaving soon," he says quietly.

It's like a deep wound. Like when I've cut myself chopping herbs, and I see my finger bleeding, but my brain does not yet understand. I have the sense that this will hurt in a moment. "What?" I breathe, hoping I misheard him.

Father still doesn't meet my eyes. "I spoke with Master Thorvald the Physician, and Master Willem, from the college, and Princes

Alaric and Coll. The consensus is that it would be best for us to stay until King Allard is well."

"But *why*?" I burst out, unable to bear the thought of more days—perhaps weeks or even months—in the Northlands. "We kept him from dying, didn't we? Isn't that *enough*?" To my shame, my voice quavers, and I clamp my lips together angrily.

"Ellin," he says, facing me at last, "when you offered to help the king, you offered to take responsibility for his life. He became your responsibility. And mine, when I came."

"But I don't want him!" I'm nearly shouting, but I don't care. "I just wanted to make him live. And we did. That's all."

"Ellin," Father says again, sounding disapproving, "I know you're underage, and you haven't yet taken the oath of a healer. But that doesn't change the fact that, in offering your gifts and applying them, *you are bound* to see this through." He sighs and takes a step closer, his expression softening. "Besides that, we've both broken the laws several times over. Even if I said we could go, we wouldn't be allowed past the city gates."

I close my eyes and grip the back of a chair. I'm almost surprised the wood doesn't splinter. "We're prisoners, then," I whisper.

"We're guests," Father corrects gently, laying a hand on my shoulder. I shrug it off and give him a nasty look, though I'm angrier with myself than at him.

"If we can't leave, we're not guests," I spit. "We'll never be guests here, where the clothes I wear are so filthy, after I've borrowed them, that they might as well be thrown away. Where I have to feel embarrassed about my damned *hair!*" I dig my fingernails into the wood and hope they scar it.

"Ellin—"

"I never should have healed him in the first place," I interrupt, glaring at the king. "I should have let him die! And I can't believe you've known about this and didn't tell me before now." That's unfair, but I'm past caring.

My father closes his eyes and rubs his forehead, pushing his faded auburn hair back and leaving it disheveled. "I didn't have a chance. I didn't want to wake you, last night, and the Keeper—

Nan—said you were off with the princes when I went to find you this morning."

"I don't care," I mumble, flinching away from his touch again. "I just—this isn't fair." Before he can reply, I hurry out, feeling sick with anger and guilt.

I wander the halls, hands clenched into fists so tight my knuckles hurt, wishing that small pain could distract me from the ache in my heart. I want to go *home*. Home, where my hair is like everyone else's. Where the grass and trees and everything are brown this time of year, but the winter rains are probably just beginning, and the air smells fresh, like decaying leaves and damp earth. Where there's at least the promise of life to come again in spring. Unlike here, where all of the Northlands are just white and frozen and dead.

I have no real destination in mind, no goals except to avoid my father until I'm less angry, and to avoid Finn and Erik, whose pitying glances earlier make sense, now. Avoiding everyone seems like a fine idea, and I'm relieved to find the great room empty when my feet, moving apparently by memory, lead me there. I drop onto one of the benches by the hearth and stare at the fire listlessly, feeling time slow to a crawl now that I'm stuck here for who knows how long.

I hear footsteps behind me but don't turn, hoping whoever it is will go away and leave me alone. Whoever it is comes closer, though, and folds himself down onto the next bench. I don't look up, but out of the corner of my eye, I can see that it is Alaric. I say nothing, because I have nothing to say to this prince who can keep me and my father here as prisoners when we only wanted to help.

"I see your father has told you," he says at last.

I look down at my lap and remain rudely silent, and Alaric sighs.

"Is it so bad, Ellin?"

I'm just miserable enough—and just angry enough—to answer honestly. "Yes," I say, clasping my hands on my thighs. "I hate it here. I want to go *home*." My voice quivers, and I clench my teeth, determined not to cry.

"You will," he replies. "When my father is well."

"And until then?" I look up, though I know my feelings must be written on my face for him to see. "Must I keep my head down in the market for fear of being spat at or shoved or called names? Must I be able to produce papers at a moment's notice, lest I be thrown in jail as a spy or locked out after dark? Or am I even *allowed* to go out," I add, as this occurs to me, "or am I to be kept in this castle like a dog on a leash?"

"I did not make the laws," Alaric says, and something flashes deep in his eyes that frightens me. Suddenly I remember that, next to the king, Prince Alaric the Golden is the most powerful man in the Northlands. And I have just dared to criticize his kingdom. Strangely, I still don't care.

"But do you believe in them?" I ask softly, and I find, with a funny jump of my heart, that I *do* care how he answers. "Do you think I'm less than you, not because I'm not a princess, but because my hair is red?"

Alaric looks at me levelly, deep blue eyes unreadable. "I believe that my father believes in the laws," he says at last.

I close my eyes and nod, adding this new hurt to the others blooming like fresh bruises in my chest. Garreth's words from the gatehouse come back to me, and I whisper them now. "I saved his life, and he hates me. He hates my people."

"Ellin…" Alaric inhales audibly and spreads his hands. "You would do well to remember that sometimes hatred stems from something else. Ignorance, or fear, or jealousy, or a dozen other things. It isn't always rational."

"That doesn't change anything."

"Perhaps not," he says, standing. A small smile tugs at his lips as he looks down at me. "But don't be too quick to dismiss all Northlanders as evil. We aren't, any more than all Southlings are good."

I roll my eyes. "You sound like my father."

Alaric shrugs, though his smile lingers. "He's a wise man."

"I know."

He starts to leave, but his boots pause before he reaches the doorway. "By the way," Alaric says, "I think your hair is lovely."

Startled by this, I reach up almost unconsciously and touch my hair. My mouth is still slack and wordless when I hear him go out.

CHAPTER EIGHT

I PASS THE NEXT SEVERAL HOURS in sulking silence, keeping to myself in the great room until Nan shoos me out. After that, I fetch a napkin full of dried fruit from the cook, a thin woman who seems kind enough, and wander the castle aimlessly as I eat. It's boring, though, since I know better than to snoop in many rooms. I do find the library, which seems safe enough, but I've barely picked up a book when I realize I'm too restless to sit and read.

So, I fetch my coat. Though I almost expect to be stopped at the door, I find that either no one notices my departure, or no one cares. Once outside, I inhale deeply, and the crisp air sears the inside of my nose and clears my head. I squint for a moment, then look around in wonder, dazzled by the sparkling blanket of snow. I've never seen it this deep before, and this snow is different from that down in the middle of the city. It's cleaner, for one thing, but also less trampled-looking.

It isn't deep here in the yard, of course. There is a big scraped area by the door with paths branching out down to the out-buildings surrounding the castle, but around this, the snow must be nearly to my knees. I decide immediately not to venture out into the unscraped snow to explore. For one thing, I'm not certain my feet, even in thick socks and boots, could handle it. Even here, where the snow doesn't reach my ankles, my toes already ache from the cold. Also, I don't dare get my borrowed dress wet. I'm not sure my own clothes are clean yet, and I've a feeling neither Nan nor the maid Bregid would appreciate having to find me another change of clothing.

The out-buildings it is, then, I decide with a nod, and I start down the nearest path.

"Ellin!" someone calls behind me, before I've gone far. To my horror, I hear the jingle of tack and pounding hoofbeats. I gasp and turn to see Garreth approaching up another path, astride one of the enormous Northlands horses. He waves when he sees me looking and kicks the beast to go faster.

My eyes dart from side to side, seeking an escape, but the nearest fence is too far to reach in time, as is the nearest tree. I can only watch, breathing shallowly, as the horse kicks up snow around its white-furred legs, turns onto my path, and bears down on me. My calves hit something cold and almost solid, and I realize I've backed up against the snowbank on side of the path. The ground seems to shake beneath the weight of those hooves, and I try not to scream.

"Whoa," Garreth says, right above me. The pounding stops, the beast huffs and snorts, and I shiver. They are just behind me, the horse staring at me with one giant, rolling eye, Garreth regarding me curiously. "What are you doing out here?" he asks.

"Walking," I squeak, and I take a sideways step down the path, away from the horse.

"To the stable? Why?"

"The—oh." I swallow, suddenly grateful he came and warned me. Well, except that his arrival has put me between one horse, up close, and probably a lot of others. I shudder at the thought, and Garreth sees it.

"Come on, then," he says, swinging his far leg over the beast's broad gray back and sliding down the side. It seems even bigger, now that I can see Garreth himself is only barely as tall as the horse's shoulder. I eye the reins in his hand warily. "I'll walk with you."

"I—" I try to think of a reason besides the truth not to go.

"Or," he interrupts, grinning, "you can ride Blizzard! I'd wager you haven't ridden a Northlands horse before, and anyway, even if you *have*, you haven't ridden one of ours."

"No!" I exclaim. I move another step back, dismayed when Garreth follows. "And please," I add, a little desperately, "get that thing away from me."

"Oh, don't worry, Blizzard's gelded, and about as old as you are. Gentle as a puppy, too," Garreth adds as he pats the horse's thick neck. "Aren't you?"

"I don't care," I reply, crossing my arms protectively in front of my chest. Not that my arms will offer any actual protection, should Blizzard decide to trample me.

"You're afraid!" Garreth bursts out, his eyes widening as he looks at my face. "Of a horse?" He shakes his head in confusion. "Why?"

"I don't want to talk about it."

"Ellin," he says, and I'm embarrassed by the condescension in his tone and on his features. "Don't be ridiculous. He's gentle. I promise he won't hurt you."

"No." I shake my head, decide there's nothing for it, and step into the snow bank in order to give Blizzard a very wide berth. "I'm not afraid. I just don't want to," I say over my shoulder, wading through the snow. Once I'm far enough, I jump back onto the path, stumble, then start to walk as fast as my dignity will allow.

"Ellin!" he calls after me, but I pretend not to hear and run the rest of the way to the castle. I could swear I hear hoofbeats thundering behind me, but when I turn from the safety of the doorway and look, I only see Garreth leading Blizzard to the stable, shaking his head.

Once I'm inside and back in my room, I close the door and sag against it. Then I close my eyes and try to slow my rapid, panicked breathing. "It was only a horse," I say to myself sternly. "Just a *tame, gentle* horse."

The words, however, don't do much good. The memories still flash through my mind, as clear as if they happened yesterday. My mother's hair flowing behind her like a banner as she tilted her face up to the sun. Her hand lifting from the mare's mane to wave, and the way she smiled as I came out of the house to see her. The way the tall summer grass smelled, all hot and yellow in the sunshine; it tickled my bare arms and shoulders as I pushed through it.

I open my eyes, but the pictures don't stop.

I remember the way her face looked, frozen and disbelieving, when the horse lurched into that hole; the way the bone in the mare's foreleg sounded as it snapped. I ran forward when it happened, was running before I even understood, but it was too late. I saw her hair fan out again as she flew over the mare's head. The grass cast shadows, making the pool of auburn look like blood on the ground. And I remember knowing that she wasn't asleep, but I was still trying to wake her up, was wondering why the mare's screaming *wasn't* waking her up, when my father came.

"Ellin?" I start and leap away from the door when I hear my father's voice and hope he hasn't been knocking long.

"Come in," I call, voice thick.

"Good, I've found you," he says as he pushes the door open. "I wanted to see if you were all—goodness!" he exclaims, catching sight of me. "What's the matter? Are you still upset about staying?"

"I…well, yes." Of course I am. "But I'm fine," I add, not wanting to upset him by telling him that my fear of horses is not, apparently, conquered as much as we thought. At least, not when the horse is up close. I force a smile instead. "Really."

Father nods, obviously relieved. "I'm glad. Contrary to what you might think, I don't *want* you to be miserable."

"I know." With a sigh, I go to him, lay my head on his shoulder, and breathe in his familiar, comforting scent of herbs and medicines. "I'm sorry," I add, though I know he already knows.

He puts his arm around me and gives me a gentle squeeze. "I am, too," he says quietly. "I do know you hate it here. And I'd take you home this moment if I could."

I nod, sighing again.

"But," Father adds predictably, "I would ask you to try and make the best of it. There's much to learn here, and I'm sure you'll find that the Northlands aren't all bad."

I smile, just barely stopping myself from saying that he sounds like Alaric. And, to my surprise as much as his, I nod as I think of some of the princes. One thing I decided in my wanderings earlier was that, if nothing else, I can't be angry about having a little more time to get to know them.

Thinking of Alaric has reminded me of something else, and I step back in order to look at my father's face. "Father?" I ask. "Do you know *why* they hate us here?"

He tilts his head and gives me a surprised, rather approving look. "Now, that's an interesting question. Why do you ask?"

"I just wondered," I reply, strangely reluctant to tell him that Alaric put the idea in my head. But now that I've thought about it, I can't help thinking that 'because we're Southlings' can't be the real reason, and I say so. "There had to be *something* that started it," I add. "Wasn't there? I mean, you don't just wake up one day and decide you hate something."

"Well…" Father steps away and clasps his hands behind his back. "I'm not sure if anyone alive knows the precise reason," he says slowly. "And at the time, it did seem as if the old king, King Derrick, woke up one morning and decided he hated the Southland. Almost overnight, the Southlings living here were unwelcome. Asked to return home, even if they had been born here in the Northlands. Those who didn't go willingly were forced. And those who dared practice healing under the new laws were arrested or executed."

"I know that," I reply, impatient. "And you were just a boy, and you remember when the Northlanders left the college at home. I know. But *why*? What happened?"

Father lifts one hand in a small, helpless gesture. "Ellin, I don't know. It just happened."

"But why did we let it?" I shake my head. It doesn't make sense. "Why didn't the Southlings just say no?"

"And risk starting a war?" Father frowns. "You know better than that."

"*They* would," I say, meaning the Northlanders. "They wouldn't let themselves be treated like that."

"They aren't like us."

"But *why*?" I roll my eyes and come very close to stomping my foot in exasperation. "It's so stupid!"

"Ellin! You don't understand," Father says, gripping both my arms and giving me a look that frightens me. "You don't understand. Yet." There's something in his voice that sends ice down my back.

"What? What is it?"

He sighs and lets go, though he doesn't drop his gaze. "Ellin," Father says slowly, then nods as if he's just decided something. "Perhaps it's fair for you to know, now, early, given the circumstances. But you must *promise*," he adds, "to keep this knowledge to yourself, until you are of age. Do you swear it?"

"I swear," I whisper, feeling the deathly seriousness of this moment. The room suddenly seems smaller than before. Colder, too. "What is it?"

"You know that every Southling healer must take the oaths when they come of age," Father says. "And it is then that the full power of healing is wakened in them. But what you don't know is that *every* Southling must take an oath when they turn eighteen."

"Really?" I look at him curiously. "Why?"

Father sighs and looks at his hands. "There is…another power," he says quietly. "A darker, terrible power. All Southlings once had the potential for it in them, and some still might. The oath we swear is to never let it be awakened within us. And if by some chance it is, never to use it. Never to speak of it, and to hope always that someday it will leave our people for good. Because of this power—this curse—and the destruction it could bring, we swear oaths of peace," he says. "Never to lift arms, lest the temptation to use this power become irresistible."

I shiver violently and sink down on the edge of the bed as my knees threaten to give out. "Do many people have it?"

"Not any more." There's a strange note in his voice, and I find that I don't need to ask *why*. I remember the time, back home, when old Padrus Miller's house burnt to the ground one night. I didn't understand at the time why no one tried to stop it. Why no one cared how it had happened or wondered if he was all right.

"And that's why they hate us," I murmur. "The Northlanders, I mean. Because of this power. They know."

"No." Father shakes his head. "They knew before. It is no secret, except to Southling children to prevent them *trying* to use it. No, it is something else," he says, frowning slightly. "But I don't know what."

He shrugs it off and shakes his head again, as if to clear it. "Regardless, now do you understand why the Southland did not protest?"

"We're oath-bound to peace," I say with a nod, feeling awful. Until now, I was proud to be a Southling. Proud of my people, known for their skills at healing and music and creating beautiful, useful things instead of making war. Now, though, I'm chilled because I know why we're this way. "And it's because we're dangerous."

"Could possibly be dangerous," my father corrects with a small smile. "But we aren't. We choose not to be."

"I see," I whisper, past the tightness in my throat. I look up at him and force my face to remain bland. "Father?" I ask as he turns to go. "The terrible power. What is it?"

"Ah," he replies, shaking his head, one hand on the doorknob. "Now that, you don't need to know until it's time."

"All right."

And in truth, I don't need him to tell me. I already know what it must be. There's no other explanation for it.

But what I don't know is how it is possible for Finn and Erik to have this dark, terrible Southling power, too.

CHAPTER NINE

I BRUSH MY HAIR AGAIN before going to dinner and smile a little as Alaric's compliment comes back to me. It's ridiculous, I tell myself. I *know* my hair is lovely. Wasted on such a plain girl, nasty Kethie Brewer back home said, once, but I suppose she was right. It's strange that a remark Alaric has likely already forgotten should help me hold my shoulders straight and my head high as I walk into the great room.

I wither immediately when I see how many Northlanders have gathered to eat. The tables are full of blond men and blonde women, the room full of the smells of food and the sound of harsh, clipped Northlander voices. I feel as out of place as I must look, and I wonder if it's not too late to hurry back to my room. My body is tense, poised to turn and do just that, when someone grabs my arm and pulls me in.

"There you are, witch-girl," Erik says companionably. "We've been looking for you all afternoon."

Though I'm relieved to have a friend here, I can't help eyeing the crowded room nervously. "There are a lot of people here," I murmur. It seems unnecessary to add that many of them are staring at the Southling trash being escorted by one of their princes.

"'Course there are. It's dinner." Erik squeezes my arm as he leads me around one of the tables. *"But you're as welcome here as any of them,"* he adds mentally.

I manage a small smile, but inwardly, I flinch at his use of the power. Erik gives me a curious look when I don't reply, though he says nothing until we've arrived at the head of the largest table, where Alaric, Finn, and Garreth are already seated. "Sit here," he says, pulling out the chair at Alaric's left.

"You can't be serious," I hiss, staring at him. "Here, with Northlands royalty? What will people think?"

"That you're our respected guest," Alaric says with a smile, surprising me. He gestures at the chair, nodding. "Please."

There's nothing for it, and I slide into the chair awkwardly. I hear a ripple of whispers and surprised exclamations spread through the room, and my cheeks grow hot. I'm suddenly very conscious of my secondhand, too-large maid's dress.

"Your da's over there with Master Thorvald," Erik says as he sits in the empty chair next to Garreth, who is on Alaric's right. "They seem to have made friends; did you know?"

"No," I murmur. I'm glad my father has made a friend, but I wish he were here, instead of sitting at a nearby table conversing with a short, bald man I assume is Master Thorvald the Physician. I look down at my empty plate, unsure what I should do. I've eaten at a few of the inns and taverns in the city, of course, and at the college, but this is a castle.

The customs seem to be the same here as they are at the college, though. For that matter, the same as they are for informal meals at home, with large plates and bowls of food from which everyone is supposed to serve their own portions. I reach for the spoon in the bowl nearest me and serve myself some of the creamy fish and root vegetable mixture, and I'm relieved when no one tells me I've done something wrong.

"Water, Ellin, or wine?" Alaric asks, his hand poised over the finely-worked carafes.

"Water, please." I blush again when Alaric pours for me. He leans closer with a small smile as he sets the carafe down, obviously sensing my discomfort.

"It's a political statement," he explains quietly. "Your sitting here lets everyone know that you are both welcome and under our protection."

"It was kind of you to allow it," I reply.

Erik pauses with his fork halfway to his mouth. "Allow, nothing," he says, sounding amused. "It was his idea."

"Oh." I study my food to avoid looking at any of them, but Alaric especially. I don't know why his kindness makes me so uncomfortable. Or so strangely, almost pleasantly, nervous. I frown slightly, irritated with myself, and begin to eat.

I've started to relax a little, half-listening to Garreth and Alaric talking about something Garreth did with a sword, when I become aware of a large, looming presence behind me. I swallow and turn to find Coll glaring down at me.

"You're in my seat," he rumbles.

My cheeks are on fire yet again, but this time, there's nothing pleasant about it. "I—" I bite my lip as I start to stand. "I'm sorry. I'll move."

"You won't," Alaric says, putting his hand on my arm to restrain me. His palm is warm through the fabric of my sleeve, his fingers gentle, and I exhale slowly—with relief or regret, I can't be sure—when he lets go. "Coll isn't serious."

Coll looks serious, and annoyed, but he shrugs one shoulder and settles himself two chairs down, next to Finn.

"How's Snowflower?" Garreth asks as he slides the wine toward Coll. I notice now that, despite Coll's clean hands and shirt, he smells strongly of horse.

Coll shrugs again. "The same. Sven's with her."

Alaric sighs. "Coll..."

"Damn it, man, I know," Coll snaps. He sets the carafe down hard before he shoves thick fingers through his hair.

Next to me, Finn touches my hand. "*His favorite mare,*" he explains. "*Coll's had her since he was a boy, and this was to be her last foal. He's afraid of losing them both.*"

I give him a curt nod and pull away, pretending not to notice his surprised, hurt expression.

"Maybe Ellin could do something," Erik says suddenly, his eyes widening with inspiration. "After all, she helped Da."

Before I can reply, Coll snorts. "As if I'd let a—" he breaks off and clears his throat at Alaric's warning look. "No," he mutters, stabbing a piece of carrot with his fork.

"Besides, Ellin's afraid of horses," Garreth says, with that mild, annoying condescension again. "You should've seen her run from Blizzard."

Erik snickers. "As if you'd need to *run* from Blizzard. That old brute is slow as sap running."

"Hey!" Garreth makes a face. "He might not be as fast as Crocus, but he's a good boy. Loyal, too."

Unlike some friends, I think. I wish I could crawl under the table—or smack Garreth for telling—as Erik, Finn, and Alaric regard me with curiosity. From Coll, I certainly don't need my new ability to sense abject contempt.

Finn reaches for my arm beneath the table to speak with me, and again, I shy from his touch. He gives me a confused look and raises his eyebrows, clearly asking what's the matter, but I pointedly turn away. I feel terrible for being so rude, but I know now is neither the time nor the place to explain why I can't use my new ability to talk with him anymore.

"Really, Ellin, you're afraid of *horses*?" Erik asks, trying unsuccessfully to hide a smile. And I'm sure it must seem strange and even funny here, where the huge, furry-hooved Northlands beasts are so prized. "Why?"

"I'm not afraid of them," I mutter into my cup. "I just don't *like* them."

"Well," Alaric says with a smile, "we'll just have to find you a good one to ride, then, and change your mind."

I force myself to smile back. Though I know Alaric means well, by all of his kindness, I can't help wishing that I could be on the way home with Father right now. That we'd never come to the Northlands at all. Then I wouldn't have a king for an unwanted patient, a dark power I don't want, either, and I wouldn't have to think about politics, or the color of my hair, or Northlander princes, or horses. Especially horses.

I sigh and concentrate on getting through dinner. I can't enjoy my food, though, because it comes to me, again and again, that the next few days—or weeks, or months—will be the longest of my life.

It seems my head has just hit the pillow when my eyes snap open. The urgent knocking on my door doesn't stop, and I groan as I sit up. "What?" I call crossly, squinting at the candlelight I can see flickering under the crack of the door.

"Ellin!" a hushed voice calls. "It's me, Garreth. May I come in?"

"Seeing as you've already woken me up, you might as well," I grumble as I swing my legs over the side of the bed. "What?" I ask again, when he comes in.

"It's Coll's horse. Snowflower," Garreth says, and I notice now that he looks filthy. I can smell him, too, even across the room. "I know what I said earlier, and what Coll said, but will you come?"

I stare, then scrub my cheeks with my hands, trying to clear my head. "What do you want me to do? And what time is it?"

"Late," he says, with a careless shrug. "Past midnight, at least."

I groan. "And you want me to go out into the cold and heal a horse."

"Precisely. Please?" he adds. The courtesy is obviously an after-thought, but he asks so earnestly that I almost can't be annoyed.

"Garreth, I hate horses," I say, though I stand and fumble in the semi-darkness for my dress and boots anyway. "I'm not a real healer, I don't know much about healing animals, and I know nothing at all about horses giving birth. And Coll doesn't want me. Turn around," I add waspishly. Even though I'm just putting the smock-dress on over my borrowed nightshift, it still seems improper for him to watch.

"Sorry. I keep forgetting you're a girl," Garreth mumbles, his back politely turned.

"Now you insult me?" I ask incredulously. I can't help adding, "And why? Because I'm a Southling?"

"I don't know. Perhaps." His thin shoulders hunch in another shrug, and I try not to be stung. "Sorry," he says again, when I don't reply. "It's late, and I'm tired. I probably don't mean half of what I say."

I think he does, but I shrug as I sit on the bed and bend to lace up my boots. "No matter. And you can turn around now."

He smiles as he watches me. "I'm glad you're coming."

I'm not sure I really have a choice, but I nod. "Why didn't you ask my father?" I ask, pulling on my shawl on the way to the door.

"I didn't want to wake him," Garreth admits.

"Oh, but waking *me* is all right." From his silence, I can tell that's precisely what he thought. I sigh, trying to resign myself to going out in the cold instead of back to my warm bed.

This late, so long after the watery sun has set, the cold is far worse than I'd expected. It's bitter outside, even worse than in the storm, though without the wind. My feet start to ache the moment I step out into the snow. It's beautiful, though. Still and quiet, with the moon turning the snow pale blue and sparkling. It's hard to believe a scene so lovely can make me feel so awful, and I shiver and dig my hands into my pockets. When I breathe, my nostrils freeze. I wish I was back inside, looking at this view from my window.

"All right?" Garreth asks over his shoulder, voice hushed.

"Hoping the stable is warm," I say honestly, as I hurry to catch up. "How do you *stand* this?"

He chuckles quietly. "We're a tough breed. Did you know that there are some men who like to sit in a hot bath, or a steam hut, and then go throw themselves out into the snow?"

I gasp at the thought. "You're joking."

"No," he says smugly. "It's something of a tradition. Supposed to be invigorating."

"I suppose jumping off a cliff might be invigorating, too, but it's still stupid," I mutter. "What is *wrong* with you Northlanders?"

Garreth snorts but doesn't reply as he leads me past the curve in the path. I can see light coming from the stable doors, now, and just the thought of warmth sends gooseflesh of anticipation prickling over my skin. I stare in disbelief when we arrive at the door and I have a glimpse of Coll's broad, pale, shirtless shoulders as he goes into one of the stalls. How could anyone be half-naked in *this?*

The stable is warmer than being outside, though, and it smells of hay and sweet grain and straw, mixed with the less pleasant smells of horses, horse droppings, and sweat. Garreth leads me further in, and I inhale sharply when I have a better look inside the big stall.

The huge white mare, Snowflower, lies flat on her side, legs extended stiffly. Her fur is steaming and dark with sweat, and what I can see of her backside and hind legs looks soaked, too.

Coll has gone to kneel up by her head, one thick hand buried in her mane, leaning close to her ear. He seems unaware of us, and I step closer curiously, surprised at the difference in him. Then Garreth clears his throat, and Coll turns his head. For an instant, his face looks gentle before he sees us. Then his customary grim expression descends as he lumbers to his feet.

"What?" Coll growls, folding dirty arms across his big, hairy stomach. He darts a glance at Snowflower before coming closer and lowering his voice. "I said you weren't needed, witch-girl. Or wanted." Then he glares at Garreth, forestalling him before he has a chance to speak. "And I told you not to bring her."

"Coll, you have to do *something*," Garreth says in an emphatic whisper, reminding me of what he said when I healed the king. I can hardly believe it was only days ago.

"And you think I don't know that?" Coll asks, his dark gold brows lowering into one long line. "There's nothing to be done. I was just..." His shoulders slump, and he lifts one hand helplessly. As he does, something shiny glints in his fist, catching the light. A knife.

"Coll!" Garreth exclaims, just as I gasp.

"Why d'you think I sent you back, boyo?" Coll asks quietly, not sounding angry, for a change, but miserable. "The foal's big, and it's got a leg back, but I can't get her up to shift it to the proper position. It's most likely dead already. And Snow can't take much more of this."

"And bringing it out her side?" I ask hesitantly. Even more than I did when healing the king, I feel unwanted and far out of my depth. "What about that?"

Coll gives me a surprised glance before he shakes his head and gestures at Snowflower's rump. "It's just inside, too far along to be delivered that way," he says. "Snow's had no problems birthing before, and this time...I thought she was having a bit of trouble, is all. But the truth is, she's too old for this, and she stopped her contractions almost as soon as they started. The weight of the foal has numbed her hind legs, so I can't get her to her feet to reposition the little one and deliver it myself. Either of these problems would be bad, but together..." He sighs. "There's nothing for it, girl. It's stuck tight, and it's killing her."

I know enough about the birthing process to know that he's right, so I press my lips together and nod.

"Coll," Garreth says again, softly, and I can hear him swallow as he puts a hand on his brother's shoulder. "I'll stay."

Coll looks as if he's going to protest, but then he closes his eyes briefly and shrugs his acceptance. "You go on back," he says to me, and I nod again in reply. Even though I'm used to seeing blood, and even though she's only a horse, I know I can't bear to watch. Besides, somehow I know that this is a private thing. I have no business here.

I look at Snowflower one more time before I go. Lying down like this, damp and shaking with exhaustion, she doesn't look as frightening as most horses. She seems utterly defeated, and I have to swallow hard as I leave, trying to banish a sudden, chillingly clear picture of her with her throat cut, the floor drenched and shiny with her blood.

I try, too, not to imagine how this must seem to her. My father has urged me to be empathetic, to try and understand what sick and hurt people are feeling, but now I don't *want* to. It's all too easy to imagine loving someone, and trusting them, then suddenly being in pain and having them hurt you more. So much worse for an animal, who wouldn't even understand why.

It must be awful for Coll, too, I realize. Having to do the right, merciful thing. I don't know if I could.

I've almost reached the bend in the path when I remember something I heard Father talking about years ago, with Mistress Saddler from the college in Whiteriver, when I was in bed and not supposed to hear. It gave me nightmares at the time, but now I understand. With a shout, I turn, awkward on my cold, heavy feet, and race back down the path as fast as I can.

I fall once, unused to running in stiff Northlands boots, but I scarcely feel the bite of snow on my hands and the sharp air in my lungs as I scramble to my feet again and hurry on.

"Wait!" I yell breathlessly as I burst, stumbling, into the barn. "There might be another way!"

CHAPTER TEN

"T̲H̲A̲T̲'S̲ D̲I̲S̲G̲U̲S̲T̲I̲N̲G̲," Garreth says, his face twisting in a grimace when I've explained my plan. "You Southlings really *do* that?"

"Sometimes. In situations like this, where the babe is dead already and killing its mother," I reply uncertainly. "I think."

Coll huffs softly in derision. "You think. But you've never done it, and you don't know if it can be done on a mare."

I reach up to twist my hair anxiously. "Right. But I *do* think I could," I add. "It couldn't hurt to try, anyway, not when you were going to—"

"I know," Coll interrupts. "Be still and let me think." He takes a few steps, pacing slowly, heavy boots scuffing on the floor. Then he turns and looks at me, his expression unreadable behind his short beard. "Would it hurt her, having it…cut out…like that?"

"I could make it so it won't, much. I think," I add, unsure of my abilities to practice true healing again, especially on an animal. "If you'll allow me to."

"More Southling witchcraft?" Garreth asks with a twist of his mouth. I nod. "I can't believe you're really going to cut it into pieces," he continues, looking a little green even in the dim light in the stable. "That's—"

"I know it's disgusting," I snap, annoyed that he keeps going on about it. "And I know it seems cruel. But the foal is already dead, and, from what I've heard, this is the only way to get it out so Snowflower can live. Don't you see?"

"She's right," Coll says, surprising me. "Now, boyo, you go on back," he adds as he claps a stained hand on Garreth's shoulder. "I don't want you to see."

"I'm not a child," Garreth mutters. "And what about Ellin? She *is* one, nearly."

I bristle, but Coll lifts his other hand before I can say anything. "If the witch-girl says she can do it, let her do it."

"Besides," I say, still irritated, "this *child* was setting bones when you were out playing with a stick for a sword and a sawhorse for your pony."

Coll snorts. "Girl, he had a real—if tiny—sword and a fine little pony."

"Of course," I murmur. Of course Prince Garreth wouldn't have played like I've seen other Northlander boys do.

Garreth rubs his hand over his face, and I can see the pinkness of his cheeks. "Enough of this. I'm going to bed," he mutters. I almost ask him to stay, still uncomfortable at the idea of being left alone with Coll and the horses. The only thing that stops me is that, in truth, I don't want Garreth to see what I'm going to do. Particularly not if I fail.

"Well?" Coll asks, and I realize with a start that I've been staring after Garreth. "What do you need, girl?"

"Hot water, soap, and clean towels or rags. And sharp wire," I add with a grimace.

"With an edge? I don't think we have that."

"A knife, then. With a sawing blade." I swallow, trying not to think about what I'm going to do. I already feel like I might be sick, and the picture of the white mare covered with blood comes back all too clearly. I close my eyes and try not to feel my stomach churning. "And I'll need you to help with—with the bones."

"Go on, then," he replies, his mouth twisting. "The soap and water and towels are there." He nods. "I'll go fetch the knife, and see about some wire."

After I've pushed up my sleeves, cleaned my hands, and soaped my arm to the elbow, it hits me like a slap to the face. I have to *touch* a *horse*. Where I have to touch her doesn't matter—I'd be a poor healer if such things embarrassed or disgusted me—but the fact remains that she is a horse. A very large horse.

"A large horse who's going to die if I don't do this," I whisper aloud as I force my feet to move toward her, irritated with myself for being such a coward. One of Snowflower's ears twitches, and I stop, swallowing hard again. "It's all right," I say softly. "I won't hurt you. And I'll trust that you won't hurt me."

Her big, dark eye rolls, watching me come closer. When I've knelt beside her on the floor, I steel myself and set my dry hand on her shoulder. To my surprise, the mare's coat is warm and soft as a cat's. Softer than I remember horses being. Gathering my courage, I stroke her gently as I move back, watching her huge, heavy-looking back hooves warily. I know Coll said she can't move them, but still. "Good girl," I whisper to her, pleased that my voice doesn't shake much. "Good, brave girl."

Snowflower doesn't seem to notice when I place my hand on her rump, and I sit for a moment, just breathing, as I contemplate what I have to do. I've never done it before. And though I've seen cats, dogs, pigs, sheep, and shaggy Southling cows give birth—and even watched my father deliver calves and sheep—this is different. For one thing, it's *my* hand that has to go…in there…this time.

"All right there, girl?" Coll asks quietly behind me, causing me to jump and tighten my fingers against Snowflower's rump, though she still doesn't flinch.

"Fine," I mutter. The last thing I want is to admit to him that I've never done this, so, with another deep breath, I screw up my face and slowly place my soaped hand where it needs to be.

"Oh," I murmur, feeling a little breathless. It isn't comfortable, by any means, but…it's strange. And oddly wonderful. I can *feel* the foal. There's a tiny hoof just inside, attached to a skinny, straight leg. On the other side is a big, knobby bump that must be the knee of the leg that's bent under, causing part of the problem. And between them, my fingers slide over a sloping forehead, then down along a straight expanse of nose. I feel the curve of a nostril, and then—

"Oh!" I gasp and look up. "Oh, Coll. Its lips moved. It tried to suckle my fingers," I whisper, past the sudden tightness in my throat.

His eyes widen. "I thought it was dead."

"So did I. I can't do this." I shake my head as I begin to withdraw my hand. "I'm sorry. I can't."

One big shoulder shrugs at me. "Fine. Nor can I. I'll just—" he grimaces and gestures at Snowflower's throat again.

"But they're both alive!" I protest, horrified. "We can't do that!"

"I'm not asking *you* to do—"

"No," I say firmly, shaking my head again and wishing I'd thought to tie my hair back. "There has to be a way to birth it alive. Coll, there *has* to."

"There isn't," he says, his face bleak as he reaches up to rub the back of his neck. "Not if we can't get her on her feet. Trust me. I wish there were." I close my eyes, heartsick, but then he speaks again. "Unless there's some Southling witchcraft that would help?" he asks, so softly I almost don't hear him. I wince at the hope in his voice.

"I don't know," I say, sounding as helpless as I feel. "This is so far beyond my skills as a healer..." Coll's face falls, and I sigh, knowing how much this horse means to him. "But...I could try?"

He nods. "Do it. If you would."

"Be quiet, then," I murmur, closing my eyes as I start to concentrate. I breathe deeply through my nose, stilling myself. I concentrate on the warmth of Snowflower's coat beneath my palm, spread flat on her hip, and reach for my healing power.

I stop trying to ignore the smells and instead embrace them: the sharpness of blood and the musk of her sweat and the cloying sweetness of birth fluids. They are part of her, part of this process.

In order to become part of it myself, I know I have to accept all of it. I feel the healer's sense again, and I understand, now, how the foal is pressing inside Snowflower's body just hard enough in the wrong spot to make her back legs limp and useless. I understand how her body was just too tired to keep trying to expel the foal, when the first few contractions only made it more tightly stuck. With my healer's sense, I can almost *see* how the foal looks inside of her, can see how its bent leg makes it too large to fit.

I fully understand the problem, now, but I don't know how to fix it. With my healing power, I can dull pain…but Snowflower, with her hindquarters numb, can barely feel the foal as it is. I can slow the flow of blood, a little, but the mare isn't bleeding abnormally. I know how to brew medicines and use herbs to soothe coughs and upset stomachs, but I don't have the slightest idea how to use healing to make Snowflower stand up.

With a defeated, frustrated sigh, I start to let go of my healing power and open my mouth to tell Coll that I can't do this, after all. And then, at the edge of my awareness as the power drains away from me, something tickles. I gasp sharply when I realize what it is.

It's Snowflower, I realize, awestruck. I can sense her mind with my other power. I can't hear or understand her, but I feel her thoughts buzzing, like the distant drone of bees. And I know, suddenly, that I *can* do this, after all.

I squeeze my eyes shut tighter and home in on her mind with my own. I remember the way Finn's mind felt the first time I touched it, like a hand gently pulling itself away, and now I do the opposite and hold on—but gently—and don't let go. With our minds meshed like this, I command her to rise. I don't know how, but I think the idea at her with all my might. And though it should be impossible, her flank shivers under my palms.

I think at her harder, more desperately, in wordless, unformed ideas. I lose track of time. Of myself, almost. I forget where I am, what I'm doing. There is only one idea. Stand. And then, finally, Snowflower shudders from ears to wrapped-up tail, rolls up onto her chest, and climbs unsteadily, swaying, to her feet. I don't know how I know when to move, but somehow I do, and I rise with her and keep my hand pressed against her hip.

In a daze, I hear Coll swear. Beside me, he says something about his hands being too big, but I'm several steps ahead of him, poised and ready. I've never done this before, and I feel as though I'm being stretched in a dozen directions at once, but I find that I don't need his gruff, murmured instructions to know just what slippery bits to pull, and which ones to press back, until the foal slides into place. Sagging against Snowflower's warm flank, I motion with a filthy hand for Coll. Speech comes slowly, as though my tongue is full and too large. "You do it, now," I whisper thickly.

As Coll pulls, slowly, with startling gentleness, I close my eyes again and concentrate on keeping the mare relaxed. Now that she has regained use of her legs, the last thing we need is for her to panic.

It seems to take forever, but at last, the foal slithers free, into Coll's waiting arms. Unable to maintain the bond with Snowflower's mind or to hold my healing sense any longer, I feel my power drain away, leaving me just Ellin once more. Just Ellin, too tired to move, legs trembling, with one cheek pressed against Snowflower's flank. I notice distantly that I'm drooling, too. I raise a limp, slimy hand to my face, check myself just in time, and wipe my mouth on the shoulder of my dress instead

"Isshaliit?" I mumble, slurring in my exhaustion. I swallow and try again, though my lips feel numb and swollen. "Is she all right?"

"They both are," Coll whispers roughly, and I feel his hand come to rest lightly—and wet—on my back.

"Good." I smile into soft, sweaty fur. Then the fur begins to slide against my cheek. Coll exclaims and, before I realize I'm falling, I feel his thick arm around me and his belly and chest against my back.

"Come sit down," he says, half-carrying, half-dragging me to a heap of straw in the corner. I open one eye and squint up at him, still oddly distant. "I think you need some healing," Coll mutters, frowning. "Are you all right, girl?"

"Damn it, my name is Ellin," I mumble. "And I'm fine," I add, feeling a little better now that I'm seated and no longer using my mind in ways I don't even understand. I close my eyes again and lean back against the partition. "I just need to rest. I don't suppose you have tea?" I ask hopefully. My throat seems coated with dust.

"It's a stable, not a kitchen," he says, "but I do have a bottle of brandy."

I shrug, too tired to care, and nod. "Fine."

Coll stomps off, and I'm feeling well enough when he returns to sit up with both eyes open, though my head still feels strange and light, my body strangely heavy. Coll sits on a farrier's stool in front of me, looking ridiculous on the small seat, and hands me a dented tin water cup part-full of some brown, strong-smelling liquid. "For you," he says. "With my gratitude."

I sip, then make a face as it puckers my mouth and burns my throat going down. The bad taste wakes me a little more, though, enough to glance across the stall and really look at the foal. It's beautiful. Pale gold except for a white star on its forehead and a white mane and tiny plumed tail, perfect and wet. It has already climbed to its feet and stands, wobbly, blinking with enormous, dark eyes as Snowflower licks it. As I watch, the little one totters after a particularly vigorous swipe from Snowflower's tongue and falls to the straw, only to start trying to struggle up again the next moment, instinctively seeking milk.

"A boy or a girl?" I ask, unable to stop looking at it.

Coll swallows a swig from the bottle, and I can hear the smile in his voice when he replies. "Look at the size of him! A boy. Her best yet. I hadn't dared hope for a golden."

"Oh. That's good?" I ask stupidly.

"The rarest color. He's a fine one."

I grin into my cup, hardly able to believe that a *horse*—even a baby one—could make me feel like this. "He's perfect," I whisper, and I mean it. "The most beautiful thing I think I've ever seen."

I finish my drink in silence, feeling a deep satisfaction, looking at Snowflower and her foal, that is only partially due to the brandy. At last, after the cup has dropped from my hand and I'm almost beginning to think that curling up here in the stable to sleep sounds like an excellent idea, Coll stands and extends a hand to me. "I've kept you long enough," he explains as he pulls me to my feet. "I'll see you to the castle."

My protest is swallowed in a jaw-cracking yawn, so I nod instead. "All right," I murmur, with one last look at the horses. I'm startled to find that the sky is pale purple and almost light with dawn, so much so that I don't notice I've forgotten my shawl until we're halfway to the castle. Coll still lacks his shirt, and though it's still more than freezing, I don't think either of us cares.

"Look," Coll says abruptly, pointing to one of the trees by the path.

I shake my head, squinting at the dark, bare leaves and branches, unsure what I'm supposed to see. "What?"

"This plant." He goes and pinches something off the trunk, then holds it out to me as he returns. "You know it?"

I shake my head again, looking down at the waxy-looking green leaves and berries. Even from a distance, I can smell its sharp, clean scent. "Why? What is it?"

"It's called Horse Ivy," Coll says, and he drops it into my hand without looking at me. "It's said that if two warriors in battle come upon it, they must lay down their arms and be at peace with one another until the next sunrise."

I blink in confusion. "Do they really—oh," I murmur, closing my dirty fingers around the plant as I realize what he means by it. I smile at him, accepting the truce. "That's a good story," I say quietly, feeling a little lost for words.

Coll smiles—the first genuine smile I've seen on him—and goes to open the castle door for me. "Goodnight. Ellin."

"Good morning," I reply, very glad that it's only now sunrise today.

Even after I've scrubbed my hands, the sharp, spicy smell of the Horse Ivy lingers when I finally go to sleep.

CHAPTER ELEVEN

"**W**E HEARD WHAT YOU DID last night," Erik says when I walk into the kitchen shortly after waking up. I nod, then wince as the movement hurts my aching, but thankfully clearer, head.

"Coll told you?"

"Garreth," he replies. "He's beside himself that Snowflower and the foal are both alive."

"And they're all right today?" I ask a moment later as I pull out a chair, waiting for my tea to steep.

He nods. "Far as I know." Then he pushes his hair out of his eyes and grins at me from across the table. "I knew you could do it."

I smile back, but before I can reply, I see my father and Finn in the kitchen doorway. More importantly, I catch sight of my father's face.

"Is it true, Ellin?" Father asks in that quiet, calm voice he gets when he's very upset.

I take a nervous gulp of tea. It's too weak, and too hot, and my face puckers as it burns going down. "I didn't mean to," I say, looking at my cup. "I mean, I didn't know what else to do! And I did a healing on the king, in a way, so I knew I could—"

Father shushes me with a sharp gesture. "I don't care about the healing. You did it—though I'm still not sure how—and what's done is done."

I frown, puzzled. "Then what?"

"I heard from Prince Garreth what you were planning to do."

"Oh." I press my lips together as guilt curdles in my stomach. I wasn't certain Father would approve of my plan, but since Coll and I didn't have to remove a dead foal in pieces from Snowflower, I wasn't going to tell him that I'd even considered it. Damn Garreth for talking too much, I think, but my anger withers under the weight of my father's gaze. "Well," I manage, "I was—"

"We need to speak privately, I think," my father interrupts, glancing at Finn and Erik, who are regarding us curiously.

I nod, and Erik gives me a sympathetic look as I stand. Finn gives me an icy look and turns away, and I remember with another pang of guilt that I snubbed him last night. In all the excitement with the horses, I'd almost forgotten. I swear again, silently.

With a sigh, I resolve to fix things with Finn later. Then I pick up my tea and follow my father from the room. He remains silent, his shoulders rigid in front of me, and I dread our talk more with every step. After what seems like miles of endless hallways, we arrive at his room, and he closes the door behind me with a too-loud thump.

"What could you possibly have been thinking, Ellin?" Father asks as he turns to me.

"I wanted to save the mare," I reply. "Why are you so upset?"

"Why am I upset?" He shakes his head and starts pacing, punctuating his speech with gestures. "You would have killed the mare and her foal, for one thing. There is no doubt of that. It would have been horrifically gruesome, not to mention horribly painful—were you really going to use a *knife?*"

"I thought—"

Father's glare silences me. "You had no business whatsoever even *thinking* about attempting such a procedure. You shouldn't even know of it."

"I'm not a child," I snap as I set the cup down hard, sending tea sloshing out onto the table. "I could have done it."

Father sighs, and I can almost see his anger draining away. Then he places his hand on my shoulder. "I suppose you aren't," he says quietly. "But with a knife and an unskilled assistant—no matter how large or strong—you would have failed. You could have cut yourself to the bone, like that. As it is, you're lucky the mare didn't start to contract again and break your wrist. What you wanted to try—Ellin, it takes hours. It's one of the most difficult, awful tasks I know. One that many healers don't *ever* need to perform. And you were going to act on a whim, before educating yourself."

"I thought I had to try," I protest, though I'm feeling smaller by the moment.

"Rather than fetching me?" One of his eyebrows quirks, though he still looks disappointed. "That was unbelievably arrogant of you."

I nod because it's at least partly true. I could have woken him, but honestly, I wanted to prove to Coll that a Southling 'witch-girl' could do better with his precious horses than any Northlander. I look at my feet, ashamed that my desire for recognition could have resulted in the beautiful golden foal being chopped into pieces and Snowflower likely dead, as well.

"I didn't do it, though," I whisper, as much to myself as to my father. "I saved them both, when they said it was impossible."

"It should have been," Father replies, his voice sounding odd. "From what I've heard, the way the foal was positioned... Either you're more talented than I knew, or you were very lucky."

"Just lucky," I say with a small, tight smile. I can't help wondering what Father would think if he knew that it wasn't healing alone that saved them. It was my power. Instead of saying anything about that, though, I step into his arms and let myself be hugged tightly.

"Please don't do anything like that again," Father murmurs, over my head. "I know you aren't a child, but there are some things I'd rather you not know about—or do—until you're older. I don't want you to get hurt," he adds when I look up at him.

"I'll be careful."

He smiles. "That's all I ask."

I wonder, a little later, if using my forbidden Southling power for something small could be considered not being careful. Hovering in the doorway of the tower, I can see Finn, head bent and his back to me as he sits at the table, reading. I bite the inside of my lip and hang back, unsure what to do. I've never known anyone deaf before, besides old Madam Maple back home, and with her I only have to shout. I can't clear my throat to alert Finn to my presence, or shuffle my feet, and I don't want him to think I'm trying to spy or sneak up on him.

I'm unsure, too, what I'm doing here in the first place. It's not as if I have to apologize for not wanting to have my mind invaded. It's uncomfortable, and too intimate, and, of course, forbidden for me. I shift from one foot to the other, hesitating, before I give up and decide to just go away.

I've just started down the stairs when I hear the chair scrape, then the book being smacked against the table loudly, to get my attention. With a wince, I turn again and find Finn with his hands on his hips, wearing an unfathomable expression.

He motions for me to come in, then to himself and the door, and I don't need anyone translating to understand, "Come in. I was just leaving." His expression conveys his sarcastic politeness so well I can almost hear him speaking.

"I'm sorry," I say, feeling wretched, "I—"

Finn shakes his head and crosses the room, then makes an exaggerated, impatient gesture at my arm, asking permission. I nod.

"*You needn't explain,*" he says, the flatness of his tone clear even in thought. "*I understand well enough.*"

"But you don't!" I say aloud.

Finn snorts. "*I thought you of all people would—well. It doesn't matter.*" He gives me a small, strange, bitter smile. "*Whatever your reasons, I'll respect this. And if you change your mind...*" he shrugs and pulls his hand away, and then he leaves before I have a chance to decide what to say.

As I hear his footsteps going down the stairs, I know I've lost a friend, and it's my fault. That thought alone shouldn't make me want to cry, but I sink into the chair anyway, feeling miserable and very much alone.

I've been sitting just long enough to get cold when I hear someone taking the stairs two at a time. I look up, hoping it's Finn, and feel myself droop a little when Garreth's pale head pokes through the door.

"I've been looking for you," he says, smiling.

"Well, you've found me." I make an effort to soften my tone and smile back. "What is it?"

He shrugs and leans against the doorpost. "I just wondered if you'd like to come out and see the little one."

"Oh! Of course. But I'll have to get my shawl."

"I still can't believe you did it," Garreth says a few moments later, as we head down the path to the stable. "I mean, I don't understand *how* you did it."

"I don't either," I reply honestly. "I just…knew how. Have you ever known how to do something without being told?"

"Well, of course." He shakes his head in awe. "But nothing like *that*. You're a strange one, Ellin," he adds, giving me a considering, sideways look. "We're lucky you've come."

I'm not, I think, but I give him a small smile as we go into the stable and head for the big stall. Once my eyes have adjusted from the blinding light of the snow, I stare.

The foal, now that he's dry and standing, looks magnificent. I don't know anything about horses, but even I know a fine one when I see him. And he is. His coat is soft, dusty gold, his short mane and tail snow white, and I marvel at the details of him. His delicate hooves, perfect ears, the way his tiny tail flicks from side to side as he drinks from his mother. And Snowflower, too, looks beautiful. Cleaner than last night, and more alert. I can see now, from her bearing, that she must be a queen among horses.

"Oh," I whisper, transfixed but not daring to go closer lest I disturb them.

"Ah, here's our girl," Alaric says behind me. Both his words and the surprise cause me to start. He gives me a grin, then claps a hand on my shoulder and squeezes it warmly. "You've done it again, Ellin."

"Well, Coll helped," I reply, catching sight of the big man over Alaric's shoulder. "I couldn't have done it without him."

"Save your praise, witch-girl," Coll says, but he's smiling. He nods at the foal, who has looked up from his mother at our voices and stands blinking at us, licking milk from his lips. "Go on, pet him if you want to."

"Snowflower won't mind?"

"Pat her, first, then," Alaric says, and he squeezes my shoulder again before taking his hand away. "Go on."

I go to Snowflower, unsure of my welcome. Despite feeling so close to her—even loving her, a little—last night, today I can't help being frightened of her big hooves and powerful hind legs. I grimace inwardly as I approach and hold my hand out for her to sniff.

"Hello," I say softly. "Are we still friends?"

She pushes her nose into my palm, which I take to mean yes. Feeling a little bolder, I carefully stroke her cheek, then her neck.

"See?" Coll says as he comes to stand at my side. He scratches beneath her chin, and the mare rubs her jaw on his hand, looking pleased. "She knows you."

"I guess." I slide my hand over her shoulder. "What a lovely girl."

"She is. Now, you'd best not make him feel left out," Coll adds, gesturing with a nod. "I'll tend to her."

I turn to the foal, who has gone to stand behind his mother and pokes his head out at me shyly. "Beautiful boy," I murmur, holding out my hand. "Come see me."

To my surprise, the foal stretches out his neck and brushes his nose against my fingers with a curious sniff. I hold still, and he comes closer, picking his way on spindly legs, until he's near enough to touch. Gingerly, I reach out and set my fingers on the side of his neck. I can't suppress a quiet gasp at the softness of his fur.

"You are beautiful," I whisper as I begin to stroke him. The foal's ears twitch, and he watches me with one dark, curious eye. He doesn't flinch, though, and so I dare to step closer and run my hand over his back, petting him as I would a cat.

"You like him, then?" Alaric asks, watching with a smile.

"I don't like horses," I reply. Then the little one nudges my side with his nose, and I feel myself melting. "But I think I love this one."

"Good," Alaric says. "Because he's yours."

My hand freezes its motions, and I look at him in shock. I'm certain I didn't hear correctly. "What?"

"He's yours," Coll repeats, "despite my protests. Damned fine horse to be wasted on a girl who'll put ribbons in his hair, I said, but Alaric insisted."

Though I don't doubt he's serious, I can tell he's fighting a grin. But I shake my head, still unable to comprehend it. "I—"

"It's a good surprise, then?" Garreth asks from Blizzard's stall. "You didn't suspect?"

"Suspect! I can't believe it," I stammer. "And I don't understand," I add, feeling my eyebrows knit as I look from Coll to Alaric. "I thought he was Snowflower's last foal. And the best. Surely you don't—"

"We want you to have him," Alaric says, his eyes twinkling with pleasure. "A gift, from all of us."

"Besides," Coll says, and he pats Snowflower's rump affectionately, "I think our girl here would be most displeased if we *didn't* give her boy to the one who deserves him."

I swallow hard. "Thank you," I murmur, though the words seem insignificant. "He's perfect."

"Now, you'll have a time riding him," Coll says a few moments later, as the four of us start back to the castle. "Unless you get a damn sight taller, that is, or if you geld him." His face twists as if the very thought is painful. "But if he's trained correctly, you'll be able to control him well enough."

I shake my head, not having even considered *riding* him. Then I frown as reality comes jabbing through my joy. "I don't know how to ride," I admit. "And…and I can't keep a horse."

"Why not?" Garreth asks, walking backward to look at me. "I thought your da said you had land."

"A bit, but the barn is falling apart."

He shrugs. "So, rebuild it."

I blush. "We can't afford it. That's what I meant, anyway. Horses are expensive."

"We're not *selling* him to you!" Garreth rolls his eyes. "Honestly, Ellin. Even I couldn't afford *this* one."

"She means feeding him, idiot," Coll explains, chucking a handful of snow at him. "And…"

"And did we not mention the rest of the gift?" Alaric interrupts. "You won't need much winter feed in the Southland, of course, but whatever you do require—grain and tack and even fencing—is yours, whenever you ask."

I bristle, though I know he means well. "I don't need charity," I snap. "We aren't *poor*. We just—"

"We meant no offense," Alaric replies. Again, he pats my shoulder. "But you should know that here, the king's life is priceless."

"Not to mention Snowflower's," Garreth adds. "Well, nearly so, to Coll and me."

"So you see," Alaric says, "no matter what we might give you, we are still indebted to you."

"Thank you," I say as we near the castle. And I mean it. "But what about the laws?" I can't help asking. "The ones that make my people so unwelcome here. Changing those would pay any debt you owe me, and more."

Garreth shakes his head as if the suggestion is ridiculous, and a strange, tense look comes over Alaric's face. To my surprise, it's

Coll who answers. His big hand grips my upper arm to pull me back as the others go on inside.

"Ellin," he says softly, following Alaric with his gaze, "the colt was in his power to give."

CHAPTER TWELVE

THE DAYS THAT FOLLOW pass slowly because I'm alone again. Not truly alone, but I feel as if I am, with Finn avoiding me because he's angry with me, Erik avoiding me because of Finn, Alaric and Coll busy with their own affairs, and Garreth back at the wall on guard duty. The cook, Nan the Keeper, and maids still ignore or insult me at every opportunity, and the stable boys, I find on my trips to see the foal, are no different.

With no other choice, I begin to spend most of my time with my father, shadowing him as he shows Master Thorvald the Physician and others from the college some Southling healing and learns some of their Northlander techniques. I assist him with the king, who, though better in body every day, has not yet returned in mind. Normally I enjoy my time with Father, but everything has changed. Now, with this new power that I ache to use every time I see the twins, I feel guilty and on edge around him. Worried that I'm going to make a mistake and reveal too much.

I'm sure from the puzzled, considering looks Father gives me that he notices. I know he knows I'm unhappy and not sleeping well, but he says nothing except at dinner, when he chides me because I only pick at my food. All the while, I just wish I could go home.

And then, one morning, I come out of my room and know immediately that something is different. It's a feeling I can't quite define, like when I woke up as a child knowing it was my birthday, or there was a carnival in town. I hurry to the kitchen without brushing my hair and find only Jana the cook, who gives me a crooked-toothed smile, as if she understands what I'm feeling, and tells me that the king is awake at last.

Forgetting that I wanted tea, I nod, not knowing what to say. I take the stairs almost running, feeling a lightness like spring in my heart at the thought of going home. Then I arrive in the hallway to King Allard's room, and I see Keeper Nan's pleased, righteous look as she sweeps the hall and listens through the door. She shifts her gaze from the floor to me, and a cold hand grabs my heart and threatens to squeeze it.

"You'd best go in," Nan says, leaning on her broom with pieces of graying blonde hair sticking to her reddened cheeks. "Your da's in there already."

I do just that, surprised that my shaking fingers can manage the doorknob. The room is as crowded as it was the night I healed the king, only this time, Alaric is the only prince present. Besides him, I see tall, white-haired Lord Erfold the Wise and short, round Lord Ivan. And my father, standing at the foot of the bed. He turns and gives me a strange look when I come in; I can't tell if he's dismayed to see me or trying to tell me something, but I go to stand beside him anyway. Only when I'm near enough to grab Father's hand (which I don't, though I want to) do I look at the king.

He's sitting up, and his hair is combed and his color is better, but these things are insignificant. What matters is the look he gives me. I'm reminded of when I'm with Alaric, very conscious that he is royalty. With the king, it's far worse. I feel, for the first time, as if I really *am* just Southling trash. Swallowing hard, I stare down at my feet.

"So," King Allard the Prudent says. Though his voice is hoarse and quiet, the deepness of it, the command, sends shivers down my back. "This must be the girl."

"Yes, your highness," my father says, and I'm appalled to hear how deferential he sounds. "My daughter, Ellin."

"Can you speak for yourself, Ellin?" the king asks. "Or is my floor too interesting for you to tear your attention away from it?"

"Yes," I say, blushing. His piercing, pale blue stare makes me uncomfortable when I raise my eyes to his face. Suddenly I remember what they say, back home, about Northlanders freezing your blood with just a look. "Your highness. I mean, no, it isn't."

"You seem timid, for a girl who so heedlessly broke so many of my laws."

I swallow again and take a deep breath. "I'm sorry."

The king raises an eyebrow. "Are you? For saving my life, by all accounts?"

"No, your highness." I inhale again, feeling like I can't get enough air. And then I don't know what strength possesses me, but I am able to force myself to straighten my shoulders, to force my voice not to shake as I continue. "For having to break the laws to do so."

My father hisses, and I can almost feel Alaric stiffen, but King Allard chuckles, a dry sound, like dead leaves on ice. "Cleverly put, child." His mouth twitches behind his beard. "I suppose I owe you thanks, do I not?"

"I was glad to heal you." It's not exactly a lie, and I try to smile.

"And, indeed, I am grateful." He raises a finger before I can reply. "Grateful enough," the king continues, his expression sobering, "to ignore my own laws, which would require me to have you put to death for your crimes."

"You wouldn't!" I gasp.

The king nods, apparently excusing my rudeness. "I should, but I will not. I cannot, however, let your transgressions go unpunished."

He turns to Lord Ivan and Lord Erfold the Wise. "Bear witness," King Allard says to them. "Rowan Fisher, called Master

Healer, has already admitted his guilt in this matter. He laid his Southling hands, not once but repeatedly, on our royal personage and practiced the Southling witchcraft of healing."

He turns to me. "Ellin Fisher, you are accused of illegally breaking into the city after the gates were closed. Of laying hands on us and practicing the Southling witchcraft of healing. Furthermore, you are accused of laying hands on one of the royal horses, Snowflower, and practicing your witchcraft on her."

The king looks at my face, and his cold eyes seem to see right through me. Though I can't feel him reading my thoughts—I'm sure he isn't—I have the uncomfortable feeling that I've been turned inside out, examined, and been found wanting. "Are you guilty, Ellin Fisher?" King Allard asks. He speaks quietly, but the words almost echo in the silent, tense room.

I know what he means, of course. And yes, I broke the laws. But—

"No," I say, lifting my chin. "I did what needed to be done. It wasn't witchcraft. And I feel no guilt."

The king nods, and I almost think that I see the corner of his mouth twitch again. "Prince Alaric," he says, not taking his eyes from me, "you witnessed this girl practice Southling witchcraft, did you not?"

My gaze darts to Alaric, and I beg him in my thoughts to say no. To speak in my defense. Anything to show the king that he is my friend, that he cares about me and won't let me be punished for breaking laws that aren't fair in the first place.

Alaric looks at me for the barest instant before turning to his father and nodding. Just a single, curt jerk of his head, but the movement thrusts a knife straight into my heart. "I did, your highness."

"And what did you see?"

"She placed her hands on your hand and your forehead, closed her eyes, and entered some sort of trance. She spoke to you. When she did this, the room felt…strange," Alaric says.

"Strange?"

"I cannot describe it, your highness. But I am certain it was the feeling of witchcraft being worked."

King Allard nods again. "Do you deny this?" he asks me.

The floor seems to tilt. There is not enough air in the room, and I'm so cold, I wonder if I am turning to ice, after all. My hands begin to shake, and my lips feel numb and clumsy as I reply. "I can't," I whisper.

"Very well." The king clasps his hands on his lap and studies them for a moment before looking at my father. "You realize that merely being banished from the Northlands is not possible."

"Yes, your highness," my father replies, his face ashen.

I close my eyes, as if not watching this happen will make a difference. I can't stop my ears from hearing, though, as the king continues.

"And," he says, "I will not have you burned. Instead, you will be imprisoned. How old are you, Ellin?"

I blink at him, not understanding, through this fog of pain, why he would ask. "Sixteen."

"Two years for you, then. Until you are of age. At that time, you will be sent home, never to return to the Northlands, under pain of death."

As if I would ever want to come back, I think bitterly. My eyes widen as I realize he didn't say how long my father will be imprisoned, and, with yet another pang of dread, I ask.

"Ellin—" Father whispers, sounding anguished, but the king interrupts.

"Child, your father is a man grown. Unlike you, he understood what he did when he broke the laws. He will remain here for the rest of his days. In prison for some time, and then, perhaps, he may work at the college."

The words "for the rest of his days" finally break me. I can't bear the thought of going home without my father, and I close my eyes again as hot tears spill onto my cheeks. I reach my hand out blindly; feel him clutch it with chilled fingers and pull me close. I bury my face in his shirt so the king can't see me fall to bits, shaking like a leaf under Father's arm.

I barely hear the king speak the formal words to sentence us. The clenching in my chest, the rolling sickness in my throat and stomach, and the cold that penetrates so deeply I can't stop trembling have dulled my ears to anything but the sounds of my own ragged breathing. Distantly, I feel my father's arm hugging my shoulders, his long fingers clutching my upper arm hard enough to bruise. It's as if he fears to lose me already.

I swallow and taste bile when the guards come in to lead us from the room. My eyes skim over the king, unable to bear the sight of him, and seek out Alaric instead. He watches me from the side of King Allard's bed, shoulders straight, his face an unreadable, unfamiliar mask.

I don't know him at all, I realize with a sickening burst of clarity. I never did. I only thought—

It doesn't matter what I thought, though. I was very wrong. And I know this, now, as I look into Alaric's expressionless eyes. Despite being a darker, more pleasant shade of blue than most Northlanders', they're still cold enough to turn my blood to ice.

I stop in the doorway, dragging against the guard who tugs at my arm. "I will never forgive you for this," I whisper. My voice is so low and hard that it frightens me. I look up at Alaric, and for once I don't care what he can see on my naked, unguarded features. "*This* hate is rational."

Before he can reply, I spit at his boots with all the force I can muster. It doesn't reach him, or even come close, but that is beside the point.

He is a Northlander. Less than me, and worthy of my contempt.

CHAPTER THIRTEEN

T HE GUARD SLAMS THE cell door shut behind me with a thud that rattles my bones. Then his key scrapes in the lock, and I hear his booted footsteps walk away, clomping on the stone floor. I wait until I think he's out of earshot before I go to the door and press my face against the small opening from where, I assume, the guards will give me food and water.

"Father?" My voice is too loud in the tomb-like silence. It echoes, ragged from crying, in my ears. "Can you hear me?"

"Ellin!" he calls, off to the right. I press my hot, swollen face against the cool wood, sagging against the door in relief. "Are you all right?"

"I—" I swallow and try not to start sobbing again. "I'm fine, but Father, I'm so sorry. I didn't know—"

"Shh," he says. "Ellin, *I* knew. I knew what I risked by coming here. By bringing you. All of it."

"But I'm the one who broke the laws first!"

"And I would have, had I been in your place." His breath catches, and when he speaks again, his voice is a hoarse, earnest whisper. I can't bear the thought of him crying. Of having upset him so much. And his next words undo me entirely. "I'm proud of you," he says. "This isn't your fault, and you didn't do anything that I wouldn't have done."

But I did, I think miserably. I close my eyes and lean my forehead against the door, knowing that I can't keep this from him. Not anymore. Not when it *is* my fault that we're in prison. After having put him here myself, how can I lie to him as well?

I take a deep, shaking breath and reach out with my thoughts. I find him easily, and it doesn't surprise me that his mind feels like my own. It is so easy to reach out and touch his thoughts, and I know, somehow, that I don't have to touch his arm for him to hear me.

"Father?" I say with my mind, feeling shy and nervous and incredibly guilty. *"I did do something you wouldn't have done."*

I expect him to be angry, or disappointed, or ashamed of me. Instead, he laughs, and I can feel with my mind that he isn't surprised at all.

"Oh, Ellin," he says softly. Though I can't see him, I can hear his smile. "Did you really think I didn't know?"

"I—" I blink, shocked. *"You aren't angry?"*

"No."

I shake my head, not understanding. "But why?" I ask aloud. "It's forbidden. And wrong. Isn't it?"

My father is quiet for a moment. "It can be," he says slowly. "But you haven't used it for evil, have you?"

"No! Of course not!"

"Well, then." He sighs, and I wish, again, that I could see him. "Does anyone know?"

I bite my lip and hesitate. On one hand, Finn and Erik trusted me with a secret, and they gave me no reason to distrust them. But on the other, I trusted Alaric, too. For all I know, all of them could have known what would happen to Father and me. They might have planned it together.

I can't believe it, not quite, but thinking this makes me feel a little less guilty when I reply. *"Finn,"* I think, strangely reluctant to speak his name aloud. *"And Erik."*

"Oh?" Before he can say anything else, something occurs to me.

"How did you know?" I ask. "I was so careful—"

"Don't you remember?" Father sounds almost amused. "You called me."

"No, I didn't."

"You did. When I was at the inn," he continues, lowering his voice, though I can still hear the note of wonder in it. "I heard you, loudly, calling for me. I knew you needed me. It was your voice that I followed through the blizzard."

"I didn't do it on purpose," I whisper, though now I do remember. I remember, too, that it was only after calling for my father that I heard Finn. "I must have…woken it, I suppose…by needing you so much. By being so afraid," I say slowly. "Father, I didn't mean to!"

"Of course you didn't. You didn't know." He sighs again, and I hear his fingers tapping against the door of his cell in thought. "Ellin," he says, after a pause, "now that you have this ability, you must not tell anyone else. You must not use it to gain an unfair advantage over another. Do you understand?"

I nod. Then I realize he can't see me. "Yes, Father."

"Good girl."

Later, after I've eaten the bowl of tepid soup the guard gave me through the door, I lie curled on my side on the narrow bed. The cell is very dark, and the moonlight that manages to creep in the window makes everything look long-shadowed and frightening. The mattress is hard and lumpy, and the lone blanket is thin. I shiver and rub my aching feet together, then pull the blanket snug beneath my chin as I think about my power and try not to cry. Again.

Surely it wouldn't be very wrong to use my power, I think. Just once, to see if I could talk to Erik or Finn over this distance. Or I could use it to escape! I could look into the guard's mind, and—

And I don't know what I would do then, I realize with a sigh. Simply knowing someone's thoughts wouldn't help at all. There has to be a way to escape, though. Even if my father said he is resigned to this, I won't allow it. I won't let us stay here in this cold, miserable place because we broke some stupid laws.

It isn't fair, I think for the hundredth time. Despite my best intentions, I sniffle. The laws aren't fair to begin with, and it wasn't fair of King Allard to punish us for helping him. It wasn't fair of Alaric to act as if he was my friend and then stand there, calmly, and condemn me to this.

I see Alaric's face again behind my closed eyelids, and I squeeze them shut tighter to make the picture go away. "How could you do this to me?" I whisper, face working against the musty-smelling pillow. "*Why* did you do it?" I don't really need to wonder, though. He is a Northlander. And, quite obviously, he didn't care for me at all. Not as a friend, and certainly not—

"Oh, you idiot," I whisper to myself, irritated even though my heart feels like it's splintering in my chest. "Honestly. He's a Northlander *prince*. What did you expect?"

It still hurts, though. All of it hurts, but I try to clear my mind, to not think about anything at all so I can go to sleep. It takes some time, but at last I begin to get tired and sag into the mattress as my body relaxes, bit by bit. And then I feel it, faint and tickling like the brush of a feather.

"*Why are you so sad?*" whispers a voice in my mind.

My eyes snap open, and I stretch out with my thoughts, straining to reach him. "*I'm in prison and freezing cold, and I can't sleep, and my feet hurt,*" I reply, a little impatiently. "*As if you didn't know.*"

"*I heard you were in prison. The other things, no. I didn't know.*"

I smile in the darkness. I can't tell if it's Finn or Erik, but I imagine both of their faces before me, and I realize how much I miss them. If they were here, I know this wouldn't seem so bad. And I wish, again, that I hadn't been so rude to Finn. Surely *this* use of my power isn't wrong. Not when it lets me talk to a friend.

"*Using your power is never wrong,*" the voice says, sounding surprised. "*Especially not power as great as yours. It's part of you, isn't it? Like your arms, or your eyes, or your ears.*"

It must be Finn, after all. It makes sense for him to think of this power as another way of hearing, I think. "*I'm sorry,*" I say. "*I was just...afraid. I was told this power was dangerous. And forbidden. Do you understand?*"

"*Of course.*"

"*I wish you were here,*" I say impulsively.

"*I will be,*" he replies. "*We're coming, my dear, but we have to make plans first. Be patient.*"

"*Plans? You mean you're going to help me escape?*" My lips part in a silent gasp even as I speak with my mind.

Amusement is clear in his tone when he replies. "*Of course.*"

Relief makes me go limp, and I almost lose our mental bond in my joy. "*Oh, thank you!*"

"*I have to go,*" he says abruptly, sounding distracted. "*But remember that we're coming. Be patient, and be ready, and be strong.*"

"*I will.*"

After he leaves, I smile to myself and hug this new secret to my chest like a warm blanket. The cell doesn't seem so frightening and lonely now. Not when I still have *some* friends. I'm still smiling, and thinking of escape, when I fall asleep.

CHAPTER FOURTEEN

IT'S HARD TO BE PATIENT when every moment is spent in a bare, cold cell. Father and I talk through the doors, but it isn't the same as being face to face. Anyway, it's hard to think of things to talk about. Since he can only hear me speaking in his mind but can't reply the same way, we can't discuss important things for fear of being overheard, and we soon run out of new things to say aloud to one another. Before now, I didn't realize how many of our conversations are about small, everyday things, like what to have for dinner, or who we saw in town. He tells me stories to pass the time, but I've heard them all before. So, while he talks, I find my mind wandering as I think about escape, and about my friends, and the foal, and all the things I could be doing instead of sitting here.

I find myself looking forward to the small, bland meals the guards bring. Looking forward to the guards' visits themselves, because they give me a chance to practice "listening" with my mind. Finn was right. Not using my power would be like closing my eyes and pretending to be blind. I don't tell Father, though, because I know he wouldn't approve or understand.

With nothing to do and nothing to read and conversations with my father wearing thin, I spend much of my time curled up on the bed, wrapped tightly in my thin blanket. Partly because it's cold in the cell, but mostly because I don't see any point in being up and about. I think about trying to contact Finn, but something always keeps me from doing it. I'm still ashamed about the way I treated him, for one thing, but I'm also afraid to send my thoughts reaching so far. Besides, he said to be patient.

And so I try to be patient. I lose track of how many days pass. With the solitary window in my cell letting in only a slender shaft of light, I barely know if it's night or day. I try to be patient, though I'm always hungry, and I'm cold and irritable and would cut off my hair for a cup of hot tea.

The days keep passing, maddeningly, slowly, like cold honey sliding off a spoon. When the nights in the cell get even more frigid, cold enough that the kindest guard gives me an extra blanket, I begin to suspect an awful thing. They aren't coming. I hardly dare to think it at first, lest my thinking make it true. But the first time I allow myself to form the words with my lips in a silent whisper, I know, with a heavy feeling in my stomach, that I'm right. I know, too, what I have to do.

"We can't stay here," I think to my father the morning after I've decided. *"I won't."*

"Ellin, it's only two years," he whispers, sounding tired.

"For me! What about you?"

"Ellin…" He sighs, and I hear him tapping his fingers on the door in vexation. "I know what you're contemplating, and the answer is no."

"But Father, I could use—"

"No."

"Fine," I snap, smacking my hand on the wall by the door. "Fine!" If I have to arrange things myself, so be it.

I wait two more days, giving myself time to plan and time to talk myself out of it. But with each hour that passes, I'm more certain than ever that I'm doing the right thing, and I brace myself to do it.

There are three guards who take turns bringing us our meals and taking away the dishes: a tall, sturdy young one who looks like a farmhand, an old one with a big nose and gray hair, and a homely, greasy one who doesn't speak to me. It's the young one on duty the evening of the second day, and I feel guilty for a moment, because I like him better than the other two.

His thick boots clomp down the hallway, and he pauses at my father's door. Speaks to him, for a moment. My father's dinner bowl clanks against the opening in his cell's door, and the spoon rattles as he passes it to the guard.

The guard approaches my cell, and my heart beats faster with each heavy footstep. He stops, and I try to control my breathing, fighting my body, which wants to pant as though I'm running.

"Finished with your dinner?" the guard asks companionably, leaning down to speak through the opening in the door.

"I—not quite," I manage. I'm grateful that my voice only shakes a little. "Just a moment." Staying to the side of the opening, out of sight, I close my eyes. Reaching out with my mind, I find his thoughts and touch them.

He's uncomfortable; his blue guard's coat is too small across the shoulders. Taking my father's empty bowl has made him think about his own dinner waiting for him in a room upstairs. He has to remember to buy cheese and tea for his mother at the market tomorrow morning.

Scarcely knowing what I'm doing, I frown in concentration and begin to search through his mind for the information I need. My thoughts pull like thread tightly stretched as I dig deeper.

At last, I find the things the guard knows but isn't thinking about. He's alone tonight. He saw the old guard heading into a tavern, and the greasy one is posted out on the wall. And he keeps his keys on a thick ring in his coat pocket.

Finished, I try to withdraw my mind from his. But it's painful. It feels like I'm stuck. I pull harder and even take a step back, and my breath quickens with panic when I realize that my mind won't come away.

The guard knows something is wrong. I hear him think it. Hear him decide to peek through the opening. He thinks his head feels strange. I groan quietly and press myself against the wall where he can't see, feeling the rough stone dig into my shoulder.

"Hey, girl," the guard says. The words are strange and echoing because I hear him think them before he speaks. "Are you all right?"

I try to open my mouth and tell him yes, I'm just finishing my soup.

"I'm fine," the guard says, and next his words send ice down my back. "Just finishing my soup."

I feel his panic, huge and dark like choking smoke as it billows around my mind and his. I'm terrified, too, and the bowl clatters from my shaking hand. I'm panting now, and I wonder when I sank to my knees on the cold stone floor. There is too much in my head, too many thoughts, and I can hardly tell where I end and the guard begins. It's horrible. I've never felt so trapped, and I tug frantically with my mind, trying to break free. With every pull, white-hot pain stabs behind my eyes.

"What the—?" The guard's key rattles as he tries to unlock the door. His big, clumsy hands are trembling as violently as mine. "Girl, I'm coming in."

I stare in horror as the door opens. I'm afraid he'll know I'm practicing "witchcraft." He'll tell the king, and then I will be burned. I think, very clearly, that I don't want to die. More than anything, though, I just want *out* of his mind. I keep trying to find my way back to myself, but he has so many thoughts, and they're all so loud, that I can't concentrate.

"What are you doing?" the guard demands, looking even younger than before with his eyes wide and frightened. "What are you *doing* to me, girl?"

I open my mouth. Shut it at once, afraid to speak, lest my words come out of his lips again. I move away, scrabbling backward on the floor, until my shoulders hit the wall.

"Girl? Ellin?" He takes a step closer, warily, fingers twitching for the heavy stick hanging from his belt. "Answer me!"

I pull harder, desperately, and feel something rip in my mind. I make a sound that's somewhere between a gasp and a scream, and jagged sparks swirl behind my eyelids. The guard shouts, too, and then there is a thump and a clatter.

Tears leak out onto my cheeks as I try to catch my breath. I've never felt pain like this before. My head hurts so much I could vomit. I swallow hard and gingerly cradle my forehead in my cold, still-trembling hands.

After several moments, I open my eyes and find that the guard is lying crumpled on the floor of the cell. He isn't moving, as far as I can see in the dimness. Then there is noise, and I stare at the guard in puzzlement until I realize someone is shouting.

"Ellin!" my father calls again, sounding frantic. "What's going on?"

I try to speak, but words won't come. Fighting nausea, I try again. "I'm all right," I manage. My voice is a raspy croak. "I—"

"Ellin! What is it?"

I don't have an answer, so I sit motionless for several more moments, feeling ill and dazed. And then it hits me. The guard is unconscious or dead, and the door of my cell is open.

This thought sends me lurching toward him, still on my hands and knees. The motion makes my head hurt worse, but I fight the pain and fumble with clumsy fingers for his throat. Then I let out a breath I didn't realize I was holding when I feel his heartbeat, strong beneath my touch. I didn't kill him.

I find his keys and stagger to my feet, clutching at the wall until the waves of dizziness pass. As fast as I can on unsteady legs, I head for the door, then lock it behind me and go to my father's cell. "I have the keys," I whisper. "Get ready."

"What?" Father's face appears in the opening, looking startled. "How? What did you do?"

I press my lips together and try a second key when the first doesn't fit. This one won't work either, and I frown impatiently and try a third. My hands are still shaking hard enough to make the metal clink and jangle, but this key turns, and I open the door and face my father.

"Does it matter how?" I ask. "Let's get out of this place."

"Ellin." He folds his arms and speaks slowly and doesn't move. "What did you do?"

"He fainted," I say, unsurprised that my voice quavers as much as my hands. "I—I went into his mind. But I didn't mean to hurt him! I was going to find what I needed and put him in a healing sleep, but then—he just—" I break off with a choked gasp as my vision wavers with unshed tears.

"Oh, Ellin." He pulls me close and hugs me tightly, and it feels so good to be comforted that I almost don't care about my throbbing head. "I told you not to—"

"I know." I draw a ragged breath and look up at him. "But can we go? Please?"

Father nods, then darts a worried glance down the hallway. "This way," he says at last, steering me to the right. "I remember where the door is."

The hallway is dim, but the stairs are pitch black. I shiver as we walk up them blindly, our hesitant footsteps seeming loud despite our best efforts to be quiet. I can hear my father breathing, but I'm grateful for this, and for his hand on my arm. Being together, even if I can't see him, is better than being kept apart by the doors and locks of our cells. My father stops suddenly, tightening his grip. "Did you hear something?" he whispers.

I shake my head in the darkness before I remember that he can't see me. "No." But then I do. Footsteps and murmured voices, somewhere past the top of the stairs. I stiffen. "What do we do?" I hiss. "We can't go back!"

"Keep going," he replies with a tug on my elbow. "If nothing else, we'll surprise them and make a run for it."

It doesn't sound like a very good plan, but I don't have a better one. We creep to the top of the narrow stairway, and I trail my fingertips along the wall to give myself some sense of where I am, since I can see nothing. I can hear the voices better at the top, and I know whoever it is is approaching the stairs. I begin to reach out with my thoughts to feel their minds, but a stab of pain makes me gasp and stop at once.

Father squeezes my wrist in concern, and I pat his hand in reassurance, knowing it's too dangerous to speak. Then he tenses. The voices are even closer now, still too hushed to hear clearly. Several sets of feet approach the door, and I hold my breath as my heart roars in my ears. My father puts his hand on the door. Then I see light shivering under the crack at the bottom, and the knob turns.

My father lets go of my wrist. With a shout, he shoves the door open and charges out. The men on the other side yell, too, as they're pushed backward. I hesitate an instant, but then I hurry after my father, eyes squinted and almost shut, bracing myself to be hit or kicked or shoved.

With a bone-jarring smack, I run into someone and stiffen as he grabs my upper arms. I struggle, attempting to claw at my captor's hands and hit him. Then I twist and crane my neck, trying to bite his fingers, and I feel a strange, feral glee when I succeed and he swears.

Then I freeze, because I *know* that voice. I raise my eyes in disbelief and find Erik staring back, looking as incredulous as I feel.

"Ellin?" Erik grins and squeezes my arms again, but in a friendly way, this time. "It's Ellin!"

"And her da," says Garreth as he comes over, massaging his shoulder.

"Sorry," my father mutters dazedly. He rubs his knuckles, and I look from him to Garreth, wondering just how hard my father punched him.

"And it's *you*," I say stupidly, grinning so broadly my cheeks hurt. "And you," I add, seeing Finn, who raises his lantern in greeting and gives me a smile from within the hood of his cloak. "You came!"

"'Course we did," Garreth says, sounding offended. "We weren't going to let you stay here, were we?"

"We started planning to get you out as soon as we heard what happened," Erik explains. "It just took some time."

"Speaking of time," my father says, "I assume we don't have much?"

Finn shakes his head, coming closer, and lifts his free hand to say something to Erik.

"Only a few moments before they know something's wrong," Erik says aloud, with a worried glance behind him, as if he expects to see angry guards charging in the door any second. "We have to hurry. Put this on," he says, shoving a cloak at me as Garreth hands one to my father. "Cover your heads. And come on."

When we're covered, Finn douses the light. Erik grabs my wrist and leads me out onto the moonlit street behind Finn, Garreth, and my father. We're free, but I'm too frightened to be relieved. I know we aren't safe yet.

CHAPTER FIFTEEN

"SHH!" ERIK HISSES, dragging me farther into the shadows of the alley. I press myself against the wall and wait, holding my breath, as the man on horseback passes and clops away down the street.

"Where are we?" I whisper. I've lost all sense of direction between the dark and the twisted route we've taken through the city. "Is it much farther to the gate?"

He shakes his head. "No. Just a bit. We're at the far end of the market street."

I nod and peer out of my hood as we go back onto the street. Up ahead, I can just barely make out the tall shadows that are my father, Garreth, and Finn.

"Careful," Erik murmurs, tugging at my elbow. "There's a tavern straight ahead where the guards go when they aren't on duty. Keep your head down."

I nod, growing even more nervous as we cross the street and walk past the tavern. I nearly jump out of my skin when the door opens, letting out smoke, noise, and light. Though I'm tense, and my skin prickles with gooseflesh, I force myself to keep walking when a burly guard walks out. I'm certain he's going to call any second and ask us what we're doing out so late, but he only belches and stretches before heading down the street, away from us.

Erik sighs with relief. I do, too, but that was too close. I walk faster, trying to ignore the pain in my head and the now-familiar aching of my feet. "Let's hurry," I mutter. "I want to get away from here."

"Don't forget, we still have to get out the gate," Erik replies, and my heart sinks a little at the reminder. "That might be the hard part."

We catch up with the others at the Southlings' gate and find Garreth already digging in his pocket for his keys. "Why aren't the guards here?" I ask in a whisper, when I scan the wall and fail to see any of their lanterns.

"Someone's outside the wall, making a disturbance," Garreth replies as he unlocks the narrow gate.

"How do you know that?"

Erik snickers. "Because it's Coll," he says, "acting drunk and bellowing that he can't get in."

I squint, trying see his face. Despite the darkness, I imagine I can see his eyes gleaming. "Coll? You're joking!"

"He owes you a favor," Garreth says over his shoulder. "But hurry—it won't take them long to tell him to go away and wait 'til morning."

"What happens if they don't?" My father sounds far calmer than I feel. "What if they let him in and resume their posts?"

Garreth snorts. "They won't. After what happened with Ellin, everyone knows that the rules are not to be broken under any circumstances."

"Except by you?" I ask.

"*We* aren't going to get caught," Erik says smugly. He tugs at my arm again when we're all through the gate, urging me to slow down. "Wait," he murmurs. "We're going to meet Coll at the gate-house, but we have to wait until the guards are—there! See?"

I look up, and only Erik's warning grip keeps me from making a noise of dismay. The guards are coming back, their lanterns gold circles bobbing along the top of the wall, getting closer. "Come on!" Erik hisses, dragging me forward. "Run!"

The five of us make a mad, almost-silent dash for the gatehouse, staying as close to the wall as we can. Running jars my head with every step, and the cold, sharp air burns, but I don't care. I think only about where I'm going to put my feet, trusting Erik to lead me. Our footsteps crunch, pounding dully on the snow, and I run even faster as we pass beneath the guards.

"Hey!" one guard shouts. His lantern sways dizzily as he leans out over the wall from a high parapet inside. "Is someone down there?"

But we just go faster, until at last we fling ourselves into the gatehouse and gasp with mingled relief and exertion.

"All right?" Coll asks quietly, from the direction of the table. There is a hiss, a spark, and a sputter of gold as he strikes a flint, then steady light once he lights a candle. He shields it with his hand, giving us just enough light to almost see by.

"They heard us," Garreth pants. "Heard something, I mean. We don't have much time."

"Didn't anyway," Coll snaps, but I know that he's short because he's worried, not because he's angry.

"Yes, well, now we have even less time," Erik says easily, as he pushes back his hood. "But we'll be fine."

"What about us?" I say when I have my breath back. "Do you have a plan?"

Coll nods. "A friend with a wagon is waiting just inside the forest to take you to the river. Do you have money for the ferry across?" he asks my father.

Father shakes his head. "I don't know what was done with my things."

"Damn it." Erik smacks his thigh with his fist. "I knew we forgot something."

"It's fine," Coll says as he stands and digs in his pocket. "I have enough."

"And we'll be all right once we're across, in the Southland?" I ask. "No one will come looking for us?"

"They can't, once we're across," Father replies. He takes a deep breath and extends his hand to Coll. "We're in your debt."

Coll almost smiles as he clasps my father's hand with both of his big ones, pressing a purse into my father's palm. "No. We're repaying ours."

Erik jabs my shoulder and gives me his quick, sharp smile when I turn to him. "Glad we got you out," he says. "We were all furious with Da and Alaric when we heard."

"I'm glad, too." And it's true, though I feel overwhelmed. I'm free, and I'm going home at last. But I know that I'll never see Erik—or the others—again, and that fact weighs heavily, dampening my happiness. "Thank you," I add, knowing that there isn't nearly enough time to say everything I want to, even if I had the words. "For everything, I mean."

Erik grins and pokes me in the shoulder again. "Of course."

"Well, Southling," Garreth says as he comes to stand beside Erik. He smiles, and I know that he, too, must be remembering our first meeting, right here in the gatehouse.

I smile back. "Northlander."

Garreth shoves his hands in his coat pockets, then apparently reconsiders and extends one to me stiffly. "I'm glad to have met you, Ellin," he says, sounding awkward.

Touched, I squeeze his hand. "Don't forget," I say quietly, "the king's youngest son was the one who brought all this about. You count for much, Garreth the Youngest."

He nods, pale hair bobbing in the faint light, and looks down at his feet. His too-large, callused hand grips harder. "I'll miss you," he says, the words mumbled in a rush.

I nod, too, feeling my throat tighten unexpectedly. "I'll miss you. All of you."

Garreth drops my hand and turns away to speak with Coll and my father, leaving me to the most difficult goodbye. I motion for Finn to join me at the table, where it's lightest, and look at him helplessly for a moment when he does.

"I can't talk with you," I say softly, making sure to face him after I've seen that Coll and Garreth aren't listening.

Finn nods, looking as though he expected this. I shake my head when I realize he doesn't understand.

"No! Finn, I want to," I explain. "But when we escaped, I—I did something to the guard." I point to my forehead and make a face. "It hurts."

Finn's eyes widen, and he nods again. Then he gives me a wry smile and makes a frustrated gesture with both hands.

"I know," I say, with a mirthless, breathless laugh. "But I—" I break off, startled, when he touches my hand and, when he has my attention, taps a finger to his lips, shushing me.

Then he stands and pulls me up and hesitantly puts his arms around me. And I realize as I hug him back that some things—some apologies and some forgiveness and even some goodbyes—can be said without saying anything at all.

"Ellin," Father says after I've pulled away and wiped my eyes, "we have to hurry."

I readjust the cloak covering me and let myself be clapped roughly on the back by Coll. "I'll look after the foal for you, witch-girl," he says. "He won't soon forget you, either."

And then Father and I are out in the snow, the princes' chorus of goodbyes still in my ears. I inhale deeply, and the crisp Northlands air sears my nostrils and bites my lungs.

"Come on," I say, taking Father's hand as we head for the forest and the wagon waiting for us there. "Let's go home."

CHAPTER SIXTEEN

A DRIZZLING RAIN AND HEAVY, gray metal sky welcome my father and me home as the cart we're riding in rolls up the muddy road into Harnon. After we crossed the dark, swollen river at the border, the deep white blanket of snow in the Northlands gave way to scrubby grayish patches and finally to cold rain and limp fallen leaves as we came farther south.

"Here we are," the farmer from Dunbarton, southeast of Harnon, says as he pulls the two shaggy brown ponies to a stop in front of Alder's inn. "You'll be all right, then, Master Healer?"

My father smiles after he's climbed down from the cart. "We'll be fine. Thank you again for the ride."

"Yes, thank you," I add, brushing bits of straw from my dirty skirt before I hop down to the road. I know I must look like a vagabond, and my father looks hardly better. Prison and travel have left us bedraggled and filthy, and I think longingly of our tub and fresh-smelling soap at home.

"'Twas nothing at all," the farmer says, rubbing his big red nose with the back of his hand. He touches the brim of his hat at my father, waves to me, then clucks his tongue and sets off down the road, wagon wheels leaving wet channels in the mud.

"Well," Father says, and I look up at him. His thin face seems years younger, suddenly, as he grins. "We're home."

"I know," I murmur, hardly able to believe it. I turn in a slow circle, admiring everything. The rain-dimpled puddles in the road, the weathered, painted sign hanging above Alder's, the wooden fence marking out the Beechwoods' front yard... I blink raindrops out of my eyes and grin back. "I know."

I breathe deeply, chilly air filling my lungs, relishing the scents of wet earth and chimney smoke. I could stand here forever and not even care if the rain soaked through my clothes. My feet might even take root like a tree, I think with a smile, because my body knows this is where I belong. I can feel it.

"You look content as a cat," my father remarks, putting his hand on my shoulder. "What are you thinking?"

I shrug and try to think how to put it into words as we begin to walk down the road, toward home. "Just that...in the Northlands, everything was so strange. So new. Here," I gesture, taking in everything, "I know this place. Every little part of it. I've been everywhere, and it just feels—"

"Comforting?" he finishes.

"Better than that. Right."

Father nods. "I felt the same way, the first time I went home for a visit after leaving to go to the college. It was as if I'd left a part of myself behind, and only found it when I returned."

"That's exactly it." I smile and look up at him. "How did you ever go away again?"

"Well, I was a young man, eighteen years old, and I wasn't about to admit that I missed my parents so much," he says, the corner of his mouth twitching. "Besides that, I wanted to be a healer. Was called to be a healer. And soon, the dormitory at college began to seem like home, as well. I made friends, met your mother..."

"And you never did go back to live," I finish, thinking of the whitewashed cottages and winding streets of Glennig, on the coast, where my father was born. We used to visit every summer, when my grandparents were still alive.

"I never did," he agrees. Then he shrugs. "Home can change, Ellin. Once I had your mother here, and you, then Harnon was home."

I nod, supposing that it does make sense that you belong wherever your loved ones are.

"And speaking of being home and going home," Father says, interrupting my musings, "we should stop at the grocer's first, if we want dinner tonight."

Though Harnon has a regular market most of the year, with stalls and tables where farmers can bring their produce, cheese, and eggs, and everyone else can bring whatever goods they make to trade or sell, in the winter, everyone purchases their food at Thystle's grocery. Master and Madam Thystle buy cheese and milk from farmers with milk cows, eggs from those with chickens, and they bake their own bread in the mornings so that it's fresh to sell. They have sweets and imported spices, too, not to mention soap and tea and flour and all sorts of other things that they sell during the rest of the year.

I've always enjoyed the smell of all the different foods jumbled together, so I sniff appreciatively when we enter the cramped, warm shop. As Father goes to talk with Master Thystle, I look around, wide-eyed. After more than two weeks on the road, this abundance of fresh, good food is dazzling. There are bins of potatoes and turnips and sweetroot, shelves with big balls and wheels of pale yellow and white cheese, both herbed and plain, a barrel of dried sunberries that smells so sour and delicious that my stomach growls... Most tempting of all, though, is the sparkling row of glass canisters full of sweets on the counter. From where I stand, I can see that one is full of dainty, sugar-covered tartmynt leaves, another contains dark, peppery spice balls, and a third is packed with brown burnt-sugar creams.

"Well then, Ellin," Master Thystle says as I approach the counter, still eyeing the sweets, "glad to be home?"

"You wouldn't believe how much," I reply with a smile.

He chuckles, reddened hands flying to wrap our food in cloth and paper. Then he glances up at my father. "Folks have wondered why you went," Master Thystle says conversationally. "There's been talk it was a matter of some importance, aye? With them from the Northlands coming down to fetch you in such a hurry, and all..."

I flinch and look up at my father. To my surprise, his normally friendly expression is cool as he regards the grocer. "Oh?" Father replies, but it isn't really a question. "Well, people talk."

Master Thystle shrugs and grimaces, as if thinking it was at least worth a try. Knowing him, though, our mere presence here at the shop will give him an excuse to gossip at the inn for hours tonight. "You know," he says, obviously not ready to give up, "I heard those Northlands bastards—"

"Ellin," Father interrupts with a rather strained smile, "why don't you choose one of those sweets for the walk home?"

"Yes, Father." I frown at the canisters but don't take too long deciding, since I know he's in a hurry to leave. "One spice ball, please," I say after a moment.

"Very well." Master Thystle drops it into my outstretched hand. "Well, good evening to you, then," he grumbles after Father has paid.

"Goodness," I mumble around the candy as we walk home. "He was even nosier than usual!"

Father shrugs. "He was merely curious, Ellin. Everyone will be. And can you blame them?"

Suddenly, even the delicious, tingling-sweet taste in my mouth doesn't seem as pleasant as it did a moment ago. "We're strange here, too, now, aren't we?"

"For going to the Northlands?"

I nod.

"Well, it isn't commonly done," my father says, "but we certainly won't be imprisoned for it."

I nearly choke, and I'm so busy staring at him that I step into a puddle. "That isn't funny."

"No?" He smiles, and I do, too, as we turn from the road and walk up the path to our cottage. Then my smile becomes a grin, because I'm home at last, and even my father's awful sense of humor is wonderful.

"I love you," I say impulsively, and I take the bundles from him so he can be the one to open the door.

Home is just as we left it, tidy except for books scattered about and a fine layer of dust covering everything. I like to sweep and don't even mind scrubbing the floor, but somehow I always forget that furniture and shelves must be wiped, too. It's cold, though, and my father kneels to kindle a fire in the stove as soon as he's hung up his cloak. After tossing my own cloak untidily on a peg and going back out to scrub my hands at the pump, I unwrap the food and begin to prepare dinner. We work in comfortable quiet, and in what seems like no time at all, the cottage is warm and cozy, and the pan of buttery eggs spiced with onion and sourgrass on the stove is cooked and ready, making my mouth water.

I hurry to slice the crusty round loaf of dark bread and set the table with plates, forks, and glasses of water as Father goes out to wash his hands. Finally, though, we're ready to eat, and we tuck in unceremoniously. The first bite, hot and savory, flavorful with rich butter and a little salt and just the right amount of sourgrass, makes me close my eyes and groan. "I could eat all of this by myself," I mumble through a second mouthful. "And everything else you bought, too."

Father nods around a slice of bread. "Tired of pickled fish and clotted cream?" he asks when he's swallowed, referring to the two Northlands foods that most disgusted me. But I shake my head.

"Tired of cold food!" I shudder. "If I never see another piece of dried meat again, I'll be happy."

He nods again, smiling. "Nor another bed of straw and a blanket in a barn?" he asks. "I imagine you'll be racing to your own bed as soon as you've finished eating?"

I pause with the serving spoon containing more eggs halfway to my plate and stare at him in disbelief. "Are you teasing again? I've been dreaming of tea—good, Southling tea, not that Northlands stuff—and a hot bath since before we left the Northlands!"

"Well, then," Father says, using a crust of bread to push some eggs into a pile, "while you're in the bath, I'll put the kettle on. I wouldn't say no to a good cup, either."

It takes some time to heat water and fill the large tub in our washroom, but at last, when I have it practically steaming and have shut the door behind me, I hear my father go out to fill the tea kettle. I undress quickly, thrilled to be rid of the filthy, travel-stained clothes that have nearly stuck to my skin from wearing them too long. And, finally, I climb into the tub.

The hot water makes me shudder and break out in gooseflesh at once, and I ease myself in slowly, assorted scrapes and bruises stinging. The water goes cloudy and grayish immediately, but, for a moment, actually washing is the furthest thing from my mind. I simply sit instead, eyes closed, head back, and feel the bone-deep cold that has been with me since entering the Northlands finally—*finally*—soak away. Scrubbing my skin and hair with fragrant homemade soap is nearly as wonderful, and I feel almost dazed with pleasure when I finally climb out, flushed, wrinkled, and utterly relaxed.

Dressed in my clean, soft nightshift and warm felt slippers, I meander into the front room. Father, in his chair by the fire with a cup of tea in hand, looks up and smiles. "Where's my daughter?" he asks teasingly. "The dirty one, just home from travel?"

I giggle. "Thrown out with the bathwater. I'm quite certain *this* Ellin never left." Still smiling, I fix my tea and go to sit in my chair across from him.

We've been so close lately, with only each other for company on the road, that we don't have much to say. Even if we did, I know I'm too tired, and I think my father is, to carry on any meaningful sort of conversation. I don't mind, though. The silence between us is comfortable. And so neither of us breaks it as we sit, warmed by the fire and our tea, home at last.

CHAPTER SEVENTEEN

A WEEK AFTER WE'VE COME HOME, it almost feels like we never left. The very morning after we arrived, widowed Jennet Maple sent her oldest boy to ask Father to have a look at her feverish, coughing three-year-old twins. Father had just come home and washed up when a farmer with a nasty gash on his leg came limping to our door, and he'd barely had *that* sewn up when Thom Alder from the inn came by to purchase some of the ointment for sore joints that Father keeps on hand. More than a few times, I've wondered if everyone in Harnon waited until they heard we were home to get sick or hurt themselves.

Eight-year-old Reed Fletcher is no exception, and I look at him sternly as I hold his arm still in order for my father to splint his wrist. "Why in the world were you trying to walk along the henhouse roof in the first place?" I ask. "Did you not think that the shingles would be slippery, with all the rain we've had?"

Reed rolls his eyes. "Miss Fisher, Brien *dared* me to. He bet Mary down the road a penny that I couldn't do it!"

"So now," I say slowly, "your brother has a penny, and you have a sprained wrist."

"Well, no." Reed grins, showing me missing teeth. "You see, Mary's just six, and she didn't have one. And *now*, Brien has to do my chores."

Father looks up from tying the bandages, and the corner of his mouth twitches. "Well," he says, "surely there are chores you can do with only the one hand. And your wrist will heal in a few days, lad."

Reed grimaces, looking from me to my father and back again. "You don't need to tell my mum that, do you?"

Father and I wait until we're out in the drizzle again, and the door of the cottage has closed behind us, before we turn to one another and exchange a grin. Then my father stretches his arms wide, sending his satchel of supplies swinging.

"Tired?" I ask. After all, he was awake and busy at his work-table long before I rose this morning. Before the sun rose, too, for that matter.

He nods ruefully, a fine coat of droplets on his hair. "I'll be glad when you take your oaths, Ellin. Then I can send you out while I stay home and keep dry."

I snort. "As if you would. You'll make me tie bundles of herbs and bottle tinctures while you go and heal people."

"And would you mind?" he inquires, with a gesture at the spot on my skirt where Reed, before receiving a healing for his pain, vomited a little on the hem.

Shrugging, I tilt my face up to the sky. "I like helping people," I say simply. "The bad bits don't bother me. Much, I mean."

He nods, and, tired, we both go quiet as we approach the center of town. We pass Alder's, and I can't miss the warm, savory smells of grease and wood smoke coming from the chimney. I sniff appreciatively, and my stomach growls. "Do you want to stop?" I ask hopefully, with a sidelong glance at my father. "It must be nearly time for dinner, and we haven't been out since we came home…"

"And if we do, you won't be asked to cook tonight," he adds, giving me a knowing look.

"Well, yes."

Father chuckles, already heading up the inn's walkway. "I don't see why not."

Grinning, I trot to catch up.

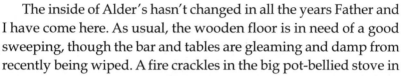

The inside of Alder's hasn't changed in all the years Father and I have come here. As usual, the wooden floor is in need of a good sweeping, though the bar and tables are gleaming and damp from recently being wiped. A fire crackles in the big pot-bellied stove in the center of the inn, and, behind the bar, Madam Alder looks up as we come in and stomp our shoes on the mat.

"Master Fisher!" she exclaims. "And Ellin! I heard you were back."

"For a week now," Father replies as he shrugs off his new coat and hangs it on one of the hooks by the door, followed by his satchel. "Are we too early for dinner, Dorys?" he asks, taking my cloak.

Madam Alder shakes her head and wipes her hands on her apron. "Goodness, no. Thom's out, and our girls aren't here for work yet, but I'll cook for you if you don't mind a bit of a wait."

"I've been waiting months for your potatoes," I say, smiling. Madam Alder minded me as a child, sometimes, while Father was called to heal someone, and I've always liked her. "A few minutes more is nothing."

Madam Alder laughs. "I'll make you a big batch, then. And what else? We're having beef and sweetroot pie for the special tonight; it should be nearly done."

"That's fine," Father says, and I nod my agreement. "And a glass of cider for me, I think." Then he smiles. "A small one for Ellin, too. She worked hard today."

"Find a table, then, and I'll have your drinks out in a minute."

Father and I settle ourselves at one of the small, round tables nearest the stove, and I sigh with contentment as the warmth washes over my back. "I missed this," I murmur, looking at Father.

"Alder's?"

"Everything." I shrug, not knowing how to explain it. "Just…us." I smile. "Back to normal."

Father smiles back, but then his face turns serious. "Well, things will have to change soon," he says. "Now that you've shown your skills as a healer, we'll want to consider—"

"No." The word pops from my mouth before I have a chance to think. At my father's shocked look, I attempt to explain. "I mean, if you're going to suggest that I should go off to the college, I'm not ready. And…I don't think I should," I finish, lowering my voice though we're the only people here.

His eyes widen. "Ah. Because of—"

"*My power*," I think, though I don't add that simply having it isn't the reason. I haven't told my father, but I'm afraid that, without using my forbidden abilities, I won't be as good a healer as he thinks I am. "Yes."

Father frowns. "Don't do that," he snaps, under his breath. "Not here."

"But I was just—"

"We'll talk later," he says firmly, just as Madam Alder sets our drinks in front of us.

"There you are," she says. "Your meal will be just a bit longer. And Ellin, you'll give me a shout if someone comes in, won't you?"

"All right."

"Good girl." She gives me a wink before bustling off to the kitchen again. When she's gone, I turn back to my father.

"What's the matter?" I ask quietly. "I haven't done anything wrong by just talking to you with it, have I?"

"Ellin," he says, and there's an intensity in his voice that frightens me, a little. "I said, we'll discuss this at home."

"Fine," I mutter into my drink.

He takes a sip of his own cider, then sighs when he puts it down and folds his hands on the table. "Regardless," Father says, "what I was going to say is that I'd like to write to Mistress Saddler at the college in Whiteriver. I want to take you as my apprentice, early, before you start your training there."

"Before college?" I shake my head, startled. "But…that isn't done!"

Father shrugs. "It isn't common, but it has been done, particularly if someone shows a talent for the healing powers very young."

I trail a fingertip along the smooth wood of the well-worn tabletop. "So, it would be official," I say quietly. "I'd be a healer's apprentice. A healer, someday."

"Of course," he replies, and I can hear the smile in his voice though I don't look at him. "Though I've never had any doubt of that."

"I know." And I never did, either, until now. But now that he's said the words; wants me to become an apprentice and go away again someday, maybe soon, to the college in Whiteriver, I feel trapped. As if my life is being laid out before me, and I don't have a choice. And I remember healing King Allard, how frightened I was, how horrified when I realized that just the healing itself wasn't enough. I remember how I was ready to kill Snowflower's foal just because I didn't know a better way. Most importantly, I remember that it was only my other power that kept both of them from dying when my healing skills weren't enough.

"Ellin? What is it?"

I look up and try to smile, because I know how badly my thoughts would disappoint him. "It's nothing. Our dinner's here," I add with relief as Madam Alder approaches with our plates.

"It is," she agrees, obviously overhearing, as she sets a plate with a thick slice of pie, thick-crusted and oozing gravy, and a pile of potatoes in front of each of us. I can smell the garlic and ashpepper in the potatoes without even trying, and my mouth waters. "Lucky for you, I didn't have to come and tend bar instead of cooking. The wet might be keeping everyone in, tonight. But it's early yet."

The door opens just as she finishes speaking, letting in a gust of fresh, damp air and a group of dripping young men, and Madam gives us a wry smile as the old Maple sisters from the edge of town totter in on the young men's heels. "Spoke too soon," Madam Alder murmurs, tucking a graying red curl back into the knot at the nape of her neck. "Do the two of you need anything else?"

Father and I shake our heads, but before we can even thank her for cooking, she hurries off to greet the newcomers and take their orders.

"Oh," I mumble around a piping hot, spicy mouthful of potatoes. "It's good."

Father nods, chewing. "Mm-hmm."

The inn fills up quickly as we eat, getting louder by the minute with the buzz of conversations, people shouting greetings to one another, and, eventually, the clanking of plates and forks and glassware. People call out and wave to my father, and a few stop by our table to welcome us home.

I'm just scooping up the last bite of my potatoes when a shadow falls over our table and a big, freckled hand smacks the wood hard enough to rattle our plates and set the cider sloshing in our glasses. "Rowan!" a deep voice rumbles. "Here at last, are you? I was wondering when you'd brave the gossip and questions for a pint."

"Donnal!" My father grins and sets his fork aside in order to clasp the big man's hand. "It seems Ellin and I chose the wrong night, after all. Another, and we might've missed you."

Donnal Marthen, the other Master Healer in Harnon, laughs loudly and whacks the table again. Then he shakes his head, copper mane flying, and gives me a white-toothed grin behind his short beard. "I see you've brought the girl back with you," he says with a wink at my father. "Couldn't find someone in the Northlands to buy her, eh?"

Father snorts. "Well. I had offers, but—"

"Father!" I blush and bury my face in my hands, but I can't help smiling. "Two pennies, and you can have him," I tell Donnal, nodding to my father. "A bargain."

"Have some respect, Ellin," Donnal says, chuckling. "You wouldn't overcharge me like that, would you?" He cuffs me on the arm, but lightly, before he settles himself into the extra chair. It creaks as his bulk descends on it. Donnal is a head taller than my father, at least twice as heavy, and as always, I marvel that such a tree of a man can be such a deft and gentle healer. He reminds me of Coll, I realize, and I sigh into my cup, wondering how Coll and the others are. Though I've tried not to think of them, tried not to think of the Northlands at all, my thoughts keep returning there despite my best intentions.

"—missed a great deal, while you've been away, Rowan," Donnal is saying when I pull my attention back to the present.

"Oh?" Father asks.

"Aye. And none of it pleasant," Donnal adds more quietly, his face darkening. He gives my father a meaningful look. "News from the Downs. They've—"

"Ellin," my father interrupts, voice as sharp as the look he gives Donnal. "Why don't you go and fetch Donnal a drink?"

I roll my eyes and would protest, but I can tell from his expression that he won't let me stay and listen. "What would you like?"

"Whisky. No water," Donnal replies distractedly. "Thank you."

I snort and head for the bar, irked that my father thinks I'm ready to be an apprentice but too young, apparently, to know what they're talking about. I can tell, watching them from the bar as Thom Alder fixes the drink, that it's serious. Both my father and Donnal lean in, faces sober as they talk, and their conversation stills abruptly when I come back to the table.

"Thank you, Ellin," Donnal says again when I hand him his whisky, the slender glass almost disappearing in his thick paw. My father says nothing, but his face is grim as he takes a drink of his cider, and his mouth puckers as if it has suddenly become bitter. I sit, feeling awkward, and toy with my almost empty glass.

"You know," Donnal says abruptly, voice still low and rumbling, "there are rumors that the Guardians have...become stricter... of late."

My father picks up his head at that, frowning. I frown too, but in confusion. "The Guardians?" I ask. "I've never heard of them."

"You wouldn't have," Father replies. "But...you remember Padrus Miller, don't you, Ellin?"

"Old Miller," I whisper, past the sudden ashes in my mouth. "The one whose house burnt down."

"The Guardians' work." Father clears his throat, and I remember that I'm not supposed to know why. "Padrus…broke a rule," Father says slowly. "Did something forbidden. The Guardians exist to discourage people from—from doing that."

I nod. "What did he do?" It seems stupid to pretend with Donnal, of all people, but the Ellin he knew—before the Northlands—would have asked. I can't help wishing I *still* was ignorant of the forbidden powers. Even if it meant not having them at all.

"You'll know when you're older."

I nod again and shrug, as if resigned. "What do you mean they've become stricter?" I ask, turning to Donnal. "Isn't burning someone's house down punishment enough?"

Donnal has been silent and still as a boulder, staring at his whisky, but now he looks up and meets my gaze. There is a sadness in his kind brown eyes that sends a flicker of apprehension to my heart. "Ellin, that isn't what I meant," he says softly. "The Guardians' methods haven't changed. It's their level of tolerance that has. They used to allow a few mistakes. But now…" He shakes his head and gives my father a meaningful look, speaking very slowly. "Now, just one time can be enough to make them act."

I see Father's hand tighten around his glass. His head jerks in a nod. "I understand."

I understand, too, and my blood runs cold at the knowledge. It's a warning.

"Good," Donnal says, and he smiles as though we've been discussing nothing at all. "Good!"

"We'd best get home," Father says, reaching for his pocket. "We've had a long day, and I'm sure Ellin is as tired as I am."

"I am," I agree, and it's true, though I'm not sure I could sleep if I had to. Donnal has rattled me, but I try not to show it as we say goodnight.

It is only when Father and I are back out on the road, getting wet again now that it has begun to rain in earnest, that I allow myself to let my breath out in a whoosh. It's ridiculous, but I feel as if I've been holding it in since I heard about the Guardians.

"You knew about the Guardians?" I ask after a moment, squinting to see him in the light of the small lantern we borrowed from the Alders.

Father doesn't look at me. "Wait 'til we're home," he says shortly, quickening his pace with an audible squelching of mud.

I sigh. "But—"

"Ellin!" he snaps. "Be still, and obey me without questioning, for once."

I nod and look at the ground, stung until it occurs to me that it wasn't anger I heard in his tone, but fear. The idea of my father being afraid makes me shiver. It takes quite an effort not to look over my shoulder or jump at shadows and regular nighttime noises.

The walk home seems to take longer than it ever has, and I breathe another sigh of relief when Father unlocks the door and we step inside. I don't even have time to enjoy being out of the rain, though, before he speaks.

"Yes," he says, sounding tired and holding his coat in his hands as if he's forgotten where to hang it. "I knew about the Guardians. I had hoped I wouldn't have to tell you yet."

CHAPTER EIGHTEEN

I LOOK AT FATHER OVER MY drawn-up knees, still feeling chilled and uncomfortable even though he has put extra wood on the stove, and I've changed into dry clothes. "So the Guardians are the ones who make certain no one uses the forbidden powers," I say dully. "And they can do whatever they like, punishing people."

He nods, studying his tea. One long, thin hand is wrapped around his mug for warmth. He has soot on his knuckles, I notice.

"But how do they know?" I press. "I mean, it isn't as if you can tell by looking at someone…"

"They just do," Father replies. The firelight glints on the new strands of silver in his hair, and I wish, for the hundredth time, that I hadn't told him about my abilities. Even if he knew without being told, if it was still unspoken between us, perhaps he wouldn't have to worry so much. "I don't know how. But my guess is that they can somehow sense if someone uses their power."

That makes sense, and I nod. Then I frown and drag my lip between my teeth worriedly a few times before asking the question foremost in my mind. "Do you think they know?" I ask, barely more than a whisper because I'm afraid to say the words out loud. "About me, I mean?"

He sighs. "I hope not. You were so far away when—when it happened. That's why I didn't say anything. I hoped—" Father swallows the rest of his words with some tea and shakes his head. "I don't know."

"But they suspect," I say. "Someone has to, or Donnal wouldn't have said—"

"No." Father's tone is so flat, so certain, that I look up in surprise. I'm even more confused by the tight, pained look I see on his features.

"How do you know?"

He opens his mouth to speak. Shuts it again and presses his lips together for a moment, then shoves himself from his chair, suddenly, and goes to poke at the fire. He stabs the bottom log hard enough to break a chunk off, sending orange sparks flying. Concerned, I climb to my feet and go to him. "Father? What is it?"

His narrow shoulders sag as he lets the poker fall to his side. "Donnal said what he did because of your mother," he says quietly, looking into the flames instead of at me. It might be the play of shadows and light on his face, but I think I see his jaw clench and unclench before he continues. "She had—she was like you. And the Guardians suspected her. Her death might have been an accident, but even if it was, it was only a matter of time before they would have—" He sighs hard through his nose. "I hoped you wouldn't be—"

"I'm sorry," I whisper, when I can find the words to speak. I'm not certain what I'm apologizing for. "Father…" I take the poker from his hand and put it away, though my own fingers are shaking. I'm not certain, either, who moves first after that, but the next thing I know, his arms are around me, and I'm clinging to him, and he's hugging me so tightly I can hardly breathe.

"I won't let anything happen to you," he says fiercely. "I promise."

I nod against his chest. Inhale and feel my breath hitch. "I know."

"Just be careful," he says as he pulls back to look at me. "Don't use your ability again, Ellin. Ever. Not for any reason."

I nod again. "I won't."

"Good girl." Father's arms go even tighter, and he rests his cheek on the top of my head as he used to do when I was small and he'd pick me up to hug me. Despite everything, despite still being stunned about my mother, for an instant I can't help thinking that everything will be all right.

When I finally fall asleep, I dream about my mother. I'm four years old again, watching her fingers get stained watery, reddish violet when she takes me out blackberry picking. She sticks the tip of her tongue out at me, showing me how purple it is, and I laugh and stick mine out, too. Then I'm in bed, and she's stroking my hair and telling me my favorite story. And I know it's a dream because I can't remember all the words, but I listen as hard as I can, hoping somehow I'll be able to hear.

Then I hear hoofbeats in the distance, and I sit up with a feeling of dread, but my mother keeps on talking as if she doesn't notice. I squeeze my eyes shut, and when I open them again, I'm standing in the kitchen doorway. The yellow morning sunlight is so bright I can barely see. I squint, and then I see her outside, riding toward me. She waves, silhouetted, and the hoofbeats get louder, drumming so hard my teeth rattle—

I wake in the dark with a gasp and sit bolt upright, pressing a shaking hand to my chest. After the worst grip of terror has passed, I close my eyes again and breathe slowly. "It was only a dream," I whisper, willing my muscles to relax. "Only—"

The pounding noise comes again, louder and more insistent, and I realize that it isn't hoofbeats at all. There's someone at the door. At the same instant, I hear my father's feet hit the floor in his bedroom. His door opens a moment later, and candlelight flickers through the crack at the bottom of my door.

I lie back down, my heart still racing. It's probably just someone wanting healing, I think. After all, that's not uncommon.

Just the same, I stay motionless and keep my head off the pillow, listening.

There are voices in the other room; my father's, and someone else's. A man's voice, low and murmured. Then another, a woman's. It's unusual for two people to come seeking my father's help, especially this late, and I creep to the door and press my ear against it.

"...have no right!" my father says, so loud that I would have heard him if I'd stayed in bed.

"We have every right, Master Healer, and you know it," the woman replies.

I frown, tempted to use my ability to find out what's going on. I promised my father I wouldn't, though. Instead, I quickly pull my dress on over my nightshift, wiggle my feet into my slippers, and wrap my blanket around my shoulders. Then I go out, trying to look as though I've been asleep instead of eavesdropping.

"Father?" I ask as I wander into the front room. "What's the—" But the words die on my lips when I see his face, bone-white and drawn with fear. I follow his gaze to the apparently healthy man and woman. And, behind them, through the open door, to the others waiting out in our yard, their lanterns dots of yellow in the drizzle and dark.

"Guardians," my father whispers. The word pierces my heart. He closes his eyes. "Ellin, run."

The woman is tall and spare, wearing spectacles, with her hair in a tight knot. I don't know her and wonder distantly if she's from Harnon or another village nearby. She clucks her tongue. "Run? Where? We'd find her."

Every muscle, every instinct is screaming at me to flee. Instead, I stay rooted to the spot. "I won't leave you," I say to my father, voice thin with fear.

"It's only the girl we want," the man says, as if he hadn't heard me. He gestures with a skinny hand and looks at my father. "Given your status, we would perhaps overlook your failure to turn her in yourself and your reluctance to surrender her a few moments ago. Provided, of course, you give her willingly now."

"She is my daughter," my father replies flatly.

"She is tainted," the woman snaps. "And you're not above the law, Master Healer. This is not a request."

As if that was permission, the man takes a step toward me, extending his grasping, claw-like hands. Time seems to stop as I stare at my father, too terrified to move, to speak, to do anything but stand helpless. Sick and lightheaded, I try to think of something to say to him, one last time, before they take me.

My father looks back. Opens his mouth as if to speak, then shuts it again and gives me the barest flicker of a smile. "Run," he mouths, and I see him tense. His hand moves surreptitiously at his side as I stand motionless and frown in confusion.

And then my father, healer, gentlest man I know, takes the fire poker and swings it with all his might at the male Guardian. "Ellin, RUN!"

His shout is like a slap to my cheek, jolting me out of my frozen terror. I toss the blanket aside and turn to run back to my bedroom before the Guardian hits the floor. There is thumping in the other room, and the woman screams, but I'm shaking with mingled terror and purpose as I leap over my bed and throw the window up hard enough to crack the glass. I fling myself out, bruising my fingers and scraping my shin on the sill, and hit the ground running.

Behind me, the woman screeches again. "She's going out the window!"

I can't go to the road because of the Guardians in the front yard, and I don't dare stay too close, lest they find me. So I sprint, blindly, as fast as I can, through the garden and the trees behind the house. My slippers skid on the wet grass; I run out of one, stumble, and kick the other off. The ground is cold and slick beneath my bare feet, the hem of my skirt soaked, but I keep racing, dragging in short gasps of air. I swear I can hear footsteps following me.

I squeeze my eyes shut and go faster, heart trying to burst out of my chest. My arms pump like windmills, and I will my feet to fly. Something collides with my ankle, and I go sprawling. With a wrenching smack that steals my breath, I land on my stomach and lie there gasping, tasting mud.

When I can, I lift my head. I must be quite a way past our old barn, on the Brewers' land, I realize. The lights of the Guardians' lanterns are far enough away, now, to be small, swaying dots. I squint in the darkness and see the black shape of a clump of bushes nearby. After I crawl to them, I wriggle under the grasping, thorny branches to the center. The branches pull my hair when I duck my head, and I hug my knees to my still-heaving chest, trying to make myself as small as possible. And I wait.

Once I have my breath back, I become aware that my clothes and hair are wet through. I can feel the grit of mud on my face and hands and taste it in my mouth, and my feet hurt. I think the left one is cut and bleeding; there is a suspicious burning along the sole. I'm cold, too, particularly now that my sweat has gone clammy and chilled. Shivering, I peer toward the house and pull my knees even closer.

The Guardians' lanterns still bob about, being raised and lowered as their owners look for me. I worry my bottom lip between my teeth and stare until my eyes water, hoping to see my father come toward me at any moment. Surely he was able to get away, I think. After he hit the male Guardian, he could have pushed the woman aside and followed me out my bedroom window, or out his own...

Then, as I watch, several of the Guardians gather together by the house, their lantern light pooling so that I can almost make out their shadowed forms. Something sparks, and a different kind of light flares, orange and living. The torch blossoms and arcs through the air like a comet. They must have doused the roof with oil because the flames spread like liquid, sweeping greedily along the thatch.

I can't move. Can't breathe. My heart drops into my stomach as I watch, transfixed. The flames engulf the roof in a matter of moments and lick red-gold tongues down the walls. In the fire's light, I can see the Guardians gathered, watching. I can see black smoke billowing up to the sky, looming over the house like some nightmare beast.

My cheeks are wet. It's only when I realize they're warm, too, that I know I'm crying, soundlessly, in small, shuddering gulps. I think of all our things inside the house, the house itself, where I've lived all my life, being reduced to a pile of ash. I try not to think about my father, except to hope that he's all right. I can't bear to think that he isn't.

Despite this, I know. I don't know how, but I feel the truth in my bones, in the bleeding hole in my heart that I don't dare examine for fear of the pain. Still, I don't take my eyes from the house as it burns. And I hope, though I feel hope withering as the flames climb higher.

Two of the Guardians apparently start to look for me again, coming closer and holding their lanterns high. I huddle against the tangled mass of trunks in the center of the bushes and don't make a sound. Don't move, though my body vibrates with the urge to run.

"—has to be far away by now," one of them mutters, sounding disgusted, when he gets near enough for me to hear. He lets his lantern swing loosely at his side and stops not far from my hiding place. "She wouldn't be stupid enough to stay. Not with her father dead."

My lips part in a silent gasp. Knowing and *knowing* are different. I clamp my mouth shut and almost bite through my cheek in an effort not to cry out.

"No. Mellry said she hit him after the girl was gone," the other Guardian replies, and I struggle to hear him past the roaring in my ears. "The girl didn't know. Wasn't on purpose, anyway, ol' Mellry says."

"Oh?"

"Didn't you hear her? He came at her like a madman. Mellry shoved him back, he fell, hit his head, and—" the Guardian sighs heavily. "Pity, that. He was a good healer."

He was my father, I think numbly. He was—

Not was. Is. He can't be dead. It can't be true.

"We'll tell Mellry we'll resume the search in the morning," the first Guardian says, catching my attention again. "It's cold, and she's only a slip of a girl. We'll find her."

"No doubt."

I watch the blurred, wavering lights of their lanterns bob away. When they're out of earshot, I finally close my eyes and feel another torrent of hot tears spill down my cheeks. I press my face against my filthy knees and sob silently, because some anguish is too enormous and jagged and gaping and horrible for any sound to express.

I cry until my face is hot and swollen and I'm gagging on tears and snot, unable to breathe. I didn't believe, before now, that you could really *feel* your heart break, but the sick, clenching pain in my chest tells me it's true. When no more tears will come, I wipe my nose on my clammy wrist. Then I just sit and stare at our house as it burns.

The Guardians have gone. Their lanterns no longer dot the yard, but I don't care. They could find me this instant, haul me up by the armpits and march me straight into the flames to be killed because I'm 'tainted' with power, and I would be limp and unresisting. I close my stinging eyes and see my father's face again, the smile he gave me that last instant before I ran. I don't miss him yet, though, not really. I can't believe that I'll never see him again. It hurts, but it doesn't seem real.

Time passes. It could be only moments, or it could be hours. At last, as my cold, cramping body protests, I crawl out of the bushes and stagger to my feet. I have nowhere to go, and I still don't care if the Guardians find me, but I can't bear to sit any longer in this place where I heard of my father's death.

My arms cling to one another across my chest instinctively, as if that pressure could stop the gaping wound to my heart. As I stumble blindly, with no real destination in mind, I focus on the icy rain and the pain in my feet. These discomforts are a welcome distraction from the bigger, terrifying hurt. Even dazed with agony, I'm not stupid, so I don't head into town or even take the main road. Instead, I cut through the Brewers' field, then another, and another, until my half-numb feet find the gravelly mud of a back road instead of wet grass and leaves beneath them. For what seems like a long time, the endless dark and cold are broken only by my sniffling and the quiet squishing of my feet in the mud.

At last, when my calves begin to cramp and my teeth are chattering so violently I'm afraid of biting through my tongue, I veer off to the side, into the trees. It's even darker in the woods than on the road, nearly as wet, but I barely notice. I walk until I think I'm out of sight of the road. Then, finally, I let my trembling legs give out and sit, hard, on the forest floor.

The damp leaves are chilled and slimy; they stick to my ankles and slither up my calves. My skirt feels waterlogged and heavy, and my hair is truly soaked, dripping rivulets of icy water down my neck and back. I rub my palms roughly up and down my arms, hoping to create a little warmth, but even that is exhausting, and my head droops toward my chest in no time. It seems only natural to lie down, so I curl on my side and pillow my face with my arm as best I can. It hardly occurs to me to worry about bandits, or wild animals, or almost anything else. I do think about my father, though, and I'm crying again when I fall asleep.

CHAPTER NINETEEN

I WAKE STIFF, STILL EXHAUSTED, and cold to my bones. For an instant, before I open my eyes, I think my father and I are still on the road, heading home from the Northlands. I hardly have time to notice that my heart is heavy as a stone in my chest before I remember, though, and I can't suppress a whimper as the truth washes over me again. When I finally open my eyes, I find that it isn't yet dawn. The small widows of sky I can see through the shadow-black trees are faint purple, only just beginning to lighten. The birds seem to think otherwise, though, and the woods echo with their whistling chatter.

I sit up, wince as the movement sends pain snaking down my back, and try to work the knots out of my neck. My stomach growls after a moment, and I realize I'm both hungry and thirsty. Dinner at the inn seems a lifetime ago.

Dinner with my father. With a groan, I cradle my forehead in my palms, suddenly sick at the thought of food. I'm still thirsty, though, so I struggle to my feet and head deeper into the woods in hopes of finding a stream.

In the pre-dawn dimness, it's hard to see my way through the trees. I go slowly, but even so, I stub my toes on sticks and rocks.

It's still cold, too, but there's nothing I can do about that except try to ignore my shivering.

As I walk, I'm reminded of the night I was locked out of the gates, back in the Northlands. I thought a night outdoors, without food or water or shelter, wouldn't be so bad. At least then, I knew my father would be waiting for me. I could have gone back to our rooms at the college the next morning, and he would have fixed me tea and breakfast, would have seen me tucked into my warm bed. Now, my filthy, sodden dress and nightshift are all I have. I think regretfully of my slippers, kicked off willy-nilly as I ran for my life, and I try not to wonder how much they would cushion my feet from the stones and cold mud.

The forest gets lighter as I walk. The sky turns pink, then pale orange, and I imagine I can feel the air beginning to warm a little. Those things are small comfort, though, because I don't find a stream. Or a path, for that matter. The deeper I go into the trees, the more it seems as if I'm the only person in the world. I'm not afraid to be alone, but the silence and the brisk morning air force my mind to be awake. I resist, wanting nothing but to stay in a numb fog of detachment, but I find myself thinking despite my best efforts.

I don't know what to do now. The words echo in time with my footsteps. Don't. Know what. To do. Don't. Know what. To do. Don't—

I sigh and shake my head, wishing that would silence my thoughts. I don't want to think about the fact that I have nowhere to go. I would be put back in prison in the Northlands. Or executed, more likely, for what I did to that guard. The Guardians are looking for me. Even if I could find a village here in the Southland without any Guardians, I don't have decent clothes, or shoes. Or any money to buy them—or food, for that matter. And, while I could practice healing to earn some coins, I'm half-trained, not allowed to do so, and I don't have any herbs or supplies.

The real problem is simple. Despite everything, I don't want to die. I know with certainty that it isn't what my father wanted. He didn't sacrifice his life for me, I think with a shudder, for me to throw mine away because I'm sad. I have to do something besides stay here in the forest and starve or die of thirst.

It is tempting, though. I miss him so much I can't breathe, and I've never been so miserable in my life. When I near the heart of the woods and still haven't found a stream, I stop to rest and flop down on the closest log, burying my face in my hands. It would be so simple to give up, I think. So simple to stay here, to do nothing, to not care at all what happens to me. I almost wish I could.

My lank, still-damp hair falls forward, making my face itch. I shove it aside halfheartedly and stare at my knees as the pale morning sun makes a halfhearted effort to warm my back. When I swallow, there is a sour, disgusting taste in my mouth, and I think longingly of a cup of water. Even a dirty handful of water would be as good as a hot cup of tea, right now.

Sitting all day won't make me any less thirsty, so, after several moments, I take a deep breath and push myself to my feet. I brush some of the drying mud off my skirt as I turn, but my hand stops abruptly when I see the large, booted feet planted not five steps away from me.

I gasp, and my gaze flies up, over his legs and middle. The blood drains from my face as I crane my neck up to meet his eyes. "You," I croak, surprised at the hoarseness of my voice, too startled to run.

"Me," Donnal Marthen agrees. He extends a hand to me, but I regard it as though his touch is poison, feeling my legs tense. Then I swallow, dry-mouthed, and wonder how fast I could run the other way. I wonder how fast he runs, and if he could catch me before I could find a place to hide. As if sensing my thoughts, Donnal steps toward me. "Ellin—"

I take two steps backward, scanning the ground for a heavy stick, a rock, a piece of bark—anything to use as a weapon. "You knew," I say, stalling for time. "You knew they were coming."

"I suspected," he replies levelly, skirting the log as he comes even closer. Again, I retreat, eyeing him warily. "But Ellin, I was trying to w—"

"Augh!" I scream when I back right into something warm and solid. Some*one* whose hands close tightly around my arms, pinning me to his chest. I struggle and kick backward, aiming for his shin, but he only holds me tighter.

"You're one of them!" I shout, straining against my assailant's grip. "I knew it! You're one of the Guardians!"

"Damn it, Mathias!" Donnal rumbles, and he frowns. "Let her go. You're hurting her."

Mathias snorts, stepping aside as I try to stomp on his foot. "Are you mad? She'll run."

"I won't," I lie, though I think I'll be lucky to outrun even one of them, let alone both.

"*You won't,*" agrees a voice in my mind, shocking me to stillness, "*because we aren't your enemies.*"

CHAPTER TWENTY

I CRANE MY NECK AND STARE at Mathias when he relaxes his grip on my arms. Startlingly green eyes look back, the only nice feature in an otherwise homely, big-nosed face.

"What?" I whisper.

Mathias rolls his eyes. *"We aren't your enemies."*

"You're like me?" I turn to Donnal, feeling a strange sense of unreality. "And you?"

"Not me, lass," he says quietly, shaking his head. "But I'm no Guardian, either. We're here to help."

"Help?"

"We've been looking for you." Donnal sighs and sets a big hand on my shoulder, and a hurt expression flickers over his features when I flinch. "Will you come?"

I frown. "Where?" I ask warily, even though the truth is that I'm too tired to care. Too hungry and thirsty, too, not to go with them. And I know it.

"A camp. Nearby," Mathias says. *"There are others,"* he adds significantly.

I look at Donnal, wanting to trust him, and he gives me an encouraging nod.

"Fine," I say at last, not knowing whether I should feel trapped or hopeful or both. "I'll go."

The camp is nearby, as Mathias promised, even deeper in the woods. I smell it before I see it, and the scent of cooking food sets my stomach to growling and gnawing itself again. I hear voices, too. Then, almost before I know it, we step out of the trees into a large clearing where several tents are pitched. There are quite a few people milling about and seated around a campfire. Most of them look over, and a few wave as we approach.

"Found her, then, Mat?" someone calls.

"Not too soon, either," Mathias answers as he heads for the fire, with a gesture over his shoulder that both takes in and mocks my bedraggled state. "She looks like a half-drowned cat, aye?"

Simply being around so many people after my night alone is almost overwhelming, and I'm tempted to run, but Donnal's solid, reassuring presence behind me keeps me from doing so. "Come along," he murmurs, with a nod at one of the tents. "We'll see you cleaned up, first, and then you can eat. Ketty!" he bellows, causing me to jump. "Keth! Have you any spare dresses?"

"If I did, they'd be a bit small for you, hmm?" a sharp voice teases. A familiar voice, and I'm trying to remember where I've heard it before when a short, curvy girl steps out of the tent a moment later with a folded armful of cloth. I stare, recognizing her pretty face and bushy ginger hair though I haven't seen her in years.

"Kethie Brewer?" I squeak incredulously, when I can find my voice. Of all the people I might have expected to find in the middle of the woods, my childhood playmate was certainly not among them.

"Keth, now, if you please," she says, making a face. Then her lips quirk in a smile. "It's good to see you again, Ellin, though I scarcely recognize you under all the mud."

I shake my head, still stunned. "But I thought you moved to Harpersfall. What are you doing here?"

"Oh, I did, and my parents are still there," she replies with a careless shrug. "But given what I am... here I am."

"What you are?" I echo, scarcely noticing as Donnal leaves, heading for one of the other tents.

Kethie—Keth, I remind myself—gives me a look I remember well from our childhood. One that clearly says I'm stupid and she's humoring me. "Gifted, of course." When I still must look as blank as I feel, she rolls her eyes. "Honestly, Ellin. Tainted!"

I can feel my jaw hanging open at the idea that pretty, snippy Kethie Brewer has powers like mine. "*You* can talk with your thoughts," I say flatly.

"*And that's just the start of it,*" she replies, pale eyebrows knitting in concentration. I'm not surprised that her thought-voice feels prickly, like a fingernail jabbing at my brain. "*You'll see.* But first," Keth adds, breaking into speech, "you'll need to wash. You're filthy, and I can smell you from here. And I've a dress for you, but it'll be too big in the chest, of course."

As I follow her to the tiny wash-tent to bathe as best I can with a bucket and sponge, I'm reminded why I didn't always like her when we were young.

While I scrub some of the mud from my skin with the sponge and a cake of harsh brown soap, Keth chatters to me from outside the tent. I listen, fascinated, as she tells me how she discovered her abilities and ran away before the Guardians had a chance to come for her.

"And you just found...these people?" I ask with a wince, as I dab away the dirt on one foot to reveal a long, reddened cut that stings. Most of the skin on my arms and legs is scored with scratches from the bushes I hid in and from tree branches, and a big bluish bump sits large and ugly on my shin where I barked it on the windowsill. The warm water does help leach the chill from my flesh, though, and I shiver pleasantly as I drip it down my bare back.

"Goodness no," Keth replies, sounding amused. "I met a boy, Brendin, in Whiteriver. He was gifted like us. He told me about Lev and the True Southlings."

Who? And the what? I wonder as I dry myself. I don't ask, though, because I assume I'll find out in time. Besides, I don't want to give Keth yet another reason to think I'm stupid.

The water in the bucket has turned nearly black now that I've swished my hair in it, but even so, the towels come away from my hair and skin streaked with traces of mud. Though I would still love a real bath in a tub, I feel almost like myself again now that I'm cleaner. Keth's dress is indeed too large in the chest, not to mention a little too short, but it fits well enough, and it's warm. Much more important, unlike the last clothing I borrowed, in the Northlands, this is a proper Southling style. The long cream-colored shift has wide, comfortable sleeves, not tight ones. And the sleeveless, leaf-brown outer dress laces only over my chest, leaving the outer skirt open. Pleased, I wrap one of the towels around my hair and poke my head out.

"I don't suppose you have extra shoes or socks?"

Keth frowns. "No spare shoes, and socks alone won't do you much good on the wet grass. We'll find something for you later. And take that off your head," Keth adds, giving me a critical look. "You look better now that you've clean clothes, but with your pretty hair covered up, you look pale and awful."

I nod and go back in for my bathwater. I debate for a moment about the towel—on the one hand, it is cold, and I don't want to go out with wet hair. On the other, if nothing else, I trust Keth's judgment about how I look. With a sigh, I unwind the towel and drag my fingers through my hair. It's useless; I know the loose curls will only tangle more tightly as they dry, and I can't help wishing for a brush.

"Much better," Keth says approvingly when I come out again, picking my way on sore feet. She shows me where to dump the bathwater, and doing so reminds me of how thirsty I still am. I'm grateful when she says we'll go eat.

A large iron pan of soup simmers over some coals piled at the edge of the big fire, and I keep a greedy eye on my bowl as I wait for it to cool. I drink my second cup of water slowly, after gulping the first and making Keth giggle at me when I told her I hadn't found the stream. I privately doubt she would have done better, out on her own, but I say nothing, in the interest of keeping peace. Impatient and ravenous, I blow on my soup to cool it faster, sip, and wince when the meaty, garlicky broth burns my tongue anyway. The soup is delicious, a little greasy and filled with grain and root vegetables gone all soft and pale and flavorful, and I'm too busy getting as much of it in my mouth as possible to take much notice of the others sitting by the fire.

When the worst of my hunger has been quelled, I look up to find Donnal, homely Mathias, Keth, and a number of others talking to each other. I wipe my mouth on the back of my hand and set my bowl aside, and, as if that was a signal, Donnal clears his throat. "Come," he says, lumbering to his feet. He extends a thick, freckled, hairy hand. "I'll take you to Levachai."

"Who is Levachai?" I ask, trotting to keep up with his long strides as he leads me to the farthest tent. "I think Keth mentioned him, too."

"He's the leader of the True Southlings."

"These people." I frown. "Why 'True Southlings?' What do they do? Donnal, I don't—"

He stops. Turns and gives me a small smile. "Patience, Ellin. You'll soon see."

I press my lips together, disliking being so unsettled. It's as if I'm wandering blind, but I've barely begun to get irritated when we arrive at the tent. The flap opens before Donnal has a chance to bellow, and a boy's head pokes out.

"This must be her!" the boy exclaims. He gives me a surprisingly formal, graceful bow. "Welcome, Ellin Fisher. We've been looking for you." As he speaks, I feel a very familiar tickle inside my head, and I yank my thoughts away and narrow my eyes.

"You know my name, but I don't know yours," I say rudely. "*And I thought you weren't my enemies here. What friend would spy on my thoughts like that?*"

The boy laughs, revealing very white, straight teeth, and holds up his hands. "My apologies, Ellin! I didn't realize you were sensitive to thought-reading. I merely wanted to make certain we could trust you."

"You could've asked."

He raises an eyebrow and looks highly amused. "Why ask for what I can easily take?"

I don't like him, I think. I turn to Donnal, who looks as if he's trying to hide a smile with the back of his hand. "I don't suppose we could stop wasting our time with this boy and talk to Levachai? Surely," I add, frowning at the boy, "your leader is more polite than you."

"Oh, I'm afraid he's just as bad," the boy replies with a grin. "Seeing as he's me."

I stare. "You're Levachai? The leader of…all these?" He looks to be of an age with Finn and Erik, surely no older than Coll. And though he is handsome in a wild sort of way, slight but well-built, with a thick head of hair so dark auburn it seems nearly black, he certainly doesn't *look* like anyone special.

He bows again, brown eyes sparkling with mirth. "Levachai Kinshield, at your service. I'll speak with her now," he adds, looking up at Donnal.

I look at the big man, too, wanting to ask him to stay, but I can see Levachai's smug, challenging smile out of the corner of my eye. He looks as if he expects me to do just that, and so I merely wave as Donnal nods and heads off.

"Come," Levachai says, beckoning me into the tent. "We have much to talk about." I follow him into the dim interior, unimpressed by the simple bedroll and two folding camp stools he has set up. It smells musty, and I wrinkle my nose. "Sit," he says. "I can fetch you a cup of water…"

"No, thank you." I smooth my skirt over my knees. "I'm fine."

"You've had a difficult night," Levachai remarks as he takes the other stool. "You're lucky to have escaped the Guardians."

"They killed my father," I say flatly. Those words sound so cold, so final, but I refuse to let him see my anguish. "You'll have to excuse me if I don't feel particularly fortunate."

His dark brows knit. "Yes, I heard. I'm sorry."

"How did you—? Never mind." I shake my head, not caring how he knows. "It isn't your fault," I mutter, looking down at my lap.

"No," he says with a sigh, "but we would have been there sooner if we'd known. We might have prevented it." His eyes gleam when he looks up. "Don't you see, Ellin? That's what we do. We prevent the Guardians from harming those like us. The True Southlings."

"Southlings with the power," I say softly, understanding at last. "Ones that are…tainted." The new word feels unfamiliar in my mouth, and I swallow. "That's where all these people come from, then? You rescued them?"

He smiles. "Rescued some. Others heard of us and came on their own."

"And the Guardians don't know?"

"Oh, they know. They just haven't found us." He winks. "It's why we move about."

"And this is how you live?" I ask with a raised eyebrow and a gesture at the small tent. Such a life would be better than being dead, I suppose, but still.

Levachai laughs. "Oh, no. This is just a small group of us, come looking for you."

I frown. "But you said you didn't know."

"We knew about you. That you were tainted," he says slowly. "We have a listener, Padrus, who heard you talking to your father. It wasn't hard to find out where you lived, and so we came this way. We didn't know the Guardians would come last night, though," he adds, frowning. "We were too late."

"Wait." I shake my head. "What's a listener? How did you find out who I was? And how did you know that the Guardians had come?"

"Patience!" Levachai spreads his hands and grins. "I forget you don't know about our gifts. Did you know they're all different?"

"What?"

"The gifts. Come," he says for the second time in a few moments, jumping to his feet. "I'll show you."

"You're not going to invade my mind again, are you?" I ask warily as I follow him.

"Not yet." Levachai gives me another grin over his shoulder, and I'm suddenly not certain whether I can't bear him or hope we'll be friends. "See Mat over there?" he asks, pointing to Mathias. "He can use thought-speech. You do know what that is?"

I nod.

"And he can read thoughts, but only on others who are gifted. I know you're familiar with that, since you recognized me doing it."

"Yes."

He nods. "Well, those are the two most common gifts. Nearly all of us can do those, to some extent. Some can read the thoughts of the ungifted, too."

"What others are there?" I ask with interest.

"Well, there's Padrus, the listener," he says. I gasp when I see the old man he's pointing to.

"That's Old Miller!"

"You know him?"

"Know *of* him," I reply, still shocked. "I thought he was dead."

"No, we got him out in time. And it's a good thing we did; he has proved invaluable. He can hear anyone using thought-speech from miles and miles away. Can't use it himself worth nuts, though."

"Is that all?"

"It's enough for now." He stops and turns to me. "And what about you, Ellin Fisher? What can you do?"

I open my mouth to tell him. Then I shut it again and narrow my eyes. "How do I know I can trust you, Levachai Kinshield?"

To my surprise, he laughs instead of taking offense. "Because you have no choice," he says at last, still chuckling. "Honestly, Ellin. We're all you have. And like it or no, you're one of us, now. So you might as well call me Lev, like friends."

"And if I don't like it? If I don't want to?"

Lev only smiles and resumes walking, utterly unruffled. "You will."

———·ooo-)◎(-ooo·———

"So," I say to Lev, when we stop circling the clearing and head for the fire, "you don't believe that the powers—gifts, I mean—are bad. And you all live together because you don't want the Guardians to catch you. And you rescue people like—like us—from the Guardians."

"Close enough," he replies. "Though we also hone our gifts, practice them, when we aren't planning a rescue." He pauses and tilts his head, regarding me consideringly. "I think you'll like it with us, Ellin. There's much we can teach you."

I nod, though I can't help wondering if that's not true. From what he has told me, it seems my gifts are as strong—or nearly as strong—as anyone's. And nothing he described sounded anything like what I did to the prison guard in the Northlands.

Something keeps me from telling this to Lev, though, and I'm relieved when we come to the others. I see Keth talking with a tall, solemn-looking woman Lev introduces as Glyn. Then there's Mathias and Donnal, a very young, fiery-haired boy named Brek, a one-handed older man named Aiddan Innys, a plump woman called Liss, and, seated a little apart, grizzled old Padrus Miller.

Padrus turns to me when I sit on the log beside him, cupping my second bowl of soup in both hands. "You're Fisher's girl, then?"

"Mm." I don't want to talk about Father. Not with anyone. So I sip my soup to avoid answering, and wince when it burns my tongue.

"That a yes or a no, lass? I can't see well enough, these days, to tell."

"I am," I say quietly. Or I was, I think.

"Aye, we heard about your father," Padrus says, surprising me. "He was a good man."

"I know."

He looks at the fire for a moment, wrinkles deepening to crevices as he squints. "Well," he says at last. "'Twas a stroke of luck we were heading this way anyway. You've been spared, girl. Count your blessings."

Before I can ask him what he means, he pushes himself to his feet with his stick and hobbles off, leaving me to frown into my soup. I feel out of place as the others talk easily to one another. With a sigh, I set my empty bowl aside and rest my forehead against my palms, intending to take a few deep breaths and collect my thoughts.

It is fully dark when I wake up, and the fire is low but still burning. It seems I slid off the log in sleep, and I'm embarrassed until I notice that someone has brought a warm blanket to cover me. Perhaps they were glad to be spared the trouble of finding a place for me to sleep, I think.

I stretch, shift to a more comfortable position, and tug the blanket closer against the nighttime chill.

"Awake, then?" a deep voice asks softly. I look up and find Donnal watching me, seated on a log on the other side of the fire with a cup in his hand.

"Only half, I think," I whisper. The camp is hushed and still, and I don't want to wake anyone. "I still feel like I could sleep for a week."

Donnal nods. "Do, if it'll help."

"It won't." I shake my head and feel a now-familiar stab of grief. I stand and go to sit on the ground beside him, then lean my back against the log. "Nothing will, Donnal."

He is silent for a long moment before he lets his breath out through his nose with a whoosh. "I know. Drink with me, to his memory?" he asks, sloshing some liquid into the cup before handing it down. "I'll have the bottle."

That reminds me of Coll, again, and my fingers clutch the cup hard enough to dent it. It seems the more I try not to think about the Northlanders, the more things remind me of them. I wonder if it will be that way with my father. If a day won't pass, for the rest of my life, without this new hurt.

Determined to dull the pain, no matter how, I take a gulp of the whisky and make a valiant effort not to cough. "To my father," I say hoarsely, holding up the glass, "who hated whisky."

"Well, no one toasts with tea," Donnal replies, with a sad half-smile. "To Rowan. The best of friends." He takes a long pull from the bottle.

"I miss him," I whisper after another moment, my attempt to feel better failing miserably. My eyes water, and my mouth puckers, and I'm not sure whether to blame the drink or not. "I keep forgetting, just for a moment or two. I can't believe he's gone—"

"Shh," Donnal murmurs, and he pats my head gently. "'Course you can't. He'll always be with you."

"That's not enough."

"I know." Donnal sighs, thick fingers stilling on my hair. "I know."

"If I'd stayed, do you think I could have helped him?"

"No. The Guardians are trained to fight, lass. You would have had no chance."

I nod and take another, slower sip. "I should've stayed. I don't—I don't have anything left," I whisper, voice quavering. "I mean—"

"Shh," he says again. "You have friends here. A place, if you'll take it."

It's small comfort, but I nod to make him feel better. "Why are you here?" I ask curiously after a moment, looking up at him. His hair is copper in the flickering light, his face shadowed. "If you can't—if you aren't gifted?"

Donnal makes a noise of distaste. "I don't need gifts to know there's nothing wrong with you."

"But why live like this, with them, if you don't have to?"

"I don't. I live where I always have, in Harnon. I just came to help them find you."

"I'm glad you did," I murmur sleepily, as I lay my head on his knee. And I am glad, and grateful. After all, I've known Donnal all my life. He was like a brother to my father, and now, I realize with a sniffle, he is the closest thing to family I have left. Donnal's cloak smells like herbs, like my father, and my tears finally spill over as he strokes my hair again.

"He was proud of you, you know," Donnal says softly. "He told me as much at Alder's. Said you would be an even better healer than he was."

My smile shakes at the corners. "Really?"

"Really. Rowan didn't tell me what happened, up in the Northlands, but he said you did something to impress him. And that's saying something, seeing as he already thought the world of you."

"It wasn't much," I reply, needing nothing but honesty between us. I have a suspicion that's from the whisky, but I don't care. "I delivered a foal, is all. Oh, and healed the king."

Donnal's hand goes still again, and he takes another drink. "Well," he says finally, "I see why he was impressed. You'd do well not to tell that to many."

"Oh, I know." I swallow a giggle and hiccup instead. "As if any Southling would want to hear that I helped a Northlander. I was fond of one, too, you know. Until—" I yawn so widely I can feel my jaw crack. "—until he put me in prison, I mean."

Donnal's chuckle is stifled, quiet, but the log still shakes. "Don't drink much, do you, lass?"

"Almost never." I frown at my empty cup. "Though maybe I should. I feel better."

"You shouldn't. And you won't feel better in the morning," he murmurs. He takes the cup before I drop it. "But while you do, sleep. The drink will help with that, at least."

"Can I sleep here?" I ask, peering up at him again. Just the idea of standing is enough to make me yawn again.

"Of course." He gives my head one last pat and smiles a little as he watches me get settled on the ground. "I'll watch over you 'til you fall asleep."

"You're a good friend, Donnal," I whisper as I pull the blanket up over my head. "Father was lucky to have you."

If he replies, I don't hear him as the merciful darkness of sleep claims me again.

CHAPTER TWENTY-ONE

THEY RISE EARLY IN THE CAMP. And noisily. Barely awake, I groan and press a hand to my ear, wishing the chorus of songbirds was quieter and the morning was less bright. When I peek out from beneath the blanket and find that the sun isn't even shining—instead, the sky is gray and looks like rain—I wince and try to remember just how much whisky was in that cup.

"Sleep well?" Keth inquires cheerfully as she bends to poke at the fire.

"I—" I clear my throat when I realize that I sound like a bullfrog. "Well enough."

"We thought about moving you, but Master Donnal didn't want to wake you."

"I'm not sure you could have, after awhile," I admit as I sit up, clutching my head.

Keth laughs aloud, and I try not to wince. "Ah. Whisky?"

"Too much of it, apparently." I squint at her, feeling a little resentful of her unwrinkled dress and scrubbed, shining face. "You're in a fine mood."

"I should be. We're moving on today. The wagons are waiting at the edge of the forest." Keth smiles. "None too soon, either. I've had enough of sleeping on the ground. At least the beds in the wagons are dry."

"The wagons?"

"Oh, the rest of the group went on the roads, since you can't take wagons through the forest. Did you think we lived in tents *all* the time?"

"I didn't know. I don't know anyth—" I break off and stare when Keth holds up a hand to shush me and frowns with concentration.

"Lev," she explains a moment later. Her expression clears, shifting to a rather smug smile as she adjusts her shawl. "Nothing important. He just likes to speak to me like this. Does it all the time."

For an instant, I wonder if I should feel sorry for Brendin from Whiteriver, but I decide it's none of my business and don't ask what happened to him. "Does it seem strange to you?" I ask instead, as I fold the blanket and try to smooth my borrowed dress. "Talking like that, I mean. Living like this. Don't you wish you were still just…regular? At home with your family?"

Keth shrugs. "I try not to think about that. I like it here."

"Yes, but—"

"Ellin, I'm not 'regular' Kethie Brewer anymore. I'm different. Gifted." She frowns. "You should be glad of your gifts. Don't fight them."

"I'm not," I say softly. "But my father—"

"—didn't know any better," she finishes, looking sympathetic. "I understand, Ellin. Really, I do. My family is the same way. But we're better than that, now. You'll see."

I can't think of a reply, so I only nod and wish I could believe her.

I feel better after I've scrubbed my face twice with frigid water from the stream and had a cup of strong, steaming tea. The others break camp all morning, taking pains to make it seem as though no one has been here. I stand about uselessly until Keth sends me to the stream to wash dishes. I'm still working, hands red and cold, when the boy, Brek, comes to fetch me.

Brek trails behind me as we leave the forest, practically walking on my heels, which makes me grateful for the shoes I borrowed from plump, motherly Liss. Mathias, who seems to be in command in the absence of Lev, told us to be quiet and walk single file. With that in mind, I pretend I can't hear Brek the first few times he tries to get my attention.

"Oi!" he says at last, just as something stings my back. I turn, glaring, and he gives me a gap-toothed grin and holds up the rest of a handful of acorns.

"What?" I hiss. "We're supposed to be quiet."

Brek rolls his eyes. "I'm not shoutin', am I?"

"*Well, why not talk to me like this?*" I say with my thoughts, still frowning. "*It's even quieter.*"

"Because I can't, you goose," he whispers, making a face.

"Why not?"

He shrugs as though it doesn't matter much and tosses another acorn off into the trees. "I dunno. Because."

"Well, what can you do?" I ask, interested. "You must have some power, or you wouldn't be here, would you?"

His grin crinkles his nose, almost making his freckles disappear. "'Course I do. Want to see?"

I blink at him in confusion. "See? What do—" I gasp and nearly stumble as I follow his gaze. Off to the side of the road stands Mellry, the bespectacled Guardian who came for me. My first instinct is to run, but Brek's small, surprisingly strong fingers dig into my arm, and as I watch, the Guardian's form wavers and vanishes.

"There," Brek says, looking satisfied. "See?"

It takes me a moment to swallow my heart back down to where it belongs, and longer still to catch my breath. "How did you *do* that?" I ask when I can speak again.

"As if I know! I just did." When I don't stop staring, he throws his hands up and rolls his eyes. "Fine. I saw her in your mind, and I reminded you that you'd seen her before."

"Reminded me?"

"Showed you your thoughts again. Made your eyes think you were seein' her. She wasn't really there," he adds unnecessarily.

I shake my head and blink, hardly able to believe it. Hearing someone's thoughts is one thing, but the power to make someone think they see something that isn't there seems even more amazing. "Is it a common ability?"

Brek laughs aloud and puffs out his chest. "Oh, no! I—"

"Quiet back there!" Mathias hisses. I blush, but when Mathias' back is turned again, Brek makes a face and a rude gesture. He catches me looking and gives me a wink and a grin, and I can't help smiling back.

We walk quietly for awhile, the silence broken only by twigs snapping beneath our feet, the sibilant brush of wet grass, and birds chirping and chattering. Bored, I watch one-handed Aiddan's pack bobbing ahead of me and try not to think about my father. From behind, Aiddan looks a little like him. About Father's age, tall and thin, though Aiddan's hair is less gray. Were it not for the others, it would be easy to pretend that Father and I never left the Southland at all. That I'm walking behind him to another village to heal someone, and the pack on his back is full of herbs and supplies, and…

I close my eyes briefly and swallow the sudden lump in my throat. Once, I didn't cry often. I remember mocking Garreth for blubbering. Now, it only takes a man who barely resembles Father, or the smell of tea, or merely the thought of him for the deep despair in my chest to writhe and ache again.

In front of me, Aiddan shakes his head, and I hear the annoyed huff of breath through his nose. "*Do you not know how to shield yourself?*" someone asks in my thoughts, and I know by Aiddan's quick glance over his shoulder that the unfamiliar voice is his.

"*I wasn't saying anything!*" I retort, both stung and embarrassed. "*If you overheard my thoughts, it's your own fault for listening.*"

"*I didn't hear your thoughts. I felt your emotions. You're making my head ache.*"

"*If your head hurts, that wasn't me,*" I reply. "*It's not my head that aches.*"

Aiddan glances back again, and I'm sure I don't imagine his fleeting look of pity. "*It's your heart. You long for your father. I know.*"

I frown, disliking the idea of someone sensing my feelings. That seems somehow even more a violation than having my thoughts read, and it makes me uncomfortable. I'm angry with Lev, again, for not telling me about these other abilities. And I can't help wondering if he's keeping me off balance on purpose.

Aiddan sighs. "*I assure you, Ellin, I'm not trying to read your emotions. In fact, I'm trying not to. Being overcome with despair isn't pleasant, particularly when it's not your own.*"

"*I'm sorry.*" I drag my bottom lip between my teeth and wish we could talk normally, without using our abilities. Despite not knowing Aiddan at all, I like him instinctively— if only because he does remind me of Father.

Aiddan stops short and turns, and the sunlight filtering through the trees makes a patchwork of fiery red and shadow in his hair. "I'm not your father, Ellin," he says, voice low. "Do not cheapen the memory of a good man by attempting to replace him. He deserves better than that."

"I'm not!" I avert my gaze, though, ashamed because he's right.

He shrugs and starts walking again. "*I'm nothing like him, you know.*"

"*I do know,*" I think quietly but, I hope, loud enough to be heard. "*He was a good man, and kind, and you're apparently nothing but an ill-tempered ass.*"

I want to make him angry enough to leave me alone and stay out of my mind. But, to my surprise, Aiddan makes a choked sound, and I see his shoulders shake with suppressed laughter. I feel a little bad for insulting him. After all, he did say my father was a good man. "*You—you knew him?*" I ask tentatively.

"*I did.*"

I nod, and I can't help glancing at the stump of his left wrist and wondering if my father helped heal him. I wonder what happened to him, too, but I know better than to ask.

If Aiddan senses my curiosity, thankfully, he doesn't say mention it. *"I could teach you how to shield yourself,"* he offers after a moment. *"For my sake as much as yours, of course."*

I smile. *"I'd like that."*

Our walk through the woods goes quicker after this. Aiddan gives me silent instructions on how to build a barrier around my mind, so I don't accidentally share my thoughts and feelings with everyone able to overhear. Building the shield is easier than I thought it would be, and in what seems like no time, Aiddan tells me that he can barely feel a thing from me.

"You realize that a gifted thought-reader will still be able to enter your mind," he adds, just as I've begun to congratulate myself on a lesson well-learned. *"Not only to converse—there's no shielding from this—but to hear your inner thoughts, as well."*

"And if my shield is too strong for them?" I ask, one eyebrow raised at his back.

Aiddan shakes his head. *"There's always someone stronger, Ellin."*

Out of curiosity, I reach out with my mind and poke at his mental shield. I can sense it, now that I know what to look for. I poke harder, testing it, and before I know what I'm doing, I've wriggled through.

I'm too startled at having breached Aiddan's shield to read his thoughts. I don't want to, anyway—I didn't even expect to get past his shield in the first place. I only have an instant, anyway, before he shoves me out.

"I'm sorry!" I exclaim, nearly stammering. "Aiddan, I wasn't—I didn't mean to—"

I don't know how to feel people's emotions, but even without that ability, I can sense his annoyance. Then he huffs out his breath, almost a chuckle, and shakes his head. *"As I said,"* he thinks quietly, *"there's always someone stronger."*

"*I don't mean to be,*" I reply, still ashamed. "*I didn't even know I could do that. I swear it.*"

"*Well, now you know.*"

But I don't, I think. The more I learn about these abilities, about what I can do, the less I feel like I know myself.

CHAPTER TWENTY-TWO

"HEY, WEARY BAND OF TRAVELERS!" Lev's teasing shout reaches us as we approach the road in the afternoon, and I'm not the only one who smiles. "Might we interest you in resting your feet and riding with us?"

"Please!" Keth exclaims dramatically, breaking out of line to hurry and giving him a brilliant smile. "Mine are going to fall off if I have to walk another minute!" I'm tempted to roll my eyes, but they widen instead as I take in the four large, painted wagons approaching.

"Grand, aren't they?" Brek asks, jabbing a grubby finger into my arm. I tear my eyes from the wagons, still gaping like an idiot.

"They're big," I admit. "But how in the world do the Guardians not *find* you in those?"

He grins. "Ellin! We're not hiding. Not really. They probably know where we are...some of the time, at least. But if we don't stay in the same spot, and if we've always got someone on watch, they can't very well plan a surprise attack, now can they?"

"But—"

"But nothing." Brek makes a dismissive gesture. "'Sides, they don't dare attack so many of us at once. They're scared."

"The Guardians are scared of you?" I echo incredulously.

Brek frowns, his freckles going all wrinkled again. "Maybe you'd better talk to Lev," he mumbles, not meeting my gaze. "He knows better than I do."

"Right," I say softly. Once again, there's something they aren't telling me. I shake my irritation off, though, when we arrive at the lead wagon's side.

"Still with us, then, Ellin?" Lev asks, eyes twinkling as he jumps down and lands, light as a cat, beside me.

"For the time being." I look around, frowning. "Where's Donnal? Wasn't he with you?"

Lev shakes his head. "Marthen left this morning. He's snug at home by now, no doubt, if he's not at the inn."

"Oh." I don't know why it should bother me that Donnal left without saying goodbye, but I feel suddenly very much alone among these people I hardly know.

"Cheer up," Lev says, giving me a pat on the shoulder. I open my mouth to snap at him for snooping about in my thoughts, but his raised palm forestalls me. "I read your face, Ellin, not your mind." Then he smiles and extends his hand. "Come. You can ride with me."

"And what about me?" Brek demands by my side, hands planted on his hips. "I thought I was to ride with you, Lev."

Lev's teeth flash in a grin. "And you, too, Brek."

"And *I* will ride with Mathias," Keth announces, looking daggers at me before she smiles at Lev. "We'll switch at the next stop."

"Perhaps," Lev murmurs, sounding amused.

"I'd be happy to," I say as I give Keth a bland smile. It's easy to guess what's nettling her. Though I think Lev is twice as irritating as any boy should be, and far too smug, I'm still smarting from Keth's remarks about my looks. Given that, I'm not about to miss a chance to annoy her a little.

Lev grins again before going off to speak with Mathias and the others driving the wagons. I look around with interest before climbing up, and I count at least ten people I don't know.

"How many of you are there?" I ask a few moments later, once we've set off down the road.

"Two dozen, more or less," Lev replies. "Why?"

I shrug. "I just wondered. Six to a wagon?"

"Some of us sleep outside. But anyway, the wagons are bigger inside than you think," Brek interrupts, poking my shoulder with a grubby finger. "Want to see?"

"Later." I say distractedly, still focused on Lev. "Only two dozen? Against all the Guardians?"

"Two dozen with me, on the road," he says slowly. He gives me a considering look before he adds, "There are others."

"Your men?"

Lev nods. "Small, scattered groups, farther south. Those who don't want to live as travelers."

I nod, too, and hook my hands over my knee. "But you like it."

He turns from the road and smiles, looking younger, all of a sudden, and less hardened. "I like it," Lev agrees. "Sleeping under the stars, cooking over a fire, the freedom—"

"Not having a home? A family?"

He shrugs. "This *is* my family, Ellin." Then he gives me a wink, carefree again. "You're a nosy girl, you know?"

"I just wondered. And where are we going?" I ask, frowning at the all-too-familiar landscape. "Not back to Harnon! I thought we were far away!"

Lev chuckles. "You came out of the forest south of the village, Ellin. Halfway to Dunbarton, almost. We're heading north, and with the wagons, we have to follow the main road."

My fingers squeeze one another hard enough to bruise, and I fight to keep my voice steady despite panic's sudden grip on my throat. "Back through Harnon, where there are Guardians who already killed my father, burned my home, and want to kill me." I stare. "Are you mad, Lev?"

"More than half," Brek says, snickering.

Lev smiles a little and cuffs his shoulder, though his brown eyes are serious and intent as they fix on mine. "You're safe with us, Ellin. I swear it."

I look at my lap and smooth the brown fabric over my legs nervously. "*Sometimes I feel like I'll never be safe again*," I think, just barely loud enough for him to hear.

Lev sighs, and he's quiet for a moment before he pushes a hand through his hair. The dark strands glisten as they catch the light. "You're safe," he says at last. "With your gifts, you're always safe."

I nod, though I'm not sure I believe it.

The wagon bumps and sways along the still-muddy road, but, warmed by the yellow winter sun, with the cool wind on my cheeks, I can't complain. I ride inside with Brek, for a while, and I am surprised at how comfortable the interior of the wagon is. There are four narrow beds along the sides of the wagon, each made up with a warm blanket. The clear space in the middle is used for playing games sometimes, Brek says, or for sitting and talking, and one big person or two small people can set up bedrolls there at night, if need be. He shows me, too, how each bed's frame has a drawer or two built into it, for storing clothing and personal things. Though it's cramped in the wagon, it is also as clean as can be expected and cozy, too. Perhaps living this way wouldn't be so bad, I think.

Brek has only just begun to show me how to play a game with some smooth, shiny stones when Lev pokes his head in. "We're stopping," he says, looking at me. "Will you come?"

I push my hair back from my face and nod. "I'm not afraid of them."

"Afraid of who?" Brek asks, glancing from me to Lev and back again.

Lev only smiles. "Good."

Something makes my heart hammer to a halt, though, when I see where it is we've stopped. It might be fear. That, at least, would explain the sudden coldness of my hands and feet. I grab Keth's elbow and pull her back, away from the rest of the group. "I can't go in there," I whisper, ignoring her look of annoyance. "Keth, I can't!"

Keth rolls her eyes. "And why not?"

I glance at the front door of Alder's inn and can almost see myself walking inside with my father, wet, hungry, and tired, but together. I remember his smile when he agreed to eat here rather than at home as a treat for me. I swallow hard. "I—Father and I had dinner here, the other night. Right before they—he—"

"Oh." Keth looks genuinely sympathetic as she gently removes her arm from my grip. "I'm sorry, Ellin. But you had dinner with him here other times, too, did you not?" she asks, giving me a small smile.

"I just—I miss him."

"Then either go back to the wagons, and we'll bring you something out, or come in and eat one last time. And remember your father."

My eyebrows knit, and I study her face. "How long have you been so wise?" I ask, only partly teasing.

To my surprise, Keth smiles again. "Told you, Ellin. I'm not the girl you knew, anymore." She gestures to the door. "Well?"

After a deep breath, I nod. "I'm coming."

It's too late for lunch and too early for dinner, so, as my father and I were, we're the inn's only patrons. Something is different this time, though. The strange tension is palpable from the moment Keth and I walk in the door. The inside of the inn looks normal; the tables are clean, the stove lit and taking the chill off the room, and I can hear Madam Alder or Thom making noise back in the kitchen. The True Southlings have seated themselves at a few tables, with the exception of Mathias and a muscular man I don't know standing guard on either side of the door.

"Girls!" Lev exclaims, waving us over. "Come and sit. We're having a good, hot meal tonight."

"What's going on?" I ask quietly when Keth and I have seated ourselves at a table with Lev, Aiddan, and dour-looking Glyn. "Won't the Guardians find us?"

"Ellin, stop worrying." Lev winks. "Order whatever you like to eat and drink, and enjoy it. That's all I ask."

"But—"

"But nothing," he interrupts with a strange smile. "Here comes the Madam, so decide what you want quickly. While I want us to enjoy a good meal, we needn't take all evening having it." Lev turns to Glyn, and his smile deepens. "You all right?" he asks, so quietly I have to strain to hear him.

Glyn arches an eyebrow and pushes her straight, faded-looking red hair behind her shoulder. "For now. She's not difficult."

Before I can puzzle out what they mean, Madam Alder is beside our table. I look up, expecting her to ask about my father or ask how I'm alive, but her gaze is fixed on Lev. "What will you have?" Madam asks, her voice oddly clipped.

She takes Lev's order, then Aiddan's, Keth's, and Glyn's, without commenting or suggesting the day's special, which seems strange. Then Madam turns to me, her face expressionless. "And for you?"

"Madam Alder?" I whisper. Cold fear knots in my stomach when she doesn't even seem to recognize me. "What—?"

"She asked what you want, Ellin," Lev says shortly. "You'd best order."

"Eggs," I blurt out, at a loss. "Two fried ones. And toast. With tea to drink."

"Very well." Madam turns to the next table, and I hear her ask them what they want in that same distant, uncaring voice.

Looking across the table, I fix Lev with a glare. "What's going on?" I demand, a little bit angry and very much afraid. "What's wrong with her?"

He shrugs. "Nothing."

"Lev, I know her," I snap. "Very well, in fact. And she acted like she didn't recognize me."

Lev looks a question at Keth, next to me, and I feel her shrug. Then he glances at Glyn, whose attention seems to be focused elsewhere, and nods as if deciding something. "There is nothing *wrong* with the woman," Lev says at last. "It's simply another of our gifts at work."

I watch Madam Alder's back as she returns to the kitchen, her footsteps slow and heavy on the wooden floor. "She's really here, isn't she?" I ask, confused. "I mean, Brek isn't—?"

Keth giggles. "No, you goose. Brek isn't working an illusion. Madam's real enough, but her thoughts are being...altered."

"I don't understand," I say to Lev, wondering why he didn't tell me about this. "Someone is controlling her? And it's Glyn!" My eyes widen as I look at the slim, pale, still-preoccupied woman. "Glyn is making her do this?"

Lev smiles. "You do understand, then. Glyn is using her gifts to influence the woman—Madam Alder?—to do what she wishes. To think we're nondescript travelers and prepare our food. She should forget us the moment we leave."

I glance toward the kitchen again, feeling sorry for her. "That's very strange," I murmur, uncomfortable with the idea. I'm uncomfortable, too, when I remember that the Northlander guard did what I wished—spoke my own thoughts, in fact—when I was in his mind. I look from Lev to Glyn and back again. "I don't think I like this."

Lev laughs. "Ellin, we aren't *hurting* her. Though even if we did," he adds slowly, sobering, "what of it? Do you think she'd welcome you in her inn, knowing that the Guardians are hunting you because they believe you to be tainted? Do you think she'd welcome any of us?"

"That's not the point."

"Then what is?" Keth asks, sounding irritated. "Honestly, Ellin, you haven't changed a bit. If we can do it, why shouldn't we? Don't we deserve to eat, same as everyone else?"

Because it seems wrong, I think immediately, though I'm careful to keep that thought to myself. I'm still trying to figure out why it seems so awful when our drinks and dinner arrive. Lev stands before we all start eating, and I pause with my fork on my eggs, looking at him.

"Eat up," Lev says with a smile, his hair falling across his forehead, nearly black in the dim light, "and enjoy the hot food and this warm room while you can. This will be our last night of comfort for some time, I think." He raises his glass of bubbling golden cider. "To the journey!"

"To the journey!" everyone echoes, leaving me confused again. Even so, I raise my mug of tea and drink with the rest.

When Lev has sat down again and everyone is busy eating, I turn to Keth. "The journey?" I ask. "Where are we going?"

Keth's eyes go wide and incredulous as she swallows a bite of food. "Why, to the Northlands, of course," she replies. "Did you not know?"

Chapter Twenty-three

FOG DESCENDS SHORTLY AFTER SUNSET, and night out on the road is cold. The damp makes the darkness seem even more oppressive, and I shiver on the seat of Lev's wagon. Even Kit's spare shawl pulled close around my shoulders does little against the chill. "I don't know how the ponies can stay on the road," I murmur. My voice seems too loud after being silent since we left Harnon.

I sense Lev's shrug. "They see better in the dark than we do," he replies. "And I can keep them on the road by the sound of their hooves."

"And you don't want to stop yet," I finish, guessing. "You want to put as much distance between us and Harnon—and the Guardians—as you can before it's light."

Lev exhales through his nose, sounding amused. "Clever girl. Dinner at the inn was dangerous," he admits, which surprises me. "Those people, coming in as we were leaving…"

"Why'd you do it?"

He shrugs again. "I was honest earlier, Ellin. I wanted everyone to have one last bit of comfort before we leave the Southland."

I press my lips together and strain to see his face in the dark. "Would we not be served at inns in the Northlands?" I ask hesitantly, not wanting him to know I've been there if he doesn't already. "Southlings aren't welcome, but—"

"We won't be stopping in towns," he says shortly. "Not until—well. You'll see."

I sigh and shift on the hard bench, wondering if Brek is still snoring in the back of the wagon. I can't hear him from outside, but from the next bed, he was irritatingly loud. I don't know how Keth can possibly sleep through it.

"I don't suppose you'll tell me why we're going to the Northlands," I say at last, burrowing my cold hands in folds of the shawl.

"A mission."

"That's vague."

"And it's good enough, for now," Lev says through a yawn. "You should get some sleep. Brek isn't snoring anymore," he adds.

"Are you ever going to stop doing that?" I ask sharply, though I'm more irritated with myself for not feeling him in my mind than I am with him for being there.

"Probably not." I imagine I can see his quick smile. "We're different. Our rules are different, too, Ellin. You'll get used to it."

A few moments later, wrapped snugly in warm blankets and hearing the soft sounds of Keth and Brek breathing deeply in sleep, I wonder if I ever will get used to it. The idea of accepting my abilities and using them casually seems so strange. I frown to myself in the darkness, thinking of Madam Alder, but the strangely comforting pitch and sway of the wagon lulls me to sleep before I have much time to worry.

My second journey to the Northlands takes longer than the first. For one thing, this time, there isn't such a sense of urgency. When Master Willem, Chief Physician at the college in the Northlands, came with his apprentice to beg my father's assistance, we left the very next day and pushed the big Northlands horses to their limits drawing our cart. Lev sets a more moderate pace, and the attitude of the Southlings is different, too. More carefree.

It doesn't take long for me to realize that their relaxed attitude also extends to laws and the way they treat other people. The first time we stop near a farm in order for Glyn to compel the farmer's wife to give us food, I'm appalled. But I'm hungry, too, and I discover with a twinge of guilt that the cheese, bread, and bacon taste every bit as good as food fairly paid for. I feel a little better when Lev points out that the simple farmers would probably be happy to watch the Guardians burn us all, and once, I even go with him to help carry pails of milk given by a slack-jawed, staring dairymaid.

With every day that passes, I miss my father more. Sometimes, I wonder if it would be better if he'd died of some natural, incurable thing and I could still be at home, in the cottage we shared all my life. At least that way, I would have his things to comfort me. I could hold his books and remember his hands on the covers, could wear his coat against the chill or curl up in his chair and pretend, for an instant, that he isn't gone. Sometimes, when heartache leaves me too listless to do anything but lie on my bed in the wagon and stare at nothing, I wonder if it would be better if the Guardians had burned me along with the house, after all.

Most of the time, though, I'm grateful Lev and the others found me and took me in. With them, life is simple. We ride in the wagons or walk alongside them, stop to steal and gather food, then cook it and eat, and we stop to rest the ponies and make camp. I don't have to decide what to cook, or when to sleep, or to worry about getting money, or wonder what I'm going to do with myself. I only have to help when asked and be reasonably pleasant when spoken to.

When we finally cross the river and enter the Northlands, the change in our group is astonishing. We set up camp early, not far from the border, where it is still only chilly and damp instead of true, biting Northlands cold. I look around at the others when we've all climbed out of the wagons and wonder at the difference in them, and in myself. It is as though we all breathed a sigh of relief the moment the wagon wheels touched Northlands ground.

And I know why. For Lev and the others, the Northlands mean a reprieve from the threat of the Guardians, at least for a little while. They might be treated rudely here, they might not be wanted, but here, no one will torture or kill them just for existing. For me, being in the Northlands again means simply being away from the place where my father died. But that is enough, and I discover that my face hasn't quite forgotten how to smile as I listen to the others laugh and tell stories at dinner.

Hours past sunset, when everyone's plates have been piled haphazardly to wash tomorrow and we all are clustered around the fire, Lev stands and brushes off the back of his trousers. "Well," he says loudly, "here we are."

"There *you* are," Mathias calls, and someone beside him laughs. "What's your point?"

Lev grins. "Here I am indeed, and what I was going to say, Master Mat, was that our first night in the Northlands deserves a celebration. A bit of music would be just the thing, I was thinking. And I was about to ask for volunteers, but since you've so kindly drawn attention to yourself..."

Mathias climbs to his feet, eyes twinkling. "Ah, well, singing I suppose I could manage," he says, so smoothly I can't help wondering if they rehearsed this beforehand. It would be just like the two of them to think of that. "But no dancin', mind."

"No dancing," Lev agrees. Then, with a flourish, he pulls a whistle out of his coat pocket. "To go with your fine singing?"

"Why, thank you." Mathias seems surprised, but even in the firelight, I can see his lips twitch. And I know from the scattered chuckles that I'm not the only one who does.

After a moment, Lev starts to play a fast, bouncy tavern song, and, to my surprise, Mathias' deep voice is pleasant when he joins in. Then Liss and Keth begin to clap along with the music, and a weak-chinned, friendly man named Jem slaps his thighs, drumming, and soon our camp is lively as a party. Lev and Mathias follow the first song with another, funny one about cider and spiders, and I can't help laughing at the faces Mathias makes as he sings and pantomimes swallowing a whole bucket of crawling, hairy things.

Breathless and chuckling, they manage to coax Liss to follow them. Then Keth, who, to my annoyance, sings beautifully and ends up with half the men making eyes at her like sick sheep. After that, Padrus sends Brek to the wagons to fetch a scuffed fiddle. Despite his gnarled fingers, the old man begins to play without faltering.

Brek plops down beside me. "You like that one, then?" he asks, pointing at Padrus.

I turn, surprised that he noticed. "The song?"

"No, grouchy old Miller." He grins. "Of course, the song."

I close my eyes and nod, listening. In sharp contrast to the others' rollicking, amusing songs, this one is slow and beautiful, and very sad. "It reminds me of home," I say softly. Though I don't know why, it's true.

"Oh." At his uncharacteristically sober tone, I open my eyes and am startled again to find Brek nodding. He draws his knees to his chest and leans his chin on them, not taking his eyes off the old man and his fiddle. "Me, too."

"Where is home for you, Brek?" I ask. I'm suddenly a little ashamed of myself for not having wondered before.

"Whiteriver."

I can tell by the look on his face that he doesn't want to talk about it anymore, so I don't press. I can't properly enjoy the rest of Padrus's song, though. Not with Brek so obviously moping beside me. But after Padrus finishes, Lev and Mathias get up to sing again and, to my relief, Brek brightens.

"They're funny," he whispers loudly. "I like it when they play for us."

"I do, too," I reply. It seems everyone does. As I look around the fire and see people's smiles, how the lines creasing Padrus's face seem less deep, and the sharp, tense look has left Keth's eyes, I realize that I underestimated Lev as a leader. He knew exactly what we all needed, tonight.

Lev has stopped playing the whistle in order to sing and clap his hands, and I watch him, head thrown back, hair disheveled and shining in the firelight, sleeves unbuttoned and rolled up despite the chill. Though hardly more than a boy, he's a good man, I think. For the first time, I feel a stirring of respect for him.

Warmed by the fire, full of good food, I close my eyes again and nod drowsily in time to the music. I don't pay much attention to the next few songs the men sing, but at last, I notice that Brek has started to chortle beside me. I crack one eye open just as Mathias sings a word that I'm not supposed to know, and then both my eyes go wide as he follows that one with some things my father would have had him chewing soap for even thinking.

Brek leans close and jabs his elbow into my ribs, still giggling. "I know what that means," he says, sounding pleased with himself.

I wince. "Brek…"

He shrugs and throws up his hands with a puzzled look. "What? I do! I know *everything* about that, because my mum was a—"

"Brek!" My cheeks are flaming as I clap my hands over my ears. I hope, very much, that he wasn't going to finish the way I thought he might. "Why don't you sing next?" I ask at last. "I've heard you whistling, so I know you know some songs."

I almost expect him to refuse, but instead, he shrugs again and marches up to the fire when Mathias has finished singing all about the lovely girls at the Weststream inn.

"You'll have to shush, now, because it's my turn," Brek announces, and I grin. He clasps his hands behind his back, but, an instant later, lifts one of them to gesture grandly. "I'm going to sing 'The Road is my Companion.'"

The camp goes quiet except for the crackling of the fire, and I see a few people nod expectantly. Then Brek resumes his position, pauses again, and looks at Lev. "Oh! And will you play for me?" Lev nods wordlessly and, still seated, begins the song.

I don't know it, and that could be why the words, sung in Brek's startlingly pure and beautiful voice, seem to pierce right through me.

"Oh, the road is my companion," he sings, "the road's my truest friend…"

A little later, nestled in my snug bed in the wagon, listening to Brek snore, I stare into the darkness. I'm tired, but two things rattle persistently in my head, making me unable to sleep. One is that, shortly after Brek finished singing, I realized I hadn't seen Aiddan all night. I remember noticing that he walked off soon after Mathias began his first song, but he didn't come back. I hope nothing bad happened to him. Though if something did, I think, surely someone would have found him by now.

The other thing that keeps me awake is the last bit of Brek's song, which haunts me. Giving in at last, I bury my face in my pillow to muffle any sounds as, for the first time since the night my father died, I begin to cry for him.

"The road is my companion," Brek sang, "as far as I may roam. And when all others fail me, the road will be my home."

Chapter Twenty-four

THE ROAD THROUGH THE FOREST to the city looks much the same as I remember it, though now thicker pelts of snow coat the squat junipers and towering firs. The black, skeletal arms of the leafless trees are bent lower than they were before, weighted by a layer of ice that glistens in the sun. On the road, the snow is hard-packed and dingy. Too cold here for mud, instead of squelching, the wagon wheels bump over the dips and ridges of snow and dirt, jarring all of us and rattling everyone's belongings.

The pale winter sun is not yet at its peak when we have our first glimpse of the wall. Brek sucks in his breath in wonder, and I inhale too, but for an entirely different reason. I remember these trees. The particularly fat juniper, left of the wagon, is the first one I went to when I looked for berries to gather for my father. The clear spot up ahead is where I set my basket down in order to wrap the twisted elm bark into a bundle. And the gatehouse, coming into sight up ahead…

I close my eyes and wish, as I have so many times, that I'd never been locked out of the city and spent the night there. If I hadn't, so many things would be different now.

"Are you all right, Ellin?" Lev asks. I turn to him, and he gives me an uncertain smile. "You look like you saw a ghost."

I shrug and look away, watching the walls of the city come ever closer. "Maybe I did," I say quietly.

Brek snickers and leans over me to speak to Lev. "Don't be stupid. There's no such things as ghosts! But, maybe I could make one for you to see, if you want," he adds thoughtfully..

"No," Lev says with a laugh. "Be patient. We'll have need of you soon enough, Brek."

"I know." Brek sighs and kicks the seat with his heels. "How soon?"

"Soon!"

"Fine!" Brek huffs impatiently, but then grins as he goes into the back, nearly kicking me in the process. "Better be soon," he mutters from inside. "I'm bored."

Lev and I exchange a smile, but my amusement fades rapidly as we approach the gates. We're close enough to see the guards milling about on the top of the wall, blue-coated silhouettes against the whitish sky.

"What is the plan, Lev?" I ask. "Isn't it past time you told me?"

His lips flatten into a thin line. "We're going into the city," he says at last. "We have someone strong and skilled at compelling in each wagon. Myself, Glyn, Cedran, and Shenna."

I nod, though I'm startled to hear that muscular Cedran—who I thought was mainly a guard—can compel people like Glyn and Lev do. Strong-jawed, gray-haired Shenna is less of a surprise. She has a way of just looking at me that makes me certain any orders from her are obeyed.

"And you're simply going to compel the guards to let us through?" I ask skeptically, with a nervous glance at the gates. There are several guards, and I remember well that they aren't likely to just let us in.

"Without any questions. Without noticing anything unusual about such a large group of Southlings traveling together."

I shake my head. "But what about all the people? Surely someone will say *something*."

Lev only smiles, seeming pleased with himself. "We'll be separating after we enter the city. A lone wagon of Southlings—perhaps a family, for all they know—is no cause for alarm."

"I don't like this," I mutter, and my gaze flicks from Lev to the gates uneasily. I'd very much like to know what the plan is for once we're in the city, but I know better than to ask.

"Well, then. It's good that no one asked you."

None of you ever do, I think. With a sigh, I pull my shawl tighter and try not to shiver as we pass beneath some particularly tall pines that cut off the sun.

Lost in my thoughts, I scarcely pay attention to Lev, or the bumping of the wagon, as we close the short distance to the gates. When the wagon rolls to a stop, a sudden burst of panic flutters madly in my stomach, and I jump. I never expected to be here again, waiting to go in the Southlings' gate. Now that I am, I'm terrified that I'll be recognized. As the yellow-haired, blue-coated guard approaches, I lower my head and fight the temptation to hold my breath.

"How many riding?" the guard asks, sounding bored. His voice sounds familiar, and I long to look past Lev to see his face. I don't, though, for fear that he'll see me.

"Four," Lev replies easily, flipping his recently-stolen, thick woolen scarf over his shoulder. "Myself and a girl, a small boy and a young woman."

I can't stifle a small, irritated noise at the idea that he thinks Keth is a woman, but I'm just a girl. She's barely a year older than me, and Lev himself can't be more than a handful of years older than that. Fuming, I glare down at my skirt.

"You'll all have to get out of the wagon," the guard says, "in order for me to search it. An' I'll have to see your papers, of course."

I frown. I don't remember them searching the wagon that brought Father and me into the city, and I wonder if the trouble we must have caused has anything to do with this. I don't have time to wonder long before Lev speaks again. "Are you certain you'll really need all of that?" he asks, and even I can hear the thread of command in his tone. "You've seen two of us, after all. And you know we have the papers."

"All right. Go ahead."

Lev clucks at the horses, and the wagon lurches forward again. As we pass through the gate, I crane my neck and catch a glimpse of the guard, staring straight ahead and not even bothering to watch after us. I do know him, I realize, from the night I was locked out. I don't know his name, but I owe him my life.

The wagon rolls down the street, bringing us closer to pointed-roofed shops and the bustle of people, and I look at Lev. "What will happen to him?" I ask softly.

One of his eyebrows arches. "Who?"

"The guard. Once everyone is through the gate," I say. "Won't he remember what happened, once no one is controlling him anymore?"

"Well," Lev begins, but he's interrupted by a giggle from within the wagon. Brek pokes his head out, still grinning.

"They took care of that," he explains. "I heard Lev and Cedran talking about it. Once we're all through, Cedran's going to compel him to go for a little swim. And he'll have to do it, of course, before the compelling stops."

"Compel him to swim in the river?" I gasp, my eyes flying to Lev's face. "You'll kill him!"

Lev shakes his head in irritation, though whether that is directed at me or at Brek, I can't be sure. "Not the river, Ellin. A lake. On the east side of the wall."

"Oh." I frown. "But isn't it frigid? And couldn't he still die?"

"What of it?" Lev snaps. "It'll keep him busy and make people think he's mad if he says what we did. Isn't that the point?"

"I—" I close my eyes and swallow. "I hope he'll be all right," I whisper, but if Lev hears, he doesn't reply.

"Cheer up, Ellin," Brek says as he climbs out to sit with us once more, dragging a blanket with him. "We're in, aren't we?"

"We are," I agree. But what now?

"Now, you sit here, try not to let that worry show on your pretty face, and follow instructions when I give them to you," Lev replies. I must look as annoyed as I feel, because he holds up one hand and gives me a teasing smile. "If you please, I mean."

I'm not amused. "You want me to follow you blindly, in other words."

Heaving a sigh, Lev puts his hand on my shoulder, and I stiffen. I imagine I can feel his palm burning through the fabric of my shawl, and I stare at his hand for a moment before raising my gaze to his face. When I do, his softer smile and the odd look in his eyes unsettle me so much that I can't even find words to ask him to stop.

"I want you to *trust* me," he says quietly. "Is that so much to ask?"

"I don't know," I stammer. "I—"

"Lev!" Aiddan's call interrupts me, and I'm grateful. He comes hurrying down the other side of the street, his cloak billowing out behind him like wings.

"All is well?" Lev asks as Aiddan clambers up to sit on the other side of Brek. This crowds the bench and forces me to slide closer to Lev, but I try not to mind.

"Fine," Aiddan replies, a little out of breath. "I left Mathias, Cedran, and Padrus two streets over. We were last. Shenna's wagon, and Glyn's, entered the gate without any trouble."

Lev nods, and I'm close enough to feel his shoulders loosen with relief. "Good."

"You've had no trouble?" Aiddan glances at me and Brek. "Where's Keth?"

Brek shrugs. "Still asleep?"

"Trying to make my face up without jabbing my eyes out," Keth says from within the wagon, sounding frustrated. "Ellin, come help me. I'll do yours."

I don't particularly want to have my face painted, but I don't want to sit with my hip pressed against Lev's any longer, either. Nor do I want any Northlanders to recognize me. With a sigh, I squeeze past Brek and go inside.

"Why are you even bothering with paint?" I ask a moment later, seated on Keth's bed and trying not to flinch as she dabs rouge on my cheeks. It's light enough to see in the wagon with the curtains tied back, but barely, which is why I refused to let her touch the sharp, charcoal-colored pencil near my eyes. "Isn't this a lot of trouble?"

Keth shrugs and presses her full, reddened lips together. "We're masquerading as performers, are we not? You and I should look the part."

"*Are* we masquerading as performers?" I ask, pulling away to look at her. "And why? Keth, no one will tell me anything!"

Keth flattens her lips again as she screws the lid on the little pot of rouge. Then she darts a quick glance at the narrow door before leaning close. "I'll tell you this much," she whispers. "We're going to the castle. Aiddan used to be a famous harpist—before his hand was chopped off, I mean—and we're going to pretend to be with him, all of us as performers, to be invited in."

A hundred thoughts whirl around my head at the idea of going back to the castle. Lost, I blurt out the first question that comes to mind. "They won't notice he doesn't have his hand?"

"That's what Brek's for."

"Oh. Right." I frown. "But, I mean, when he has to play. How—?"

Keth sighs and looks at me as if I'm stupid. "He's not going to play, Ellin," she says, very slowly. "We aren't really performers, are we? There's…a plan. Lev's plan."

"And you won't tell me any more of it," I say, knowing I must sound as bitter and confused as I feel. "I see."

With a shrug, Keth puts the small wooden box containing her cosmetics away. After a long moment spent fussing with her things, she turns and looks at me again. "I'll tell you one more thing," she whispers, so softly that I have to lean even closer to hear. "Part of the plan. The others have gone to rescue someone. A Southling, gifted like us. A girl."

I'm suddenly grateful I'm wearing rouge. This way, she can't see the color draining from my face. "What?"

Keth nods. "They're keeping her prisoner here," she explains. "Lev sensed her. He said he could tell she's very strong—maybe as powerful as he is. And I guess he needs her, for what he's going to do."

CHAPTER TWENTY-FIVE

"**T**HIS IS NEVER GOING TO WORK," I whisper, gripping my knees with white-knuckled fingers as the wagon rolls to a stop in front of the castle. Brek, between me and Lev on the bench, makes an indignant noise.

"What? You think I can't do it?"

"Not you," I say shortly. "All of it. We don't look like performers! We *aren't* performers!"

"And they won't believe we are, if that's your attitude," Lev murmurs. "We're playacting, Ellin. Surely you can play along?"

As people come out of the castle and outbuildings to see us, I take a deep breath, unable to meet Lev's eyes. "I'm afraid," I admit. "I've been here before. Recently."

He swears quietly, though he's careful to keep his face unworried and looking straight ahead. "And you didn't tell me?"

"I didn't know we were coming here!"

Lev breathes hard through his nose. "Brek, can you do something?"

"Not if I'm not with her," Brek replies, squinting in thought. "Not *and* Aiddan's hand."

"Damn." Lev sighs again and looks at me, for an instant, as he taps his thumbs together. "Was your face all painted?" he whispers, voice urgent. "Was your hair the same?"

Without thinking, I reach up and touch the fancy braids Keth put into my hair. More complicated than any style I could manage on my own, they circle the back of my head before merging into an elaborate knot at the base of my skull. "No," I reply, remembering that everyone in the castle saw me most often with my hair down and tangled, or, at best, tied into a single braid down my back. "And no," I add. "I was never made up."

"Good." He nods. "That's different enough, then. But try not to speak to anyone, just the same." Then Lev looks at the men and woman approaching and smiles wide, showing his teeth. "Hail!" he calls, and I'm startled to hear the difference in his voice. Far from his normal tone, now he sounds somewhere between self-important and greasy. "Have you use for a traveling troupe of musicians, good sirs and madam?"

"Who comes asking?" Nan the Keeper asks, putting her hands on her broad hips. Seeing her, I duck my head and hope fervently that she won't recognize me.

"Aiddan Innys of Summerwood," Lev replies grandly. "I trust I don't need to introduce *him!* And with him, his four singing companions."

"Singing?" I whisper to Brek, horrified. He shrugs.

"You're right," Keeper Nan says at last. "Aiddan Innys needs no introduction here. Though your presence is a surprise, I'm certain your music will be welcome, my good man…?"

"Lev," Lev says with a small, seated bow. "Lev Kinshield at your service, madam."

Once we've all climbed out of the wagon, and the castle servants have gone to take our horses and carry a few bags we packed for believability, Lev makes a show of presenting Aiddan and Nan to one another. Then he introduces Keth, Brek, and me. He calls me "Bess Tailor," Brek's sister, and I pretend to be overwhelmed and shy—maybe a bit simple, too—as I stare at the ground and shuffle my feet. I hold my breath, too, but Nan only welcomes me as she did the others before ushering us inside.

We only have to wait a few moments while she goes to get permission from the king for us to play. "It's all settled," Nan says, sounding excited as she bustles toward us, blue skirt swaying. "You're to perform this evening in the great room, with permission to play each night this week, should it please you and your music please the king."

"It would please me greatly," Aiddan says formally, inclining his head. He smiles at Nan but, looking up at him, I wonder if anyone else can see the tense, pained look around his eyes. It *would* please him greatly to play, I realize. Without thinking, I glance down at his hands—seemingly two of them, now—hanging at his sides. "And I can only hope my offering this evening will please his majesty."

Nan nods. "This way to your rooms," she says. "I'm sure you'll want to rest and freshen up after traveling." She leads us to two rooms upstairs, across the hall from one another. I see when she opens the door to the room Keth and I are to share that it is furnished a little more richly than the maid's room I had when I was here before.

"Go down to the kitchen if you get hungry," Nan says when she's finished showing us about. "His highness said you're to play after dinner. Someone will give you notice later on. Is there anything else?"

"This will do nicely," Aiddan says with another nod. "Thank you, Madam Keeper."

When Nan has gone, the five of us gather in the room the men and Brek are sharing. Lev flops backward onto one of the room's two beds (Brek was given a pallet) and flings his arms out with a flourish. "Perfect!" he exclaims in a whisper, his grin stretching from ear to ear. "Just perfect. Master Bard, girls, Brek...my hat, were I wearing one, would be off to the lot of you."

"It went well," Aiddan agrees from the window, his back to us. There is a strange note in his voice, and I can't help noticing that he has his arms crossed, pulled up so we can't see his hands. Or hand, now, I suppose.

Brek grins broadly from his seat at the foot of Lev's bed. "Better than well," he says firmly, sounding pleased. "You all saw! I didn't have any trouble at all. The fat lady never looked twice at Aiddan's hand!"

"You were wonderful," Keth replies, surprising me. She ruffles Brek's hair, causing him to make a face at her, before looking past him to Lev. "And now?"

"And now, we wait," Lev says. He pushes himself up onto his elbows. "Go to your room, or get something to eat, and rest, for awhile. We can't do anything until the others contact me."

With that, he flops back down and closes his eyes without even bothering to remove his boots. Seeing him this way, it occurs to me that I can't remember the last time I saw him sleep. Keth nods and wanders across the hall, and Brek fishes some twigs, polished stones, and acorns out of his pocket before kneeling beside his pallet.

"Want to play?" he asks over his shoulder as he begins to pile the stones in some sort of game.

I shake my head and look past him to Aiddan, who still hasn't moved from the window. The part of me that is still Rowan Fisher's daughter, a healer, wants to tell him that someone does see he's in pain. But another, newer part of me, the part that has been alone and been in pain and knows that some things are too deep to be shared, keeps quiet. I frown and watch him for another moment before I turn and go.

I stop in the doorway of the room I'm to share with Keth just long enough to tell her I'm going to find something to eat. Though I'm not very hungry, and I know it's dangerous because I could be recognized, I have to do something. Being here makes me restless. I can't even contemplate sleep. And, I have to admit, I want to wander about.

I do head for the kitchen, since it's the only room I have permission to visit. Despite wanting to wander, I don't want to arouse suspicion by being where I'm not supposed to be. To my relief, I only pass a maid I don't recognize on my way through the halls. As I approach the closed kitchen doors, I begin to think it might be safe for me to go in and have something to eat, after all. Then I hear voices, and I realize my mistake. It's near noon. Of *course* there are people in the kitchen, and probably in the great room as well, ready to have lunch!

I'm about to turn and hurry back to my room when one of the voices carries out into the hall and freezes me in my tracks.

"Southlings," Coll says, obviously answering someone's question. "Musicians."

Another voice says something, too quietly for me to make out the words. Then my heart twists as I hear Erik laugh. "Don't know," he says, "but I heard one of them is Aiddan Innys. I thought he didn't play anymore. And there's a boy—or two, I'm not sure—with him, and some girls."

I tiptoe to the doors, but, for a moment, I can't hear anything except some pots clanging.

"I don't know," Erik says again, at last. "If there are girls—Southling girls—Coll, do you think—?"

"No," Coll says immediately. Something heavy scrapes on the floor, and there's more noise. I can almost see Coll pushing himself up to loom over Erik at the table. Probably glowering at him, too, I think with a small smile. His next words make my smile fade quickly, though. "No," Coll says again. "She's not coming back. You know that."

My lips part in surprise when I realize they're talking about me. I have the sudden, insane urge to push open the door and tell them I'm here, to rush in and give Erik a hug and ask Coll how my little foal is. I've missed them, I admit, my palm itching to reach for the doorknob. I've missed *being* here.

But now that I'm here again, I'm here as "Bess Tailor." Here in secret. And, for that matter, not supposed to be here at all because I'm an outlaw.

I bite my bottom lip, tasting the waxiness of the paint Keth put there, and stand with one hand on the door, my feet wanting to go in two directions. And then I hear heavy, booted footsteps approaching and imagine Coll reaching out to shove the door open...

And I run back down the hallway and up the stairs and slam the door of my shared room shut behind me. Breathless and trembling, I stand there with my back pressed against the wood, wishing that keeping the door closed tight could shut out the memory of Erik's voice, sounding so hopeful.

CHAPTER TWENTY-SIX

MY HEART SINKS CLOSER to my stomach with every hour that passes. As I sit and watch the window, the sky clouds over, blue turning to flat, pale gray. Something begins to fall, but I don't know what to call it. The wet, bastard child of icy rain and snow, perhaps. Whatever it is, it drizzles, half-frozen, down the glass, leaving quivering tracks.

After awhile, Keth leaves off fussing with her hair and goes across the hall. I don't have long alone, though, before the hinges squeak as the door opens again. "Back so soon?" I ask, my breath fogging the window when I speak. "Were they asleep, or just boring?"

"Ellin," Lev says behind me, in a low, ominous tone that sends fear skittering up my neck. "We need to talk."

I turn at once, eyebrows knitting with worry. "What's the matter?" I ask. "They haven't found us out, have they?"

"It isn't that." He walks toward me slowly, with odd, measured steps. "I've just thought-spoken with Shenna," he continues. "She's at the prison, you see."

"Oh." The word is little more than a release of breath. I shiver, feeling trapped between the cold window at my back and Lev's dark, colder eyes.

"Oh, indeed," he says softly. "You see, Shenna and the others went to rescue someone. A Southling like us, being held captive." Lev tilts his head, still giving me that level, considering look. I suddenly miss the mischief that's usually in his eyes, the sly smile that usually twists his mouth. Now that those things are gone, this new Lev is older, far older, and intimidating. "But do you know what they found instead?" he asks.

Words don't want to come. My voice has shriveled, but even if I could speak, I don't know what to say. "I—"

"They found no gifted Southling," Lev snaps, cutting me off with a sharp gesture. "No one like us, with power, perhaps, to match mine. Only guards, who remember a red-haired girl and her father. A girl named—well, you know your own name. Don't you, Ellin." It isn't a question, and I know there's no use lying about it. Not now.

"Lev, I didn't know what to tell you," I whisper. "I didn't think it mattered…"

"Didn't think it *mattered?*" he echoes, dusky color staining his cheeks. I notice with shock and more than a little fear that his slender hands have curled into fists at his sides. "Half the reason we *came* was to rescue you! And you were already with us. All along! You've endangered everyone with your silence," he hisses furiously, obviously remembering that he can't be too loud, keeping himself in check with a visible effort. "An explanation. Now!"

I take a deep breath and stand, even though doing so takes me too close to him. I've faced the princes of the Northlands. And the king, and the Guardians at home. Who does Lev think he is, to order me this way?

"How dare you speak to me like this?" I ask aloud, feeding my growing anger in hopes that it will devour my fear. "I've done nothing wrong. If you wanted me to tell you that you were going to rescue a girl who wasn't there, you should have *told* me your plan in the first place! I had no way of knowing!"

My own clenched fist finds my hip, and I feel my jaw stiffen and my cheeks heat as I glare upward. "And if rescuing me was so damned important," I snap, "if you need me so badly for this mysterious mission of yours, then maybe you should have seen that power in me when you met me."

Lev stands motionless, looking as though my words pierced him more deeply than I intended. His throat bobs as he swallows. Then, to my great discomfort, he steps even closer, and his booted toes bump against mine. "I saw you," he whispers hoarsely. "I couldn't see your power, for seeing you." As he speaks, one of his hands rises and fumbles like a blind man's toward my cheek. My eyes widen as I watch it come closer, not touching, but I can almost feel the tips of his fingers brush my skin.

"But I can now," Lev says, louder. As if that was a signal, his hand drops back to his side, leaving me strangely off balance. Though whether my body was poised to lean into his touch or pull away, I don't know at all. "Now I know it's you," he continues. "It's no matter."

I swallow the lump in my throat and blink at him stupidly, unable to comprehend what just changed between us. "What— what do you want me to do?" I ask at last. "What is the mission?" In the pale, faded dimness, I notice that the light is back in his eyes.

"We're going to change the world," he says simply. "And we're starting here."

"How?" I shake my head. "Lev, there are so few of us!"

He smiles. "With our gifts, a few is all we need. *One or two* are all we need, if they are powerful enough. And *we* are, Ellin. *You* are." This time, when he reaches out to take my hand, he doesn't falter. His hand is warm, I note distantly, as I stare down at my pale fingers trapped in his strong, tanned ones. I raise my eyes to his face again, feeling lost.

"What are we going to do?"

"Find the king. Compel him to do our will. To change the laws." It's darker outside now, and the wind has picked up, but his eyes still sparkle like they hold the sun. "Then we'll have him use his army, the Northlands army, to invade the Southland."

"And get rid of the Guardians." I can see it, laid out clear as a map. "Making it safe for us."

"Yes." Lev's fingers tighten, and his face is serious, suddenly, so close above mine. "We'll all be safe, in both the Northlands and at home. No one will hate us. No one that matters, anyway," he adds, with a familiar twitch of his lips. "It's what I've dreamed of, Ellin. What you've wanted—I know your thoughts. I remember when you were in prison, so afraid that using your powers was bad. Now, it won't be. Not ever again."

"It was you," I realize, as the thing he said sinks in deeper than the rest. "When I was here, in prison. I thought it was—" I cut myself off. Speaking Finn's name here would seem wrong, now that I know what Lev plans to do to his father. "It was you."

Lev smiles. "I know. I couldn't believe it at first, either. It was you! All this time, the girl I was—"

"—looking for," I finish in a whisper. He grins and squeezes my hand again. Then his thumb strokes the back of my hand gently, almost tentatively. Gooseflesh prickles along my forearms, even though I'm not cold at all. If anything, the room suddenly feels too hot.

I look into his eyes and feel my breath catch in my throat at what I see. "Lev, what—?" And then his other palm cups my cheek, and he leans down, and I really don't need to ask. His lips brush mine, warm and soft. I don't know what to do, but when I don't move away, Lev's hand slides from my cheek around to the back of my neck and urges me closer. Clearly, he *does* know. My free hand finds his shoulder almost of its own accord, and I'm not certain whether I want to shove him away or keep kissing him until I'm as skilled as he is.

When we finally pull back, I'm so confused and flushed and breathless I can't speak. I feel lightheaded. My lips tingle, and I have to fight the urge to touch a fingertip to them to make sure they aren't as swollen as they feel.

Lev grins and pushes his hair back from his face, seeming utterly at ease. I find that I can't meet his eyes, can't think, don't know what to feel at all. I jerk my hand from his grip and turn away.

"Well. What about the princes?" I ask after a moment, trying to seem casual. "There are five of them. Won't they know that something's wrong with their father?"

Lev waves my question aside. "I've thought of that, of course. The king is most important, and after him the oldest one. The Golden, or whatever they call him. Controlling them will require the two strongest of us. You and me."

"And the others?"

"Glyn, Cedran, and Shenna will take them, of course. Along with Keth. She's quite good at compelling, you know."

I didn't know, but I nod slowly, sluggish. Somehow, I think the icy rain outside has replaced my blood. I try hard to keep my thoughts shielded. To not think at all, actually. "One of us for each of them," I say, attempting to sound impressed. "And the rest? Aiddan and Padrus and the others?"

"A few will go home to raise more to our cause. Some will join the army here." He shrugs, smiling. "Don't worry, Ellin. I have it all planned."

"I believe you." I close my eyes for an instant, afraid of what Lev might see in them. "Tonight, then?" I ask at last. "When Aiddan is supposed to play?"

"Tonight," he agrees. "We'll meet before, so I can give everyone instructions. You'll be ready?"

I try to smile. "I will."

When he has gone, I go back to the window and press my forehead against the cold glass. My cheeks are still burning, and I imagine I can still feel Lev's lips and the pressure of his hand around mine. My hands were supposed to learn how to speak with Finn. My hands helped Coll deliver a foal, and once held a sprig of Horse Ivy given as a gift of peace. I took the leaves with me all the way back to the Southland, wrapped in a handkerchief. They burned along with my home and my father.

My hand once held Erik's as he ran with me along the dark streets, saving my life. It grasped Garreth's long, big-knuckled fingers when we said goodbye. And now Lev would have all of the princes' hands clutching weapons in a war that isn't really theirs to fight. And they would fight, but not willingly, controlled by someone else like puppets.

I close my eyes and rub my forehead, trying to relieve some of the tension there. "I don't know what to do," I whisper. But it isn't true. I know exactly what to do.

Even though I remember the way the Northlanders treated me when I was here before, and the way some of them have looked at me this time, even though apparently Aiddan's reputation has given us some sort of status, it doesn't matter. It doesn't matter now that King Allard put me and my father in prison because we dared use "witchcraft" to save his life. It doesn't matter that Garreth was rude to me once, or that people on the streets might have spat at me and called me names.

Those things don't matter right now, because I remember the conversation Father and I had when he first told me about the Southling powers, about why the Northlanders hate us. Even when I thought our only power was to hear people's thoughts, I realized we could be dangerous. My father said Southlings aren't dangerous, though, because we choose not to be.

"Lev is choosing to be," I whisper to myself and the empty room. And I see why. Of course I do. I understand his plan, why he thinks it's right, so much that it frightens me. Before now, I never thought *I* could be dangerous.

But that's not true either, I realize, because I remember thinking something similar, my first night here at the castle. I thought about killing the king—well, letting him die on purpose—in hopes that Alaric might be a better, more just king.

"But I *didn't*," I say aloud, and I turn from the window to pace. "And now I know better, anyway," I add with a bitter snort. Though I've tried to forget, Alaric's betrayal still stings whenever I think about it.

His brothers didn't betray me, though. They offered me friend-ship and saved my life.

But then, so did Lev. I would have died in that forest, had he and the others not come looking for me. And *he* has been a friend to me, too. Perhaps even more—

With a groan, I stop pacing, squeeze my eyes shut, and grab the back of my neck with both hands. My head feels as though it could burst. At last, I take a deep breath and head for the door, hoping that I'm doing the right thing.

CHAPTER TWENTY-SEVEN

ONCE I'M OUT IN THE HALL, two things occur to me. One is that I still should take care not to be seen. The other is that I haven't the faintest idea where to go.

"Damn," I mutter, and I look first one way down the hall, then the other. I don't even know where I am in the castle, really, compared to where I stayed before. Not that that information would help anyway, I think, frustrated. I do know how to get to the kitchen, though. And from the kitchen, I remember how to get to the great room, and from there—I squint in concentration—yes, I do remember my way around. A little, at least.

With a curt nod to myself, I head for the stairway and hope I won't run in to anyone. Getting to the kitchen is simple, and I know I have a reasonable excuse for being there if I'm caught. After I pass the kitchen doors, though, I start to feel even more nervous, so I slink close to the walls and keep my head down.

I should have borrowed Keth's new cloak, I think as I tiptoe past the great room. It has a hood. I could kick myself for not thinking of this sooner. Even a hood indoors would attract less attention than my hair. But, thankfully, I don't see anyone.

I'm just congratulating myself on my good luck when booted footsteps sound in the great room, coming toward the doorway. My eyes widen, and my gaze darts around the hall ahead, like a rabbit looking for a hole. There aren't any more doors! Just walls with sconces and tapestries. Heart racing, I look behind me. The footsteps are louder now. Another few steps, and whoever it is will be in the hall. Will see me.

I look ahead again, truly panicked. But, now that I look closer, I realize that the wall on my right doesn't meet the wall straight ahead. It's a corner. Without sparing a thought for who might be coming around it, I dash ahead, feet flying, and fling myself around the corner. Just then, someone shouts, "Hey, what's the rush?" behind me…and the footsteps quicken.

I don't have time to catch my breath. I barely have time to notice that this isn't another hallway; it's a narrow staircase. My shin hurts where I smacked it against one of the lower stairs, and my hands are scraped, but I scramble to my feet and half-run, half-stumble upward. There's a landing at the top, a door straight ahead. Trapped, my heart pounding in my throat, I shove the door open, rush inside, and slam it behind me. It is only when I look up, chest heaving, that I realize I'm not alone.

Relief makes me dizzy. All at once, I feel a wild urge to either laugh or start crying. "I was looking for you," I manage, panting. And then I do giggle, because Finn, who jumped up when I slammed the door, looks as though a stiff wind would knock him over.

Finn stares, and I would swear I can *see* the moment when he realizes that I'm really here. Then his eyebrows draw together. He points at me, then his mouth, and makes an "I don't understand you" sort of gesture.

I nod and take a deep breath, sure that my gasping made my lips impossible to read. "I was looking for you," I say again, more clearly. "I—augh!" The door being thrown open shoves me forward, and I trip over my own feet and land with a dull, ungraceful smack on my hands and knees.

"What's going on in here?" Erik demands as he barges in. "You better not—" He stops short and gapes. Again, I fight an urge to giggle even though this second fall hurt my already-scraped palms. The twins' incredulous stares are identical, though Finn is staring at Erik instead of at me.

"Ellin?" Erik manages, sounding as shocked as Finn looked. "*Ellin?*"

"Ouch," I say succinctly, climbing stiffly to my feet.

"Sorry!" Erik exclaims. I wave him off as he moves, too late, to give me a hand up. "I didn't realize—" He shakes his head. "You're here!"

And then my eyes are wet as I look from him to Finn—now grinning identically—and feel an answering smile spread across my own face. "I know. I—"

This time, I'm interrupted when they move forward at the same time and squeeze the breath out of me all over again.

"*I've missed you,*" Finn says when we've pulled apart a moment later, though he's left his hand on my shoulder.

Still fighting tears, I can only nod that I have, too. "*But we have to talk,*" I think, loudly enough for both of them to hear. "*That's why I came looking for you. It's important.*" Finn nods and gestures to the table. When we've settled around it, I begin to talk, and Erik shapes my words with his fingers for Finn.

I tell them everything as quickly as I can. About going back to the Southland, and the Guardians, and my father, at which point Finn takes my hand across the table and squeezes it. And I tell them all about Lev and the True Southlings—what they did to Madam Alder, and what they did to the guard, and what Lev plans to do.

"You can't understand how bad it will be," I say, looking down at the table to avoid meeting their eyes. "He's going to have people—have *me*—controlling what you do. What you say. Not all the time, but just enough so the part of you inside, the part that's *you*, will be so lost and confused that you'll be terrified to say anything about it. You'll almost be dead," I finish tonelessly, "but your body will still be pretending to be you, and no one will know."

When I've finished speaking, the tower is so quiet I can hear the freezing rain drumming on the window, even above the roaring wind. Finn and Erik look at one another for a moment, but I don't think they're conversing with their thoughts. I don't think they have to.

After a long moment, Finn sighs and clasps his hands on the table. Erik looks at me. "How many?" he asks.

"How many can compel, or how many total?"

"Both."

Counting silently, I gnaw on my bottom lip and taste the waxy paint again. "Five who can compel, though there may be more. I don't know. And if the others all come..." I pause again, thinking. "Fifteen others, give or take a few. A boy who can make you see things that aren't real. And—oh!" I gasp, dismayed. "A listener. Old Padrus. He can hear people speaking with their thoughts for miles, at least, if he's trying to."

Finn makes a sharp, angry gesture, and Erik smiles a little, but without real amusement. "Damn it," he translates for me. "And I agree," he adds with a frown, "that's not good."

"I know." I sigh. "I don't know what to do. Even if we knew how to fight back like—like that, with our minds, there's just the three of us."

At that, Erik and Finn exchange another long look, and this time they talk back and forth with their hands for a moment. Finally, Finn looks at me and begins to move his fingers. "It's not only the three of us," Erik says for him.

Then he turns to me and adds, "Well, he means only the two of us here, without you, and not anymore, anywa—ow!" he mutters, as Finn elbows him. "Fine."

Erik goes back to watching Finn's hands. "After you left, Erik and I talked. Then we talked to the others, all together. We were angry at Alaric for what he did, for not defending you, and we wanted him to know that there was nothing wrong with you. That you weren't the only one who had powers. That his own brothers do, too."

"You *told* them?" I gasp. "Your brothers? And the king?"

They both snort. "Of course we didn't tell Da," Erik says, no longer translating. "We're not stupid. Alaric was enough of a risk."

I lean forward, on the edge of my chair. "And?"

The twins look at each other and grin before they turn back to me. "And...nothing." Erik replies. "They weren't angry."

Finn says something, smiling a little, and Erik laughs. "Right. They were hardly even surprised."

"That's wonderful!"

"It's not even the best part!" Erik exclaims. "Do you know, Garreth and Coll can hear us, too! Garreth can even talk, a little. He's weak at it, though."

I can only stare. "You're joking," I manage at last. "Garreth... and *Coll*?"

Finn exhales through his nose, sounding amused, and Erik snickers. "I know," he says. "We couldn't believe it, either."

I scarcely hear him, focused on Finn. "But...that's better than wonderful," I say. "Now you can really talk with them."

He gives me a wry smile and says something, very precisely, with his fingers.

"He says he *has* really been talking with them." Erik sounds as if he's trying not to laugh. "This is just different. Not better. Harder, even."

"Right," I mutter, embarrassed. I'm sure my cheeks are flaming when Erik nudges me.

"He's just teasing," he explains quietly, and I notice that he's not looking at Finn, and his hands are still. "He wants you to learn."

I grin. "Oh."

"Anyway," Erik says, heaving a sigh, "the *point* is, now there are five of us with abilities of some kind. Even if two can't really do much. But Coll and Garreth can fight," he adds brightly. "And five against twenty—"

"—is bad," I finish, depressed again. "They're strong, Erik. Too strong." The wind howls outside and rattles the windowpane as if emphasizing my point. I shiver as I'm reminded of the night I was locked out in a storm like this. And then, thinking of that night gives me an idea. "We need the others," I say, sitting bolt upright. "Alaric, as well. And the king. Your physician—Master Thormand?—too."

"Thorvald," Erik corrects, looking interested. "Why?"

"I'll explain when we're together," I murmur, thinking so quickly my head spins. "Will the king be angry I'm here?" I ask worriedly. "Will he listen? Will any of them?"

Finn and Erik exchange a glance. Finn says something with his hands. And I need little more than the look on their faces to understand, even before Erik speaks.

"It doesn't matter. We'll make them."

And that gives me another idea.

CHAPTER TWENTY-EIGHT

I PACE NERVOUSLY FROM ONE SIDE of the tower to the other. Again, I regret that I didn't bring a cloak or shawl. With all the windows and no fire, it's freezing. My feet begin to ache a little, apparently remembering their first time in the Northlands, and I know that if I'm still for any length of time, my barked shin and bruised knees will start to hurt in earnest, too.

I've only been waiting for Erik to go and find his brothers, the king, and Master Thorvald for a few moments, but each one seems to last an hour. It's worse because I'm afraid even to *be* here. Instead of Erik, I half-expect the guards to slam open the door any second and haul me back to prison. Lost in thought as I try to smooth the wrinkles out of my plan, I jump when Finn touches my shoulder.

He gives me a small smile, looking apologetic, and points to me, then to himself. Then he makes an exaggerated, worried face and a fluttery motion with his hands.

"Sorry," I say, when I figure out what he means. "I didn't mean to make you nervous, too."

Finn shrugs, but he also gestures to one of the chairs and raises his eyebrows meaningfully. I shake my head.

"I can't sit! Not now." But I do stop pacing. I try to content myself with peering out the window into the near-darkness and drumming my fingertips on the sill impatiently. Luckily—or unluckily, I'm not certain—I don't have long to wait before the door opens. I turn at the sound, hoping to see Erik, and my knees threaten to buckle. "Alaric." His name is a breath, unintended.

Alaric's eyes widen, and he opens his mouth to speak just as Erik squeezes in around him.

"Got them all," Erik says triumphantly. He elbows Alaric aside to reveal Garreth and Coll and, behind them, Master Thorvald the Physician and King Allard himself.

For an instant, I don't even care about the king and the physician. "Garreth!" I exclaim, grinning again. "And Coll!"

Garreth stops somewhere around the middle of the now-crowded room and stares, his face going blotchy red. "I thought Erik was playing a joke," he stammers at last. "But—"

Coll chuckles. "Move aside, if you're just going to stand and gape at her, boyo," he says as he lumbers over. I extend my hand but instead am shocked to find myself wrapped in a quick, bone-crushing embrace. "So, you're back, witch-girl," he mutters when he releases me.

"Yes," says King Allard, in an entirely different tone. "You've returned, Ellin Fisher."

I glance at Erik, who's come to stand next to me. "Did you get it?" I whisper. In answer, he presses a small sprig of leaves into my palm, and I exhale with relief and look up at the king. "Your majesty," I say nervously, "before anything else, I offer this." With that, I hold out my hand, and the three leaves of Horse Ivy, to the king of the Northlands.

King Allard is silent for a moment as he studies the shiny, wet green leaves. Then a small, slow smile—much like Finn's—tugs at the corner of his mouth. "Horse Ivy? Now, whose idea was that?"

"Mine," I reply, and it's true. "But Coll—Prince Coll, I mean—told me about it. When I was here before, I mean."

"I know what you mean," the king says, sounding almost amused. Ice-blue eyes meet mine. "You would have us be at peace until sunrise, then, girl?"

Of course I would, I think. He put me in prison the last time I was here, and what I'm about to propose is illegal several times over. What I say aloud, though, is simply, "Yes, your majesty. Please. Your safety depends on it."

"So I've heard," he says, regarding me intently. "Though I do not yet have the full tale. Nor, of course, do I know what it is you wish to propose."

That is, I suppose, the best answer I'm likely to get. When King Allard, Alaric, and Master Thorvald have seated themselves at the table, and the others have gathered around, a quick glance out the window tells me that we have an hour—surely not more than two—before dinner. Even if the king agrees to my plan, I'm not sure we'll have enough time. So, as quickly as possible, I tell them all what I told Finn and Erik.

When I've finished, King Allard looks at his clasped hands for a moment. "Well," he says to everyone, "the obvious answer is, we will not allow ourselves to be overcome."

Alaric frowns. "I don't see—"

"No," I interrupt. "I don't think you do. Not any of you. This is not a force that can be fought with an army. Not with strength. Lev—several of them—could have control of your mind before you raised a weapon. They could make you use it on yourselves, instead. That fast."

The king looks at me. "And you know this because you, too, are capable of such things?"

I nod. Then I curl my hand into a fist at my side, wishing that could give me strength to face him about this. "I am. As powerful as Lev, if I'm to believe him. But this—these powers—are the real Southling witchcraft. Not the healing. You were right to fear us," I add, more quietly, "but not all Southlings, your majesty."

King Allard makes a dismissive gesture, though whether that's meant to brush aside the formality or my argument, I'm not sure. "I fail to see your point regarding this matter."

I nod again, take a deep breath, and get to it. "The point is," I say, looking past him to Master Thorvald the Physician, "we can't fight them with weapons. *You* can't fight them with your minds, and we—" I glance at Erik, remembering that the twins didn't tell their father, "—I mean, *I'm* not powerful enough to fight them all. Even if I had help."

"Then it's hopeless?" Garreth asks, sounding very young.

I shake my head and attempt to smile at him, but I don't think I succeed. "No. We just have to outsmart them. Use something they'd never expect."

The king raises an eloquent eyebrow.

"Southling healing." This time, I do smile. "I mean, Southling healing *power*, but used backward. With herbs. To make you seem very sick."

"Oh, good girl," Master Thorvald murmurs. He sounds so much like my father—even with his Northlands accent—that my heart twists. "You'll make him seem ill enough that his mind is damaged, but yet, not dying anytime soon."

"Exactly," I reply. "I don't think a mentally damaged, ailing king would declare war. And Alaric, as his successor, *couldn't*. Not if he wasn't king yet, and the king wasn't *entirely* without his senses." I bite the inside of my cheek and look anxiously at King Allard, hoping he isn't angry with me for daring to suggest harming him.

To my surprise, he laughs so hard he starts to wheeze. I suddenly recall that, not long ago, he was nearly dead in truth. He looks strong and healthy now. "Ellin Fisher," the king says at last, and his cold eyes seem almost kind, "I believe I'm beginning to understand why my sons spoke so highly of you."

It's strange, but I can't help smiling at this man who once put me in prison. "Then, I have permission?" I ask hesitantly. "You will feel ill, and I will have to make you delirious and feverish with herbs," I add, warning him. "We can't risk you not looking and seeming believable."

He nods. "You have my permission to do what is necessary."

"Good." I look around and meet all of their eyes in turn, even Alaric's. To my surprise, Alaric looks back with something like respect, which, I suppose, is something. "Good," I say again. "But we need to work fast." And we do. As if my last words were a signal, everyone starts talking at once, adding things to my plan and offering to do various jobs.

In the end, the king, Master Thorvald, Finn, Erik, and I go down to the physician's workroom to make the king seem sick. Garreth goes to tell the castle guards to play along; Coll, to tell the stable boys. Alaric goes to explain the situation to the king's advisers and Keeper Nan, and to tell Nan to warn Aiddan and Lev that the king has been ill for some time, so they should not play too late. Nan is also to give Lev the message, if asked where I am, that "his girl Bess" was last seen near the stables, apparently exploring. I can only hope Keth doesn't remember how much horses used to scare me.

"It's not enough time," I mutter a little later, as I grind dried roots, berries, and a little water into a paste. My scraped, abused palm cramps in protest, and, resting it a moment, I glance at the king. "How do you feel?" I ask.

Somehow, his shrug seems elegant rather than careless. "Warm. And my throat is beginning to feel tight."

"Good." I wince at his expression. "I'm sorry. But I'm glad it's working."

He ignores my apology and peers curiously into the mortar bowl. "What is that?"

"Madder root, mainly. It will make your skin flushed and blotchy, as though your fever is worse than it really is."

"It smells dreadful," he says, and one thick, pale eyebrow arches in skeptical distaste. "I'm to drink it?"

Finn, at my side and busy shredding leaves into his own bowl, pauses long enough to lift his hands and say something. I frown because Erik is on the opposite side of the room and not here to translate, but the king startles me by barking a laugh.

"I think I won't do that instead," he replies dryly, shocking me again when he shapes the words—very slowly, even I can tell—with his big-knuckled, blue-veined hands. "But thank you for the suggestion."

Finn shakes his head and grins down into his bowl, and I look from him to the king in confusion. "What's so funny?"

"It isn't something to be repeated to a young woman," the king says, but not unkindly. I can only shake my head, amused and amazed at the change in him. How different he seems from the cold, indifferent man who sentenced me, I think.

"Well, you do have to drink it, your majesty," I say, when I've added enough water for the paste to become thick soup. "It won't taste good."

"I would be startled if it did," he says. When the king has drunk both the madder and an infusion made from Finn's shredded leaves, designed to make him stink as if very ill, I turn to Master Thorvald.

"How long will it take?" I ask, with a nod at the steaming bowl he has waiting at the counter.

"To make his majesty delirious?" The bald physician purses his lips. "The symptoms should begin almost immediately."

"Good, because dinner's in a few moments," Erik says. "I asked, when I went to the kitchen to get the garlic."

"All right." I clasp my hands together in front of me, braiding my fingers nervously. Then I take a long, slow breath. "Are you ready?" I ask the king.

He nods and gives me the ghost of a smile. "Work your witch-craft, child."

I take a few more deep breaths in a useless attempt to calm myself. Then I reach for my healing power. Ignoring the others in the room, I take the king's hands in mine, as I did once before. This time, my touch doesn't soothe him, and it doesn't heal. Doing this makes me feel wrong, unclean, but I brace myself and shove through the walls in my mind and his body. And I make him feel almost as bad as he looks.

Master Thorvald gasps, and Erik swears when I finally pull away from the king and slump forward with my hands on my knees. With a groan, I push strands of hair off my sweaty forehead and look at the king. I'm both pleased and horrified to see that he looks even worse than before.

"How do you feel?" I ask.

King Allard stares back with wild, bloodshot eyes. His breathing is fast and shallow, and spots of bright red stand high on his sunken, sallow cheeks. "They're coming," he whispers hoarsely, and he claws at my arm with a half-curled hand. "They're coming. They're coming."

I nod slowly as I look at the wreck we've made of the Northlander king. "Good."

CHAPTER TWENTY-NINE

"**W**HERE HAVE YOU *BEEN*?" Keth demands the instant I open the door to our room, panting from my race through the halls. "They've started dinner by now, you goose, and we're to be there. Lev's furious with you. Going to the stables? What were you *thinking*?" She says all of this very fast as she drags me across the hall.

Irritated, I shake my arm away from her grip. "I wanted to be outside. By myself," I snap. "Where I go is my business. And I'm not very late, am I?"

"Late enough," Lev replies coolly, waiting just inside the door of his room. "The others are downstairs already, eating with the Northlanders. I wanted to make certain you know the plan."

I make a show of biting my lip and looking guilty. "I'm sorry," I murmur, staring at the floor. "I was looking at the horses. I lost track of time."

"No matter. It's lucky your part in this is simple," he says with a shrug. "After dinner, when they are ready for the music, follow my lead. Take control of the oldest prince, Alaric. He has yellow hair and—"

"I know," I interrupt, and I brush at my dress as if to rid it of straw and dust. Actually, I remove a clinging bit of silverleaf and hope he doesn't notice. "I've seen him. What am I to do with him?"

Lev's smile is wicked. "Whatever you wish. I don't care. Nothing suspicious, though," he adds, raising a finger. "Put him to sleep, if you like. Pretend he's drunk."

"And then?"

"I will have the king dismiss everyone, and we will take the royal family aside and explain that their lives will be forfeit if they resist."

I shake my head in disbelief. "It sounds so simple," I whisper.

Lev smiles again and gives my shoulder a squeeze. "Well, we're powerful, Ellin. It should be easy."

"Besides," Keth adds, "once you have control of one, you'll realize it's easier than it sounds."

"I can't believe you're trusting me with this," I say when Lev shepherds us toward the door. "What if I can't do it?"

"Then you look like an idiot," Keth mutters, but I can hear the nerves jangling in her tone and know she's as frightened as I am.

"You can do it," Lev says smoothly. "You both can. Keth, the youngest boy will be no trouble at all. Trust me."

For half a second, I look at his warm, excited smile, and I almost want to.

The great room looks much as I remember it, except that King Allard is present. He is already seated, slump-shouldered, at the high table when we enter. Alaric and Master Thorvald are seated at his sides, and the two of them are making a show of helping him eat, I'm pleased to see. At a table near the royal family are Brek and Aiddan, their red and auburn heads looking out of place in the sea of shades of blond.

"Come," Lev murmurs. He takes my elbow with one hand, Keth's with the other, and escorts us formally through the room.

Though I want to look at the princes, I keep my head bowed and don't meet their eyes as we pass.

The meal goes by all too quickly. I'm so nervous that the meat with sour berry sauce—my favorite dish, when I was here before—turns to ash in my mouth. My hand shakes violently when I pick up my glass of water, and I put it down without drinking, afraid of spilling it all over myself. It doesn't help that Lev, Keth, and Aiddan are quiet and on edge, too. Of all of us, only Brek seems to enjoy himself, heaping his plate with second servings of everything.

"Are the others here?" I whisper at last to Lev, who has spent the meal watching the king.

"Hmm?" He shakes his head and turns to me, his disapproval clear. "Yes, of course. But hush."

"Right," I murmur, feeling ill. I'd give anything, I think, for this meal never to end.

I can't eat, and I can't look at the princes for reassurance, and so I watch the others at my table. Brek chatters happily to Keth, whose fork rises stiffly to her mouth at precise, measured intervals. I have a feeling she doesn't taste her food any more than I did. Apparently deep in thought, Lev continues to watch the high table. And Aiddan, silent and ignoring all of us, keeps his left "hand" beneath the table while he eats with only his right.

"*It's time,*" Lev says suddenly, startling me, as a maid goes to take the king's plate away. "*Be ready.*"

Brek finally stops talking, and the rest of us stiffen. And then, at the high table, Alaric stands and raises his palms for silence.

This is it, I think. This moment matters. What happens next, I realize with a thrill of horrified anticipation, could very well change both the Northlands and the Southland forever.

"There will be no music tonight," Alaric says loudly. "His majesty the king wishes it so."

"No, no, no," mutters the king. His hoarse, petulant voice carries throughout the room, and everyone shifts uncomfortably.

A pained look tightens Alaric's face, and I would swear I can hear him swallow. "Please, go about your business. Go home, and

⬩

good night." He seems to force a smile. "And friends," he adds, looking at our table as most of the Northlanders begin to leave, "Master Bard, please accept our apologies and our continued hospitality. Perhaps another evening."

Lev says nothing. Aiddan, after a moment, gives Alaric a nod.

Please, I think, and I squeeze my hands beneath the table so hard my knuckles pop. Please let this work. I glance at the high table and see the princes apparently talking amongst themselves, darting anxious looks at their father. Acting normal, I suppose, for men whose father is supposed to be very ill.

A moment later, we Southlings, the royal family, and Master Thorvald are the only ones remaining. Just go, Lev, I think, but I'm careful to keep my thoughts shielded from him. Just go. Believe he's sick, and your plan won't work. Lev stands, his dark eyes never leaving the high table, and every muscle in my body tenses. Turn and leave, I beg him silently. Please, just—

And then he brings his hands together once. Twice. Again, and a few times more. Applauding.

I close my eyes and wonder if I'm going to vomit up the meal I just ate.

"Well played," Lev says softly, but his voice fills the room like a performer's. "Oh, very well played. Almost convincing. But did you really think to fool me like this? Ellin?"

I taste bile when I swallow. "I don't know what you're talking about," I mutter, though I have a feeling my chalk-white face betrays me. "I certainly didn't—"

"Ellin had nothing to do with it!" Garreth interrupts, shooting to his feet.

Lev laughs aloud as Erik, looking pale, yanks Garreth back down. "So, she *was* involved," Lev murmurs. "I thought so." He looks past Keth and Brek's shocked faces, down at me, and smiles. "Well, this changes very little."

It changes enough, I think, and anger begins to simmer alongside my fear. I stand. "You can't do this," I say flatly. "I won't let you."

Lev snorts, eyes flashing. "I'd like to see you stop me."

"Ellin!" Brek hisses as he tugs at my skirt. "Don't—"

"Lev, please!" I exclaim, ignoring Brek. "Please. You know it's wrong. You have to!"

He's quiet for a moment. And then he turns, very slowly, to look at King Allard. "I know it's wrong," Lev says, his voice low. "Wrong, for all Southlings to be treated like we have the plague, here in the Northlands. Wrong, for this man—" he points at the king, "—to have kept his father's laws in place. Laws based on *fear!*" he shouts, cheeks going dusky again. "Fear of us, when we are not inherently evil. Not just for being born in the Southland, or having these gifts."

I can only stare, clutching the table with shaking hands.

"It's wrong," Lev continues, "for everyone at home to be *so afraid* of us, based on these Northlanders' laws and *their* fear, the burnings and unfair laws, that they set up a force to hunt us down like animals. So that they might be safe," he spits. "Safe. Tame. Like dogs."

I shake my head, feeling as though Lev and I are the only ones in the room. When I blink because the light is suddenly too bright, I realize my eyes are full of tears. "But what do you want?" I whisper. My voice is thin, faltering. "To kill everyone who isn't like you?"

Lev looks at me, and there is real anguish in his attempted smile. "What do you think I am, Ellin?" he asks quietly. "I want to be free. To be *safe*, to keep *us* safe, from these people, all of them, who think *I'm* the dangerous one."

"Lev," I whisper, but Coll interrupts.

"And you think this is the way to go about that, boy?" he calls mockingly from his seat near the foot of the high table. "To prove you're harmless by making us all your slaves?"

Whatever softness was on Lev's face disappears as his gaze shifts to Coll. "Oh, no," he says. "I'm not harmless."

Suddenly, King Allard begins to laugh, like something scraping ice. My blood runs cold when I realize that Lev has won already. "Not harmless at all," croaks the king, speaking Lev's words, as he pushes himself to stand. "Not to you, anyway."

His wrinkled, bearded face twists in a warped parody of Lev's mocking smile. And then, as Lev's youthful grace wars with an old man's ailing body, the king lifts his arm with a stiff, awkward jerk. Everyone is too frozen with shock to stop him, and so we watch, transfixed, as the silver blade in his hand catches the light.

Alaric moves then, crying out, but he's too late.

The king throws the knife.

CHAPTER THIRTY

THE KNIFE SPINS THROUGH THE AIR, but Lev underestimated Coll. Faster than anyone would expect the big man to move, he turns, half-ducking, and the blade plunges into his shoulder instead of burying itself in his neck like Lev intended.

And as Coll looks up at his father, seeming dazed, with crimson soaking through the sleeve of his shirt, Garreth shouts and throws himself out of his chair. The chair clatters backward, and Garreth begins to run, snarling, toward Lev.

"Now!" Lev shouts, sounding strained. "To me!"

I stare, too horrified to move, as Keth leaps to her feet and Glyn, Shenna, Cedran, Mathias, grizzled old Padrus, and all the rest burst through the doors, startling Garreth enough to stop him in his tracks. The other princes jump up, and Coll rips the blade from his shoulder and crouches, ready to fight.

Feet hammer on the stone floor, and they meet in the center of the room, in the clear space between the dining tables and the benches circling the hearth. It is only when I see Garreth draw his dagger and leap at Mathias, and Erik duck Cedran's club only to dart in close and punch him in the gut that I realize it: the Southlings aren't compelling them! And not for lack of trying; I can see it on Shenna's face, and Glyn's. They *can't* compel the princes.

"Stop!" I scream. It's useless, though. My voice is lost beneath all the shouts, grunts, and dull noises of blows. Frantic, I jump to my feet and scramble up onto my chair to try and get their attention. "Stop it!" I cry. "Alaric! Coll! They can't—"

"STOP!" shouts Alaric, and he strides slowly, majestically, right into the middle of the brawl. His voice rings like steel. His tone vibrates with command, and, to my surprise, he is obeyed. Even by the Southlings.

And then I see the smug smile on Alaric's face and the dead-looking flatness in his eyes, and my heart sinks. Suddenly, I know why the Southlings obeyed him.

Slowly, as if underwater, the king takes another meat knife from the table and lifts it to his own throat. Alaric's smile deepens, chilling below his fixed stare. Then he turns to his brothers, who stand, flushed and breathing heavily, obviously confused. "Now. That's better...*boys*," he sneers.

I close my eyes. In the sudden silence, it sounds very loud when Erik swears.

"Sit," Alaric snaps, pointing at the benches around the hearth. "Ellin. Join them."

Feeling everyone's eyes on me, I climb down shakily from my chair and walk across the room. Somehow I manage to keep my head high, even though my knees are trembling. I can't suppress a shiver, however, or stop myself from walking a little faster, as I pass Alaric. I sink down next to Coll, facing the room, and try to resist the almost overwhelming urge to bury my face in my hands.

Actually, Coll's elbow digging into my side is the only thing that stops me from doing just that. "What's going on?" he mutters under his breath, leaning close.

"They can't compel you," I whisper back. "Only Alaric. But I don't know who is, and I don't—"

"—know why?" Lev finishes as he saunters over to stand before us. "Nor do I. But it is no matter."

I marvel at his power. Anyone else would have to spend all their energy controlling the king, and yet, other than a faint line between Lev's eyebrows, I can't even see any signs of strain. But the king remains a slave to Lev's will, frozen at the high table with the knife pressed below his chin. Ready to die at a thought.

"Shenna! Cedran! Barricade and guard the doors," Lev calls over his shoulder. Then he turns back to us. "Now," he says softly. "You have seen what we can do to the others. That, I think, is sufficient reason for all of you to keep quiet and do as I say."

"What do you *want?*" Garreth asks, pressing a hand against a bleeding cut on his forehead. I think he adds, "you bastard," under his breath, but I can't be sure.

"Want?" Lev echoes. He makes a bland face. "I *want* you to shut your mouth and listen. All of you. Speak out of turn again, and we'll see how well your 'golden' brother Alaric likes gouging his own eye out."

Garreth swallows audibly and nods, his face pale as bone, making the scarlet trickle stand out even brighter on his skin.

"When we leave this room," Lev says, clasping his hands behind his back, "your brother Alaric will go to everyone you might have told about this, everyone who might have heard suspicious noises, and he will tell them that the threat has been dealt with. There are no magical Southlings, he will assure them. It was nothing but a lie from an unimportant, stupid girl who escaped from your prison and came back, with a few of her friends, intending to poison the king."

I'm as good as dead, I think, but I'm too angry to care.

"You all," Lev continues, "will go about your business. You will agree to whatever the king and your brother Alaric seem to decide. They will declare war, and you will fight. All of you. You will not speak of this," he says, looking at each of the princes in turn. "You will not so much as breathe a single *word* about anything you have heard tonight, if you wish to remain alive."

As he speaks, as I follow his gaze and look at my friends, I suddenly understand something. Lev hates the Northlands as much as I used to. Like me, he didn't take time to learn anything before coming here. I know for a fact that he knows almost nothing about the princes, which means that he doesn't know Finn is deaf and mute. If Lev did, surely he would realize that there is one prince who *can't* really fight in a war and *can't* ever speak of this, even if he wants to.

Lev doesn't know that the princes can speak with their thoughts, either, but that doesn't help us. Not with old Padrus in the room, who would hear any of us try. But Lev *doesn't know* about Finn, and he doesn't know that there are other ways to speak besides his precious gifts. Keeping my thoughts very tightly shielded, I begin to form a plan.

Old Padrus can hear thought-speech, I think, hardly listening as Lev goes on. But Lev told me that Padrus can't read people's thoughts. Surely he wouldn't know if I just reached into someone's mind, carefully, so they didn't even know, and extracted information. I don't *think* he would be able to tell, I amend, and I bite my lip as I glance at the old man, who stands with his arms crossed, leaning against the far wall.

But I don't have a choice. It's the only plan I have, and there's the barest chance it will work. I inhale through my nose, look down at my scraped, sore hands clasped tightly in my lap, and reach out. I choose Erik simply because he's closer.

I have to be careful. It's like sneaking through a room full of people, in the bright light of day, and hoping against hope that they won't see. My thoughts snake out, the thinnest possible thread, and I have to exert all the control I have to enter Erik's mind gentle as a feather. Gentler, even, so he won't feel and give me away by acting surprised or, worse, speaking to me with his thoughts and alerting Padrus.

At last, beads of nervous sweat wetting my forehead and clammy in my armpits, I'm in Erik's mind. Lev drones on, something about how the war will progress, I think, but I don't listen. I hunt through Erik's thoughts as fast as possible, not even bothering to look closely at anything, until, finally, I've reached the things he knows how to do but doesn't even think about. I find what I'm looking for after a moment, and my hands grip one another even harder.

Armed with the knowledge, I leave a link from Erik's mind to mine and go back to myself. It feels strange to split my concentration this way, to be in my body and his thoughts at the same time. But if Lev can do it with the king, I can, too.

And then, I wait. I still don't pay much attention to Lev; I'm too busy watching Erik's face, and Finn's, waiting for one of them to look at me. But they don't. Their focus is elsewhere. Finn watches Lev, frowning intently, no doubt looking at his mouth to see what he's saying. Erik looks beyond him, to Alaric and the king, seeming as anguished as I feel.

"And you!" Lev says loudly, drawing my attention as he turns to the group of Southlings. There's fire in his voice now, dark and dangerous and consuming. "You have stayed by my side. Have not betrayed me. Tonight, my friends, your future begins."

Though Lev's back is turned, several of the other Southlings are still facing us. But I have no choice. It is now or never. Recklessly, I move my arm and elbow Coll. He glances down, out of the corner of his eye. With the barest nod of my head, I motion to the others. I feel Coll shift as he nudges Garreth, and Garreth elbows Erik, and soon, all their eyes are on me.

I can't stop shaking. Even my hands tremble as I lift them, discreetly, and begin to use my fingers to talk, drawing on Erik's mind in order to know how.

We have to fight, I signal to them. At first, Garreth and Erik look confused. Not expecting this, they don't know to look. But then Finn, eyes wide, touches Erik's knee surreptitiously and nods toward my hands.

We have to fight, I say again. My fingers are clumsy. Despite the basic knowledge from Erik, my hands aren't used to this. I don't think it matters, though, because Coll nods.

How? he asks, holding his hand close against his belly.

I bite the inside of my cheek, hoping what I'm about to suggest isn't terribly stupid. *I'll start. Fight Lev's mind*, I reply. *When I do, Erik, Finn. Use your thoughts to fight, if you can. If not, just fight.*

They nod. Then Garreth points to himself and makes a questioning face.

You fight, too, I sign. *Knock them out.*

Then Coll elbows me again and, with a glance at the still-conversing Southlings, shows me the bloody table knife concealed in his sleeve. *Should I kill the boy?* he asks, with the barest nod at Lev.

I shake my head immediately. *No. He's mine. You get Alaric. Fast. Don't let them hurt him.*

Erik looks at me and raises an eyebrow as Lev begins to approach us again. "Well," Lev says. "I suppose you—"

And, even though I've let go of Erik's mind, I lift my hands again, where all four princes can see, and form the one word I made sure to remember.

Now!

CHAPTER THIRTY-ONE

THE INSTANT I FORM THE WORD with my fingers, I send my thoughts flying out, fast as an arrow, to plunge into the king's mind. I feel Lev's shock, see his dark eyes widen, and begin trying to wrest control of the king away from him.

Mere seconds later, the bench beside mine sails backward, hard enough to splinter, as Coll shoves himself up. He runs across the room, boots pounding like drums, and throws himself at Alaric. They crash to the floor, arms locked, and begin to grapple with one another.

Still seated on the other side of the hearth, Erik has his eyes shut, and Finn stares at nothing as they try to fight the Southlings with their minds. But they are weaker than me, probably weaker than the Southlings, and untrained. And then, too suddenly for me to shout a warning, Glyn throws a pitcher of wine at Erik's head. But Finn is even faster, watchful, and he grabs Erik and pulls him off the bench. The pitcher misses them both by a hairsbreadth and smashes into a hundred pieces and a wet spray of red, dripping down the wall.

The great room is in chaos. Caught up in my struggle with Lev, wrestling with his mind as violently as the others are fighting with their bodies, I can only pay a little attention to my surroundings. Even so, I see some things. Across the room, Garreth shoves Aiddan aside roughly and jumps up onto the Southlings' table. He runs along it, stepping in food and knocking bowls and cups aside. Then he leaps onto the high table, over it, his feet barely touching the wood, and dashes to the wall behind. Jumping again, Garreth tears down the two crossed swords and shield that decorate the wall, and I wince to see him cut his hands on the blades. With both hilts in one hand and the shield in the other, he races back across the room and shoves one sword at Erik, then pivots and slides the shield across the floor, spinning and clattering, to Finn.

A moment later, I gasp with horror when I see Erik and Cedran begin to fight near the door. Erik is fast with his blade and quick on his feet, but Cedran is bigger by far, muscular, and strong. Their blades catch the firelight, glinting and flashing, and the ringing sound they make is almost beautiful. The men themselves are almost beautiful to watch, transfixing, as they circle one another in a deadly dance. After several moments, though, I can see that Erik's hair is darkening with sweat, while Cedran looks barely winded. They pause, swords crossed. And then, quick as a snake, Cedran twists his blade, sending Erik's arm wrenching back. Cedran lunges forward, orange hair fanning, and plunges the point of his blade into Erik's thigh.

I scream and turn away as Erik falls, clutching his leg. My frantic gaze lands nearby, on Coll and Alaric. Flushed and sweaty, they remain locked on the floor with Coll practically on top of his brother. Alaric has his right hand near his face, thumb pointed toward his eye, and I can see the strain on Coll's features, the way his neck looks as if it might burst, as he tries to prevent Alaric from blinding himself.

Panicked, I wonder who's compelling Alaric. It can't be Lev. Even he couldn't possibly control two people at once. I don't think it's Shenna or Cedran. They're both fighting, and I doubt they have the control to do so much at once. Mathias lies motionless beside the high table already, and I'm sure he's at least unconscious, maybe dead.

I don't have long to wonder about Alaric, though, because a sudden burst of agony spreads inside my head like flame. Lev laughs, and, squinting, I blearily see him grin. "*Is that really all you're capable of, Ellin?*" he murmurs silkily with his mind.

And there is another swell of pain. Hot and red as blood, it burns through my skull. My thoughts are ashes. I close my eyes, place shaking hands on my knees, and will myself not to vomit.

But I cling to my link with the king. Deep within the king's mind, I can see Lev. I can sense his presence all over the king's thoughts, pulsing like sickness. But I can't possibly be as strong as he is. For every strand of his thoughts I pry off, two more grow up in its place, like worms or twisting, poison vines.

My body is shaking. Rocking, more like, and I know I'm moaning, maybe screaming, and I can't stop. I struggle with Lev's mind, trying to strike back when his thoughts rake mine like talons. I want to hurt him. I want to kill him. I shove hard, once, and feel myself pierce something. Instead of Lev, though, I hear the king cry out, at that.

But I only manage it once. I barely know what I'm doing, I haven't trained my gifts the way Lev has, and I can't be so many places at the same time. Fighting for the king's mind, trying to hurt Lev, and trying not to lose myself are just too much. I feel myself slipping, being dragged ever closer to a black and gaping abyss.

Swaying where I sit, drunk with pain, I barely notice when a blond boy—I think it's Finn—places himself in front of me. Protecting me. I can't be grateful, though. I can't even tell who it is. My vision is blurred, the room spinning, and I close my eyes again and keep fighting.

I don't know how much time passes. It could only be moments, but it seems like forever. I don't know where my friends are, or if they're winning, or if they're even alive. All I know is that it takes every bit of my strength to keep Lev off-balance, to keep him from swallowing my mind and the king's whole. The abyss is beneath me, now. I am hanging onto the ledge with only my hands, fingernails digging fruitlessly, muscles quivering.

I try to claw at Lev's thoughts again, but he takes advantage of my distracted, weakened defense and thrusts into my mind instead. A white-hot knife scores behind my eyes. With a ragged scream, I fall off the bench and land with a bone-jarring smack on my hands and knees. The pain makes me lose the battle with my body, and I gag and retch, then spit, tasting blood. I don't release my hold on the king, though. I can't. If I let go and give him up to Lev, he'll die. We both will.

There is nothing but pain. I exist to cling to the king's mind. I can't remember a time before this battle, before this purpose. I can't remember who I am, or where I am, and the sudden cry of triumph across the room means nothing. Footsteps race toward me, but I don't—I *can't*—care.

"Ellin!" someone shouts. I think that word used to be important. But it isn't. Not now. I exist to cling to the king's mind. And I'm slipping. Lev knows it. I feel his surge of excitement, feel him retreat into himself to gather strength for the killing blow—

And then someone pushes past Finn-or-Garreth and drops to his knees at my side. Hands grasp my shoulders, pull me back, and cradle my trembling body against a broad, firm chest. Whoever it is grips harder, palms warm and reassuring. And I remember.

I am Ellin Fisher. I am as powerful as Lev, or nearly so. I healed this king, once, and I had a father who would be proud of me, and I have friends who will die if I don't succeed. I must cling to the king's mind, and I must not fall into the dark, beckoning chasm, but that is not my only purpose. That is not all that I am.

All of a sudden, the hands supporting me grow even warmer. A tingling sensation of power flows from them down my arms, over my body, and fills me with new strength. The pain in my head abates, and my nausea disappears. With a soft noise of mingled joy and relief, I bask in the healing being offered. For the barest instant, I almost expect to see my father when I open my eyes and blink into the light. And then my vision clears, and, again, my lips part in wonder.

"Alaric," I breathe.

No longer blinded and made stupid by crushing agony, I gather my strength. Like an icy flood against Lev's single bright candle, I move in to wash him out of the king's mind. I have never felt such power flowing through me. For an instant, it is like *I* am a weapon, not just my mind. Trembling with the desire to act, I look at Lev.

I see the shock on his face when he senses my recovery. Then a flicker of fear. Then his eyes seek mine, and there's something else, something important, but it's too late.

I shut my eyes, unable to look at him while I do this. And I strike.

I was right. It is like a flood, roaring in my ears and boiling my blood, overwhelming. Though my eyes are closed, with this much power, I can feel Lev crumple to the floor as his mind is crushed mercilessly and swept out of the king's. The power batters me, too, and, when it has passed, I sag like a limp cloth doll in Alaric's arms.

Alaric stiffens, clutching my arms. "Ellin!"

I want to reply, but my mouth is dry and empty as the black chasm swallows me whole.

Chapter Thirty-two

I REGAIN CONSCIOUSNESS TO THE SOUND of someone calling my name. Then they slap my cheek,
which is more startling than painful, and I groan. "What?" I
grumble, squeezing my eyes shut more tightly as throbbing pain
in my head returns. "I don't want to."

"Ellin!"

I dare to crack one eye open. Then the other, slowly, blinking in
the too-bright light. But when I see Erik and Finn hovering over me,
and become aware that I'm still sprawled on top of Alaric, I remember—very abruptly—where I am and what just happened.

"Oh!" I gasp, sitting bolt upright. Doing so makes me feel almost
like fainting again, and I bury my face in my hand. "Oh," I repeat,
much more weakly.

"Are you all right?" Erik asks, putting a gentle hand on my
shoulder.

Teeth clenched against nausea, I can only nod. I take a deep
breath, then take a slow, careful sip from the cup of water Finn
wraps my fingers around. "I'm fine," I manage, raising my head
to look at them. Something tickles above my lip, and I wipe at it

absently. Only when I lower my hand to my lap again do I realize that the smear of blood means my nose is bleeding.

"I'm fine," I say again, relieved that I sound more believable this time. And then I look at Erik, remembering the sword stabbing his leg, and notice now that his thigh is dark with blood. "Are *you* all right? All of you? What happened?"

"We were hoping you'd know," Erik replies. "Alaric came running at you, and that one—Lev—just fell over a moment later. After that, the others didn't take long to give up. They're with Garreth," he adds, pointing.

I look, and see Garreth holding the utterly defeated-looking group of Southlings at the point of his sword in the corner. "But what happened?" I whisper. I turn to Alaric. "I remember you healed me. Like a Southling would! But how?"

Alaric shakes his head, looking as drained as I feel. "I did nothing. The girl—Finn said he hit her on the head, and she collapsed," he says quietly, with a small, helpless gesture. "That freed me from her control."

"The girl?" I echo. Then my eyes widen, and I swear under my breath—at myself, for underestimating her. "Keth. Of course."

Alaric shrugs again. "Whoever it was, once I was free, I saw you fall. I grabbed you. But that was all. I don't know how I possibly could have—."

"You healed me," I whisper, certain of it. It's impossible that I only imagined being healed. Before I know what I'm doing, I've taken his hand. "You saved me."

Alaric smiles, warm like sunlight on a cold winter morning, and squeezes my fingers back instead of arguing. Then he opens his mouth, but before he can speak, a hoarse cry from Coll breaks the stillness in the room. Immediately, Alaric is on his feet and running, and Erik pulls Finn up with him an instant later. I don't understand, not at first. Not until I look across the room and see that Coll, bleeding from half a dozen places, is sitting on the floor by the high table with his father's head in his lap. And then I run, too.

Heedless of my own pain, I drop to my knees beside the king and take one of his hands in both of mine. He's still hot with the fever I gave him, but his eyes, when they open and look at me, are clear and lucid. "Where does it hurt?" I ask softly, the first question I ever learned as a healer.

"I don't—" King Allard begins, voice weak. He tries to swallow and grimaces, obviously in pain. Even so, he manages to sound almost amused as he continues. "I don't think that question matters much, now."

I shake my head, even though I know it's true. I remember, now. I felt him slipping away while Lev and I were fighting, and somehow I knew that every blow that Lev and I struck against one another hurt King Allard, too. And the king's ungifted mind couldn't withstand it. "Please," I say, even with that knowledge. "Let me try."

But the king shakes his head, and I hear his breath rattle in his chest as he inhales. "Ellin," he says. "Be still. You've done enough."

"But I—"

"Shh." He turns his hand beneath mine, squeezes gently, and I close my eyes and feel tears spill down my cheeks. "Let me speak, child. I won't see the sunrise, but this peace between us needn't end with it. You are welcome here, Ellin, whatever the laws." Then he groans, and I look at his face worriedly, hoping he isn't in too much pain. "You are no Southling witch," the king whispers, so softly I have to lean close to hear. "Not when you've proved yourself so, to me. Northlander girl."

Blinded by tears, I stumble to my feet so that Finn and Erik can kneel at the king's side, since they have far more right to be there than I do. And then I go to get Garreth, to replace him with my hand trembling on a sword I don't know how to use, because the king's youngest son should be with his father when he dies.

I don't have long to stand there alone, with a sword pointed at people I once called friends. Just long enough to see that Shenna is dead, and Jem is dead, and the others are bruised and bleeding and either staring at nothing or glaring at me. I cannot bear to look at Lev, curled on the floor like a child, shaking uncontrollably and staring, with dark blood from his nose dripping onto the floor.

It's only when I feel a hand on my shoulder, steadying me, that I realize I've been swaying where I stand. Crying silently, Garreth takes the sword from my numb, unresisting fingers, and Erik puts his arm around me and, limping, leads me away.

We've only gone a few steps when I hear someone sobbing, and I stop short when I catch a glimpse of bright red hair beneath the farthest table.

"Brek?" I call, ducking Erik's arm to hurry to him. "Are you hurt?"

He answers by sobbing louder, and I bend over, peering beneath the table. Brek is curled up with his knees to his chest, but he raises his freckled, tearstained face when I call his name again. "Please don't kill me," he gasps, edging away. "Ellin, I didn't know what you could d—"

"Brek," I say softly, realizing for the first time, with horror, that he can't be more than nine or ten at most. "Oh, Brek, no one's going to hurt you."

He shakes his head, face crumpling. "But I saw—I didn't think—"

"I know." I reach out and take his hand even though he flinches. "But you were here all this time?"

Brek nods warily as he allows himself to be pulled out from his hiding place. "I got scared."

I nod again. "So did I," I admit, barely more than a whisper. "But I promise, you're safe now."

Erik and I give Brek over to Keeper Nan before he leads me to a chamber down the hall from the great room, where Alaric, Coll, and Finn are seated around a small table, waiting. Garreth follows on our heels and shuts the door with a stiff, too-careful movement.

"The guards are with them?" Alaric asks dully, not bothering to lift his head from his hands. His elbows are wrinkling stacks of maps, I notice, but I don't think he cares.

Though Alaric doesn't see it, Garreth nods as he slides into a chair between Erik and Coll. "I warned them, but I don't think anyone will try to escape. They seemed to give up when Ellin did…whatever you did," he finishes, looking at me.

"I killed your father," I whisper, clenching my hands together in my lap. "That's what I did."

At that, Alaric does lift his head, and he fixes me with those blue eyes that seem to see right through me. "No," he says firmly. "You saved him." He looks a question at Coll, who sits beside him with one big, still-bloody hand on Alaric's shoulder.

"It's time," Coll says. He grimaces. "Past time, if you ask me."

"I do." There is a strange, new note in Alaric's voice, and his mouth twists in what might be a smile. "I always will," he adds quietly, and I'm aware, all of a sudden, that now he will be king.

Coll's mouth quirks, too, but before he can reply, Erik interrupts. "Time for what?"

"Time for me to tell you a secret I swore to keep," Alaric replies. "Until now, this was known only to the king, his successor, and *his* successor. When King Derrick, our grandda, died, Da and I told Coll. And now—" he takes a deep breath and spreads his hands. "Now, after tonight, I think you all should know."

Alaric looks around the table, at all of us. "This will sound strange," he begins, "but when Da was a young man, he had a dream, and he knew it would come true."

"A dream?" Garreth echoes.

Finn gives him a wry look and moves his hands.

"After what you've seen tonight, you're questioning a true dream?" Erik murmurs, for my benefit. Despite the horrible things that just happened, I can't help smiling a little, because Finn has a point. After tonight, I don't think I'll doubt anything ever again.

"A dream," Alaric repeats, at last. "And in it, he saw the Southland as a great beast for which he had no name. The beast rose from sleep and caught the Northlands—a fierce wolf—unaware, and swallowed the wolf before it knew what had happened."

"Lev," I breathe, my eyes going wide. "The king saw this. He knew."

"He knew," Coll agrees, voice rough with emotion. "That's why Southlings aren't welcome here. When Da told *his* da, the king, about the dream, and convinced him it was real, they decided that the safest way would be to keep many Southlings away, and keep track of the ones who did come. And to forbid any use of any witchcraft."

Garreth swears violently. "But that's why *these* Southlings were angry in the first place!"

"But they failed," Erik says wonderingly, seeing the point better than all of us. Though his eyes are red-rimmed, his face seems alight, suddenly, as he smiles. "They didn't swallow Da. They didn't count on us, or on Ellin, fighting back."

The maps on the table rustle as Alaric pushes himself up to stand, leaning forward with his hands still spread across the pages. "They failed," he agrees, and that new note is in his voice again. "When—when Da died tonight, he told me he'd been pulled from the mouth of the beast. He was grateful," he says, looking right at me. "He died free of the fear that ate at him all his life."

"He called me a Northlander," I whisper, and it's only when my voice catches that I know I'm crying again. I wipe at my eyes, but I smile as I look around the table, at my friends. "At the end, he knew that all Southlings aren't evil."

"No." Coll sighs and pushes his hand over his hair. "Not all. But we have a room full of ones that are, more in the Southland who want to kill their own for the wrong reasons, and laws here forbidding abilities that we all seem to have."

"You're right," Alaric says slowly. "The laws, as they are, cannot stay in place. It's stupid to forbid healing such as Ellin performs, and it is unfair to treat all Southlings as if they are a threat. We will change things," says the new king, with such conviction in his voice that I shiver.

And then he yawns so widely that his beard seems to split and cradles his forehead in both palms. "But not tonight," mumbles King Alaric of the Northlands, sounding like himself again. "Now is not the time for making plans."

I fully intend to go to bed after I've bathed and changed into a shift and dress borrowed, once again, from the maid Bregid.

But despite the fact that the hot water soothes my sore muscles, it does little to relax me. I don't want to be alone, either. And so, instead of heading toward the room where I stayed before, I go down the stairs to the kitchen. I'm not surprised to find Alaric, Coll, and Garreth already there, sitting silently at the table. When my father died, sleep was the farthest thing from my mind, too.

I hesitate in the doorway, feeling strangely shy. I don't mind any of them seeing me in slippers, with my hair wet from the bath, but I do wonder if I'm welcome. After all, the king was their father, and, no matter what Alaric said, I am the one who failed to save him. But then Coll looks up, sees me, and jerks his head at the stove. "Kettle's hot," he says, "if you want tea."

"Where are Finn and Erik?" I ask when I come to the table a moment later, hands wrapped around a warm mug.

Garreth pushes out a chair for me with his foot, though he doesn't look up. "Erik went to see Master Thorvald about his leg. Finn went with him."

"Is he all right?"

"He'll be fine," Alaric replies, clutching a cup of liquor, "but that cut was deep, and he thought it might need to be sewn shut."

I nod, but I don't know what else to say. I can't think of anything that might make them feel better—there *isn't* anything—and it would seem wrong to talk about something trivial. I sigh and stare into my mug, watching a few stray tealeaves float aimlessly. As I'm beginning to wonder if I should go up to my room after all, Erik limps into the kitchen, followed by Finn.

And Erik swears. "You aren't sitting here and crying into your drink, are you?"

I look up, shocked, and see Alaric's icy glare. "What would you have us do?" he snaps. "Celebrate our victory?"

Erik shakes his head and sinks down, stiffly, next to Coll. "Be glad that Da wasn't forced to live as a slave, made to wage a war he would have hated," he says quietly, reaching for the bottle as Finn places empty cups in front of both of them. "He died free, at peace, months after we thought we would lose him."

"He's right, Alaric," Coll says, voice low and gruff. "We should be thankful."

Alaric looks up, and even in the dim light of the single lamp, I can see that his face is wan and more lined than it was an hour ago. "Thankful?" His mouth twists. "None of you is going to be king."

Next to me, Garreth shakes his head. "Not going to be," he murmurs. "Is."

"And you'll be a good king," I add, surprising myself. I look at Alaric and try to smile, though it shakes at the corners as I continue. "You might not do what your father would have done, but I'm sure he was proud to have you follow him. To have all of you," I say, and I glance around the table at each of them in turn.

"He was a great man." Erik shakes his head and takes a gulp of his drink before turning to me. "I wish you could have known him. How he was around us, I mean."

"Then tell me," I reply. My smile comes a little more easily this time, though I'm still afraid I might cry. Even if I did, though, I wouldn't be ashamed. After all, Garreth already is. "Tell each other. Remember what you loved best about him."

I sit back in my chair and listen, warmed by the stove and snug between Garreth and Finn, with one hand still clutching my cup. My other hand lies on the table between me and Finn, just in case.

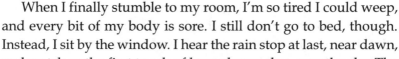

When I finally stumble to my room, I'm so tired I could weep, and every bit of my body is sore. I still don't go to bed, though. Instead, I sit by the window. I hear the rain stop at last, near dawn, and watch as the first touch of lavender washes over the sky. The birds start singing, and slowly the dark silhouettes of trees and rooftops become visible as the sky turns lighter, streaked with pale pink and yellow.

"Sunrise," I whisper. But my peace with the Northlands holds.

CHAPTER THIRTY-THREE

THAT FIRST WET STORM, the night King Allard the Prudent died, signaled the end of snow and the beginning of the cold spring rains. It has at least drizzled every day since then, as if the Northlands themselves are mourning the passing of their king.

The old king was laid out for three days, so that everyone could honor him. At King Alaric's command, Master Thorvald the Physician and I left the evidence of false sickness upon his body. Alaric and his advisors, Lord Erfold the Wise, Lord Ivan, and Coll Horse Master, decided it would be best for the people to think their king died of sudden illness, to keep the True Southlings' part in his death secret. This way, the people of the Northlands won't hate all Southlings even more, once the new laws are in place.

The new laws, I think wonderingly. I can scarcely believe what Alaric plans. Months ago, when I asked him if he would change the laws to pay his debt to me, what I meant was that I thought Southlings should not be required to have papers and a curfew. I didn't dare hope that practicing Southling healing would ever be legal, but now, under King Alaric, it will. And more than that. The other gifts—all of them, except compelling—are to be allowed, as well. After all, the king said, it wouldn't be fair to outlaw powers that all of the royal family and their friend from the Southland possess.

The day after King Allard died, Alaric, the princes, and I sat in the study for an entire day, just talking. To my surprise, after I told them all about how my father died, and how Lev and the others saved me, none of them wanted to kill the remaining True Southlings. I'd been ready to plead for their lives, and I was relieved not to have to argue about it. Instead, Alaric declared that Mathias, Liss, Aiddan, Padrus, and anyone else who cannot compel will be free to stay here and make new lives for themselves in the Northlands, or go back to the Southland, as they please. I was glad. I know the Southlings aren't evil—not all of them. They were just desperate. Even Lev didn't mean to be evil, really. He wanted to be free.

Keth, Glyn, and Cedran, the only Southlings who can compel people, were placed in prison, with several guards—too many to control—watching over them. When Alaric sentenced them, he warned them that if they ever try to escape, I will do to them what I did to Lev. I'm not sure I could if I had to, but the threat, I hope, will be enough.

Lev himself still hasn't come back to his senses, and Master Thorvald and I doubt he ever will. He, too, was placed in prison, with guards and a young physician from the college to care for him and feed him. I didn't watch when they took him away, though Alaric and the others did. I didn't think I could bear to see him this way, shackled in his own mind the way he wanted to imprison others.

I sigh and pinch the bridge of my nose. Thinking about the new laws and the True Southlings—and especially, thinking about Lev—still makes my head swim.

"You're worrying again, aren't you?" Erik asks from behind, as he comes out to join me on the balcony attached to my new, richly-furnished bedroom.

"You always come outside to worry," Garreth adds, plopping down companionably on the bench beside me. I consider warning him that his trousers will get damp, as my skirt is, but I doubt he'll mind any more than I do.

Instead, I smile at him and Erik, and then at Finn, who's been seated on the other bench in friendly silence for awhile, watching the sky. I looked up when he first did but found nothing unusual or interesting in the flat, endless expanse of gray and white. But then, maybe that blankness is what he's looking for, right now.

"Not worrying," I say with a shrug, and I trail a fingertip along the carved edge of the bench, herding droplets. "Just thinking."

"But about what happened," Erik presses. He jabs my shoulder affectionately on his way to sit with Finn. "Again."

I shrug again and spread my hands. "Can I help it?" I ask. "They *were* my friends, for awhile. I've known Keth since we were children," I add, shivering as I remember the bitter, hateful look she gave me when the guards led her away. There was a promise in her eyes and in her thoughts, and I know, deep within me, that she will consider me an enemy for the rest of her life. I never would have expected that thought to make me sad.

"*But, for the others, it will be better now,*" Finn thinks, speaking with his hands, too, to help me learn. "*Particularly the boy, Brek.*"

"I know." I smile, remembering the enormous, gap-toothed grin that lit up Brek's face when we told him Aiddan was going to take him back to the Southland, very probably to live with Donnal. I sent a long letter with them, and Alaric sent money, and I know the arrangement will thrill Donnal. He has always wanted children, and he was always good to me. Brek is lucky.

With a sigh, I push my damp hair off my cheeks and look at Finn, whose hair is cobwebby with raindrops, too. "It does give me chills, though," I say, "thinking how close we all came to being dead, or nearly dead."

"You're chilled because it's cold," Erik replies, and he gives me a quick, reassuring grin. Even that has changed, though. His grin used to be full of mischief, almost dangerous, but now, instead, I just see a quiet sort of strength. "We could have died, but we didn't, Ellin. That's what matters."

"Besides," Garreth adds, digging his hands into his coat pockets, "you shouldn't be moping out here at all, anyway. It's enough to make anyone shiver. Not when Alaric's coronation feast is tonight, and Coll sent me up here to ask if you want to visit Snowflower's little one for a bit, beforehand."

"Have you decided what to name him yet?" Erik tilts his head to look at me curiously. "Coll's been calling him 'boyo,' but then, he calls all babies that."

"Hey!" Garreth exclaims, but he's laughing, and I do, too.

I close my eyes and take a deep breath. The air is cold, of course, and thin like snow. But even so, I imagine I can almost smell a hint of freshness, of damp earth and growing things. Spring isn't here yet, not quite, but the worst of winter is over.

I've thought about 'Winter' as a name for my foal, and 'Sunrise' and 'Silverleaf.' Even 'Road'—half seriously—since he will be my companion. But nothing has seemed quite right. "I don't know yet," I reply at last, and I look over at Erik. "I've thought about it, but choosing a name for someone is harder than you think."

"*Not always,*" Finn says, giving me the wry, unfathomable smile he's worn so often since the night his father died. Finn has changed, too; become more difficult to understand even as I've started to learn to speak with him properly. As I take his hand and let him pull me to my feet, I can't suppress a pang of regret that we've all grown up these past few days. Grown different. None of us more than Alaric, though, as he's begun to take his place as king. "*Sometimes,*" Finn continues, "*choosing a name is easy, Ellin Fisher Healer.*"

I feel my lips twist in a bittersweet smile, too, as I follow the princes inside and out of the cold. Ellin Fisher Healer, they call me now. Both a Southling name and a Northlander one, but not really either.

And names in the Northlands might not be what one would wish, but they're always true.

THE END

ABOUT THE AUTHOR

MEG BURDEN has been writing and reading fantasy and science fiction since sometime around kindergarten. In true science fiction fashion, but in real life, she graduated from college when she was 18 and shortly afterward, began writing when she wasn't waitressing, bartending, tending parrots (really), and teaching as a graduate student at the University of Virginia. Nowadays she lives in a small Nebraska town with no stoplights and more cows than people and works part of the time on a farm. She breeds and raises Siamese cats when she isn't involved with online science fiction fandom. If you'd like to write to Meg, her address is *meg@megburden.com*.

ALL THE CATS OF CAIRO
by Inda Schaenen

EGYPTIAN CAT-GODDESS AND AMERICAN TEEN JOIN IN EPIC BATTLE

Maggie, an American teen living in Cairo with her diplomat parents, is given a small bronze statuette of the ancient cat-goddess, Bastet, which mysteriously grows hot in her hand. Bastet has awakened from her millennia-long sleep to chaos in modern-day Egypt and is attempting to communicate with Maggie through the goddess's disciples, the multitude of cats who wander freely through Cairo's streets, markets, cemeteries and mosques, the cats who seem to be seeking out Maggie.

Maggie puzzles out the goddess's message—that her ancient temple and cemetery are due to be defiled in a joint American-Egyptian development project—and that the new factory will abduct and force Egyptian boys to work in near-slavery conditions. But what can 13-year-old Maggie do to help? She speaks almost no Arabic and she doesn't know her way around Cairo. In an epic battle, with the help of an Egyptian boy who has befriended her, with the aid of the myriad Cairo cats, and with the power of Bastet herself, can Maggie rescue the land from powerful enemies—some strange, some all too familiar—that threaten the very life force of Egypt?

An exciting, suspenseful story and a vivid picture of modern Egypt for young adults from 10 up.

"...ALL THE CATS OF CAIRO comes alive with its vibrant setting and its harmonious blend of twenty-first century modernity and mystic wonder. Highly recommended..." Midwest Book Review

"...easy for kids and teens to understand...eloquently covers one of the most important international issues in the world today from multiple perspectives and adds an abundance of Egyptian culture into the mix to create an authentic experience..." *YA Books Central*

ALL THE CATS OF CAIRO by Inda Schaenen
ISBN: 978-09768126-5-4
trade soft cover, 232 pages, $8.95, ages 10 up.

available from your bookseller

THE GHOST IN ALLIE'S POOL
by Sari Bodi

Eighth grade goes from fun to disaster when Allie's best friend, Marissa, dumps her for the popular crowd. Suddenly, Allie finds herself sitting alone in the middle-school cafeteria with no one to call on her new cell phone. In a moment of frustration, Allie flings Marissa's friendship necklace into her pool, and to her surprise, the ghost of Dorothy May the ancestor she's been researching for English class—appears. Problem is, Dorothy May is as depressed as Allie, because she fell off the Mayflower 400 years ago. Worse: if Marissa finds out Allie's talking to a ghost, she'll never want to be Allie's friend again. But is it possible that Dorothy May is exactly who Allie needs to help her fit into eighth grade?

"Bodi's affecting debut novel balances a familiar fictional theme with an inventive historical premise. When Marissa abandons Allie for two new best friends, Allie muses, 'They're beautiful and great lacrosse players. They're also kind of mean. In our school, you can't get any cooler than that.'" *Publishers Weekly*

"Just wait until you meet Allie and her mysterious friend in this imaginative, satisfying story. Heart stopping and unusual, I couldn't put it down. You won't be able to either."
   —Patricia Reilly Giff, Newbery Honor Book author of "Lily's Crossing" and "Pictures of Hollis Woods."

THE GHOST IN ALLIE'S POOL by Sari Bodi
ISBN: 978-09768126-6-1
trade soft cover, 184 pages, $8.95, ages 10 up.

available from your bookseller